OVER THE HIGH SIDE

Sacred Hearts PNW Chapter - Book I

A.J. DOWNEY

BOOK ONE

COPYRIGHT

~

ISBN: 978-1-950222-24-7

Editing & book design by Maggie Kern @ Ms.K Edits

Cover art by Dar Albert at Wicked Smart Designs

DEDICATION

To Carrie. You know why.

*D*ump Truck…

I looked back over my shoulder, doing a double take as I waited behind some blue-hairs to get their geriatric asses out the way. The woman behind me was a looker. Tall and slender, what a lot of guys would call a cool drink of water. Except she was a citizen through and through. Her shapely legs ensconced in a prim pencil skirt to her knees, paired with smart hose in a pair of expensive-ass pumps. The skirt matched the jacket, the blouse straining over her tits, a light cream – both the blouse and the exposed skin of her throat.

Boy howdy did she have a rack. I wished for a better look, but those tits were hidden behind the book she had clutched to her chest. A familiar title that I happened to own.

So, she may be a citizen but maybe not *a prude. Interesting.*

"Next please!" the guy behind the counter called and I stepped up, the old fart that'd been in front of me putting himself between me and his wife with a hostile stare. I chuckled inwardly and gave the old-timer a polite nod. I had no interest in the Q-tip in front of me. Just the woman behind me. I didn't make a thing out of the disrespect. He was a Vet. One of those blue trucker hats on his more than likely balding head declaring his station and whatnot. I didn't have anything against

Vets. Had several in the club I belonged to. It was the only reason he got a pass.

I set my purchases on the counter and the guy behind it let his eyebrows shoot up.

"You kidding me?" he asked, and he was either fearless or that fucking dumb.

"No," I growled simply and leaned in. He predictably leaned away from me – afraid – which is as it should be. I had enough respect for the old-timer given his age and record of service to the land I loved, but this hipster douchebag didn't have anything going for him to get him into my good graces. At least, not yet.

"You able to look up an author and title in that damn thing and ring it up for me, even though I ain't got the book?"

"Uh, yeah, why?" he asked.

I jerked my head back and he looked over my shoulder, his eyes falling on the book tucked against the woman's chest, her dark eyes otherwise occupied by the screen of her phone which was in her other hand.

"You know what it is?" he asked. "I can't see it from here."

"That I do," I said. *"Love In Purgatory* by Timber Philips."

"Thanks." The guy clacked keys on the register's keyboard, a few mouse clicks and done. He reached for my books and I shook my head.

"Ring that up first on its own then I'll pay for these."

"Right, okay. Whatever you say."

"Customer is always right," I agreed and put some menace in my tone.

I think the guy may have shit himself and that amused me.

I handed over the cash for the book in the woman's arms and got a receipt, paid for my purchase, let the guy bag the titles I'd picked, and took the bag from him.

"Thanks," I muttered and turned, walking up to the woman stopping in front of her, jerking my head at the dude behind her in line to go around and go ahead.

"Hey!" She frowned at him as he went past, then looked up at me. She had to be five foot nine, maybe five ten easy, but that was nothing against my almost six foot seven.

"Your book's paid for," I said, handing her the receipt. She took it and blinked at it like she didn't understand while I plucked a pen out of the front inside pocket of my cut.

"Why would you do that?" she asked.

I plucked the book out of her arms and flipped it open to the front page and wrote my road name and number in it. I closed it, made a great show of putting my pen away and handed her the book back.

"Figured my odds might be more improved buying you a book rather than a drink," I said.

Her mouth dropped open in a tiny 'o' of surprise and I would be lying if I said I didn't picture that lush mouth of hers wrapped around my cock. I smiled at her, winked, and said, "Gimme a call," before limping to the set of stairs leading to the doors out onto the street.

I missed the Westwood Village Barnes & Noble. My usual go-to was the Tukwila location, but they hadn't had the book I'd wanted. Downtown Seattle's Pacific Place had, so here I was.

Hopefully she'd get intrigued, call me, and it would make this my lucky day for having to go out of my way.

CHAPTER ONE

*B*ianca...

I was crazy.

I'd called the biker from the bookstore, admittedly intrigued, and now, here I was, seated in Caffe Ladro in Kirkland, waiting for him... to talk? To flirt? I didn't know what.

I'd called him. It'd taken me a couple of days, but I'd eventually picked up the phone and dialed and lo and behold, he'd picked up the phone. I still couldn't fathom *why* I would call a man like him. Especially considering all he had written in my book was 'Dump Truck – (206) 555-2122.'

I mean, what the hell kind of a name was *Dump Truck*? Other than, you know, the sheer size of him.

I had stared at the patch on his back as he had stood in front of me in line, out of place in the elegant downtown bookstore location. On the top had read '*Sacred Hearts*', the middle a red human heart, veined in blue, wrapped in barbed wire, the valves of the heart morphing into what I supposed was supposed to be tailpipes. Beneath the grisly colorful patch was another curved patch that declared '*W. Washington*.'

His long brown ponytail had interrupted it all, hanging just past the middle of his back in this strange black leather sheath, snaps all along its length holding it closed. I hadn't wanted him to catch me staring so I'd buried myself in my phone, answering messages, committing to dinner with my father by the end of the week, although he was the last person I wished to see right now.

Maybe that was why I was doing this. The fact my father had practically brokered me to the highest bidder to save his floundering real estate ventures. Marrying me off, quite literally, like chattel to a rich and admittedly handsome real estate mogul out of Las Vegas. I mean, at least he was my own age and wasn't botoxed to within an inch of his life. Still, he wasn't as authentic as the man who'd been in front of me only two days ago, who had bought me the latest book by my favorite author and who had flirted with me because… well, I didn't know why. All I knew is that I couldn't get his warm brown eyes out of my head. How he looked at me as though he could actually *see me*.

The door to the coffee shop opened and the heavy tread of booted feet against the polished concrete floor brought my head snapping up. He scanned the room, deep dark eyes alighting on where I slowly stood from my seat by the window. He waved me down with one hand and went to the counter, ordering a drink for himself in that deep bass voice of his. The timbre of it somehow soothing.

He paid in cash, and I caught a glimpse of a great wad of green in his wallet. I wondered about that – although not too hard. I'd learned a long time ago that you didn't want to think about or wonder too loudly about that kind of thing. It just wasn't something you did. You could find yourself in entirely too much trouble if you weren't careful. Another bitter lesson learned at my father's knee.

I took a sip of my latté and its velvety foam and waited for this bearded, and admittedly sexy, hulk of a biker to join me at my little table.

"When you said to choose where to meet, I half expected you to say 'not Kirkland' when I said here," I told him.

He set his coffee down and hooked the chair behind him with a boot, pulling it forward up under him as he sat. It was actually kind of impressive considering he hadn't taken those deep dark eyes off of me. His lips curved into a smile, hidden in his dark beard and he considered me.

"Why'd you pick it then?" he asked and I felt myself pale.

Good going, Bianca. Now you have to admit to living or working near here.

"Seemed like a good idea at the time," I said, letting out a slow breath.

"If you're trying to catch me off guard or whatever, it won't work," he said, raising his coffee to his lips and taking a sip. "Been judged my whole damn life, coming someplace where the judgy rich folks like to hang ain't gonna bother me none. Sure is going to draw a lot of attention to you, though. Although, I have to guess that maybe that was what you were going for." His chin came up slightly as he fixed me with those deep brown eyes of his, calculations of social projections and trajectories sliding behind them.

"Then again, maybe not. Maybe I'm judging a book by its cover here… because now I'm not so sure. In fact, by the look on your face, I'm pretty sure you didn't tell anybody you know you were meeting a Sacred Heart. How am I doing?"

"Um…" I didn't know what to say. I mean, he was right about a lot of it. I kind of *was* one of those judgy rich people – at least my father was, and at twenty-six, I hadn't exactly rushed to find my own way out from under his roof or anything. I was pretty much the epitome of a spoiled little rich girl, so…

I sighed, reminding myself, *and that is exactly why you're in this mess with father and Guy.*

My thoughts were disrupted by Dump Truck, since I didn't know what else to call him, when he chuckled and shook his head.

"It's all right. Not the first time I was called for a thrill ride," he said.

"I'm sorry?" I blinked and sat back, taken aback.

"It's okay," he soothed. "You ain't gotta pretend. All you gotta decide is bike or dick and let me know."

He sat back too and hooked his thumbs in his belt loops, staring at me openly, waiting me out. I took it partially as a challenge, but there was something else there. I mean, his eyes, they hadn't left mine, even though my cleavage was out, somewhat on display.

I'd run here, and so I was in my athletic gear which consisted of skintight leggings, a sports bra that showed off the girls, under a skintight jacket, zipped halfway up.

"Your name isn't really Dump Truck, is it?" I asked, attempting to change the subject although his proposition was still turning in my mind's eye. *Why else* did *you call him, B.?*

"That's what people call me, if you don't like it you can always go with D.T. Everybody else does."

"They shortened your nickname? I mean, they gave you the nickname Dump Truck and then decided that it needed to be shortened too?"

He laughed and it was a good sound, rich like dark chocolate, coating the senses and sending a shiver through me. I would be absolutely lying if I said the way he looked at me didn't appeal. The way he ran his tongue over his bottom lip and that same lip between his teeth was seriously enticing.

What is wrong with me? I wondered, but even as I did, I knew the answer. I was about to be married to a man I didn't know – an arranged marriage – and I didn't know if he would be any good… Dump Truck sure as hell looked like he knew exactly what he was doing and like he had several things in mind that he wanted to do with me.

I'd never, not once defied my father. I had never taken that walk on the wild side and I wasn't likely going to get the chance once this marriage business transaction thing went through so…

I swallowed hard and took a breath to try and talk some more when he asked me, "Did you like it?"

"Like what?" I asked, a little derailed. He seemed like he was really good at that – keeping me off center. I hadn't decided if I liked it or not.

"The book."

"*Love in Purgatory?*" I asked.

"Yeah."

"I did… thank you."

"Was one of my favorites of hers," he commented dryly.

I blinked in confusion again. "You read romance novels?"

He laughed, low and deep, and I suppressed a shudder of delight at the sound.

"Long story, but yeah."

I glanced him up and down and meeting his eyes said, "A little odd, given the packaging."

"Don't make the same mistake I did," he warned and winked at me.

"What's that?" I took another drink of my rapidly cooling latté and considered him coolly. Or at least what I hoped was coolly.

"Judge a book by its cover," he returned.

We sat in silence, each silently considering the other, eyes roving and with a satisfied sigh after his next sip from his drink he said, "Dick it is, then," and leaned forward. The pen reappeared from inside his vest pocket. "I'm not even going to ask your place or mine. I already know the answer." He pulled the napkin I had by my drink closer and flipped it over, writing out something on the back. He slid it to me, capped his pen and took another drink of his coffee, his eyebrows raising as in *your move.*

"When?" I asked, without looking.

"Tonight. Be at my place or don't, it's up to you. I ain't got any other plans."

"Staying in and reading?" I asked.

"Something like that."

"And if I show up? What happens?"

"Whatever you want, I'm not picky when it comes to the company of a beautiful woman."

"And after?"

"Whatever you want that to be, too. I'm easy."

"Apparently so," I murmured with a grin and he laughed, louder, more complete this time.

"What if I'm married?" I asked, curious.

"Not my problem," he said, then after a moment of silence, "Are you?"

"Not yet," I said, deciding I should be completely honest.

"Lucky guy," he commented sardonically.

"It's more of a… business transaction, I guess you could call it."

"Sounds like a bad idea," he answered.

"For who?"

"By the looks of it, for you. Again, ain't none of that my business."

He stood up, favoring one leg as he had at the bookstore, and taking up his coffee said, "See you around, maybe."

"Yeah," I agreed, faintly and belatedly adding a similarly faint, "Maybe."

He raked me over with a final keen-eyed glance and we both knew there was no maybe about it. As soon as he left the coffee house, the atmosphere lightened somehow. Like the very air I breathed thinned back out, and it was less of a struggle to drag it into my lungs.

Dump Truck was a very intense man.

I slid the napkin toward me as soon as he was out of sight and sure enough, it was an address.

I checked the time. I had just enough to finish my coffee, go home and change, and to fight my way through traffic.

I didn't want to give him the satisfaction of not showing up. I didn't want him to think I was afraid. It was suddenly like if I could do this? I could do anything… including marry Guy Evans.

I went home, selected a very nice bra and panty set, a particular favorite garter belt and some lace-topped nude stockings.

I wasn't a virgin, though the set I'd selected was white. Still, Dump Truck looked more than a little experienced and I was certain, that by far, I would be downright virginal by comparison so the white was fitting.

I picked out a pair of nude patent leather heels out of my shoe closet and a camel coat that belted at the waist. The closest thing that I had to a trench coat or raincoat.

Am I really going to do this? I wondered, staring down at the items laid out on my bed.

I couldn't stop thinking about those piercing dark eyes, of how they seemed to see right through me. How they seemed to see *me*, and I wanted that. At least once. To be with someone that saw *me* and not what being with me could do for them.

I took a deep breath, held it, and let it out slow.

I was going to do this.

I showered, carefully shaving everything. When I got out, I moisturized with my favorite lotion, dried my hair and straightened it before I carefully did my makeup. I kept it light and natural the way *I* liked to do it and dressed in the lingerie set carefully.

I felt sexy, cool, and confident when I stepped out of my townhome's door and locked up. I had a condom in my coat pocket, my license and a credit card just in case, and the napkin wrapped around it all. In my other pocket I had my phone and my keys. I went down to my car, a sleek silver BMW, and got in, putting my phone in the cradle and bringing up the navigation screen to put in his address.

He lived in Burien, around thirty-eight minutes away without traffic, but the traffic was stretching that drive to fifty-seven minutes or more via 405.

"Just more time to talk yourself out of this crazy idea," I muttered to myself as I pushed the button to start the ignition.

The car purred to life, and I backed out of my space, heading for the freeway.

Traffic was hell, but I slid into a sort of road hypnosis. Calm, not really thinking about anything. Just stopping and going with the flow.

I followed my GPS's insistent directions, I-405 to Highway 518, Highway 518 to Highway 509, getting off on the 128th street exit. I turned left on 128th, right on First Ave, then finally a left on SW 117th.

"The destination is on your left! Arrived!"

I slowed and turned on my signal at the sign on the street corner for the Arbor Heights Apartments. It was a light off-white, the letters in a muted sea blue. The building was likewise painted in the same color scheme. An off-white with the same blue for the trim, doors, and railings. I immediately knew which covered space was his.

It was the one with the motorcycle, carefully parked deep and against the back wall in anticipation of my car parking in the spot with it.

Wow, Bianca, he really does have you pegged.

There was something exciting, arousing about his arrogance. The man had bad boy etched in every line of his being, and that was pretty much why I was here, right? To let him do bad things to me.

I pressed my thighs together, locked my phone in the center console along with my license and debit card, and taking just the condom, my keys and the napkin with me, I exited my car.

Raising my hood, self-conscious of the type of neighborhood I was in – which wasn't the most reputable – I found the entrance to the building and went up, hesitating only briefly outside his door.

With one last cleansing breath, I raised my hand to knock. I immediately plunged my hands into my pockets and waited, hoping their shaking would remain hidden. I heard his voice through the heavy door and my spine tingled with anticipation that I barely could hold in check.

He opened the wooden slab and stared down at me for a moment, and I *loved* how tall he was. How he made me feel small even though I was almost five foot ten. Turning to the side, he let me slip past, shutting and locking the door behind us.

I swallowed hard before he turned to rake me with that wild gaze of his. I almost didn't register that he was shirtless with the intensity of the look he gave me.

"Am I going to find out what's under the coat?" he asked.

Wordlessly, I pulled the sash and unbuttoned the jacket, letting it fall open.

"Now that's what I'm talking about," he muttered, reaching for me and I for him. He kissed me fiercely and it felt so good, his skin against mine, all that hard muscle pressed against my softer curves as he gripped my ass through the lace of my panties beneath the hem of my coat.

"Come this way." He growled the command and I would follow him wherever he would have me go as long as he kept touching me. His touch was unique. Something else. Somewhere between commanding and fierce, yet at the same time gentle and considerate. He led me straight to his bedroom, a king-sized bed for a king-sized man waiting within.

"Kick those off," he demanded and I did as he asked, slipping my feet out of the killer heels and losing several more inches in the bargain. I felt positively petite next to D.T. and that was a feat in and of itself.

Suddenly it occurred to me, "Don't you want to know my name?"

"Maybe later, right now I just want that mouth on mine."

He bowed his head, hair shrouding our kiss, making this a hundred times more intimate, and I kissed him with every begging ounce of need I had, desperately begging him to make me feel good, wordlessly, soundlessly.

I pushed my hands into his hair, which was slightly coarse where the strands tucked into the slight webs between my fingers. He helped himself once more to twin handfuls of my ass and we kissed, the passion ramping into an inferno that threatened to devour any shred of common sense we had left.

I drifted my hands down the front of his body and undid his belt, liberating the button from its denim prison, lowering his fly.

Holy shit, he was *huge*. I mean, his length was impressive, but that wasn't what I meant by huge. What I meant was, I couldn't get my fingers all the way *around him*. They wouldn't meet and I suddenly had my first doubt…

"What's wrong?" he whispered, pulling back from the intense kiss we shared.

"I don't think the condom I brought is going to be big enough," I whispered breathlessly.

He chuckled, sultry, dark, and deep. The sound made me close my eyes, made me wish I were nude. The type of sound that felt like sable soft fur against the inside of your skull. Erotic, sensual, making me crave more of him.

"I got you. I special order 'em. Bedside table." I glanced over and sure enough, there were several round, white and black foil packets on the nightstand.

I let my overcoat slip from my shoulders and down my arms, the warmth it provided leaving, the cool air of the room caressing my exposed skin, his eyes replacing the heat that was stolen by the fabric's departure, replacing it and surpassing it by tenfold.

"Fuck yes," he whispered, taking me in, his hands gentle against my stomach in a light caress. He wrapped around my sides, pulling me close, his cock like a branding iron against my stomach where it peeked through the parted denim of his jeans.

I hooked fingers in his waistband and thrust the stiff material down, and he chuckled again, lightly, pleased by my eagerness, backing up to the bed, sitting down when the jeans were clear of his ass and letting me pull them off the rest of the way to drop them to the floor.

"Take a step back," he ordered and I did.

"Touch yourself," he purred and I did – cupping my breasts, squeezing and massaging them. Raising my chin, looking at him, looking at me, and God it was so hot, the heat in his gaze, the way his eyes were rapt upon me, traveling over my breasts, over my stomach, following my hands as I slid them against my skin.

My panties were soaked, and he just half sat, half lay there watching me, cock straining, throbbing slightly with what I imagined was every heartbeat.

"God, woman. You're so fucking beautiful."

I slipped my panties off, sweeping them down my legs, my clit throbbing, begging for attention. The hungry look in his eyes edging me toward him, urging me closer, within reach.

He reached over and slid one of the condoms off the table, eyes still fixed to mine, tearing it open with his teeth, his eyes twin burning coals in his face, hypnotizing, transfixing me, as he worked the condom down his length.

I moved on him, stepping forward, light on my feet, putting a sultry little sway in my hips as I put my nails against his thighs and scraped up the tops of his legs lightly scratching, a different sensation, meant to tantalize and by the sound of his groan, succeeding at the endeavor.

I put one knee to the bed beside his hip and his big hands engulfed my hips to aid me so I could get the other up there as well. I didn't come quietly, backing off so I could lick a wet line along the length of his dick from root to tip, the chemical taste of latex unpleasant but tolerable, soon to be erased by the taste of his mouth. I kissed my way along his stomach, over the crisp smattering of hair on his chest, until I could dip my tongue past his lips.

His hands gravitated from my hips to my back, massaging me, encouraging me, as I slid my sex over his wrapped length, dry humping him, lubing him up slightly, still wondering how I would take someone so long, so wide, inside me.

He was certainly and easily the biggest man I had ever been with and daunting in more ways than just *how was I going to fuck his cock?*

"Take it slow, baby. One inch at a time if you have to," he whispered in my ear, his hand wrapped in the back of my hair, holding my body down against his.

"Help me," I whispered back, and he reached between us, his big hand holding himself out from his body at a better angle for me to take him at.

I felt him at my opening and gasped as I sat back slowly, the head of his cock penetrating my grasping pussy. I lowered myself onto him by the first few inches, panting slightly as the width of his cock began to flare out, desperate to take more of him but doing it slowly, so slowly… I wanted this to be good. I wanted to take him all, and if I did things too quickly, if I didn't give myself enough time to stretch and become acclimated, it wouldn't be nearly as good as it could be.

"Oh, yeah, that's it, baby. So good, take that dick," he murmured passionately, his breath hot against my ear, sliding down my neck in a tingling rush.

I worked him inside further, and soon, my ass met the tops of his thighs and he was fully seated.

Fuck, that was good. So good. I felt myself throb and pulse around him, my pussy spasming in ecstasy, a gentle thing; a warm up, a preview of what could come.

It only grew in intensity the more he murmured encouragement in my ear, the praise sweet and dirty at the same time. My pussy throbbed and fluttered against him and I went limp, giving myself over in surrender to the sensation. God, *fuck*, that was the sweetest and gentlest orgasm I'd ever had and *I wanted more.*

"Take your time, baby. That's it. *Fuck yeah.*"

I pushed up off his chest and seated myself more firmly on his cock and his mouth worked. Open and closed, his cock throbbing once inside me as I simply sat astride him. Him so deep, as far as he could go, the both of us staring at one another, equally as deeply in the eyes, each of us simply *feeling* the other in the most intimate of ways possible.

I rode him, slow, sensual, and I watched nameless emotions play out over his face as I did it. Whatever they were, they ran deep, moving him as much as the sight of it moved me… my soul crying out, begging me to see more.

"Tell me," he growled, but before he finished, he took one of my nipples into his mouth, working it with lips, tongue, and teeth.

Tell you what? Oh, God! I would tell you anything, my mind cried but my voice wouldn't couldn't form words.

"Tell me your name!" he gasped, releasing my breast from his mouth.

I pushed up and looked into his eyes, into the bottom of his soul and answered him, "Bianca."

"Bianca…" He rolled my name like candy on his tongue and lifted his hips ever so slightly to meet my downward motion.

I threw back my head and cried out, and his hands gripped my hips mercilessly as he drove up into me again with a determined grunt.

"Scream for me, Bianca," he ordered and drove up into me again.

I gasped, my voice betraying me, slipping from my lips in a feral surprised cry that was half begging, half surrender.

"Come for me, Bianca. Come for me and scream," he urged and slipped his thumb against my clit and I would do anything, *everything* he asked just to feel the flood of what came next.

I howled my pleasure to the heavens even though he quickly dragged me into the burning pits of hell. The sensation like burning, crawling over my skin, the orgasm brutally efficient, lighting me ablaze, cooling ripples dousing those flames as quickly as they could ignite. It was intense, a complete lack of control as I shuddered and shook, all the while he held onto me, crushing me to his chest, whispering sweet nothings, voice soothing as I came completely apart.

That voice, that soothing voice, stitching me back together as quickly as I came undone.

"That's it, that's a girl. I got you… I've got you, now."

And I wish you never had to let me go…

CHAPTER TWO

------

*D*ump Truck...

 I happened to be laying on my couch, doing a re-read of Love In Purgatory *when the light knock fell at my door. I raised my head up off the arm of the couch and set the book aside on my worn out coffee table I found out on the curb one day.*

I didn't think she had it in her. Looked like I was wrong.

I heaved myself up, coughed and called out, "Gimme just a minute here!" *to let her know I was coming. My leg didn't always want to cooperate in the transition from sitting to standing and hurt like an SOB the first couple of steps.*

I'd come by my broken wings honestly, and I'd have them forever.

When I opened the door, she was on the other side in a pair of those sexy ass heels and a tan raincoat that hit her at mid-thigh, the hood up, covering all that luxurious straight ebony hair. I turned sideways to let her pass and she slipped into my place, lowering her hood.

I shut the door and threw the lock and turned as she turned around to face me.

"Am I going to find out what's under the coat?" I asked.

Wordlessly, boldly, she untied the sash and unbuttoned the jacket, revealing a real nice lingerie set.

"Now that's what I'm talking about," I muttered, pulling her into me with an arm around her waist.

She tipped her face up to mine and I kissed her, the feeling of her hands on my face, pulling me to her rather than pushing me away, heating my blood. I was already shirtless, my jeans suddenly constraining and way too tight in the crotch region.

"Come this way," I growled against her mouth and hands to her hips, guided her past the dining area and kitchen, past the bathroom and linen closet doors and into my bedroom. Her chest heaved, tits practically busting out of the white lace straining to contain them, her light tan, patent leather heels muffled by the crummy carpet of my shitty apartment, but that was okay. She'd have them off in a second.

"Kick those off," I demanded and she did as she was told.

"Don't you want to know my name?" she asked.

"Maybe later," I told her. "Right now I just want that mouth on mine."

She twined her fingers in my loose hair this time and I helped myself to twin handfuls of the globes of her ass, pulling her tight up against my body. She moaned and it was a sweet sound.

I didn't get a chance to go for my belt. She was already there, sliding it through its buckle, releasing the little metal tongue out of the hole that held it closed. She had my button and fly open before I could blink and goddamn did her hand feel good wrapped around my shaft.

"Mm," the first slight sound of protest. I pulled back, her lips swollen from my kiss, and petted the side of her face, stroking over the soft skin and asking. "What's wrong?"

"I don't think the condom I brought is going to be big enough," she said breathlessly.

I chuckled. "I got you, I special order 'em. Bedside table."

She let me go just long enough to let her jacket slip off her shoulders and down her arms to land discarded with her shoes somewhere behind her.

"Fuck yes." I was vaguely aware I whispered it as I took her long, lean, yet still curvaceous body in. A body made for sin. A woman ready to sin with me. Jesus, fuck, she was hot. So beautiful... I pulled her right up against me, torn

as to whether I wanted to just look at her or feel her and desperate for both at the same time. She kissed me like she'd been made for me, my dick standing at attention, weeping pre-cum at the sight of her, twitching at the feel of her soft skin pressed against it.

She boldly hooked fingers into the waistband at my hips and thrust the thick material down. I chuckled at her eagerness, backing up to the bed; sitting down when the jeans were clear of my ass. I leaned back, letting her pull them off the rest of the way to drop them to the floor.

"Take a step back," I ordered and she did as she was told. So sexy, so obedient, it made me that much harder. So hard it hurt.

"Touch yourself," I growled and she did, cupping and squeezing her tits together through the lace cups of her bra.

She looked down at me, but not down on me, her hands sliding against her flesh, her nipples stiff peaks beneath the lace, areola's barely peeking through the gaps, slightly duskier than the surrounding skin. Her manicured hands sliding over her flat, toned stomach, fingertips dipping so slightly into the waistband of her lace panties, which were visibly soaked from here.

"God, woman. You're so fucking beautiful," I groaned and she slipped her panties off over her stockings and garter, letting them fall to the floor. Her pussy shaved smooth except for a tantalizing landing strip, dark, perfect, slightly curling at the top of her sex.

I liked that. I didn't dig clean shaven women. It made me feel like a fucking pedo. I liked fucking women, I didn't dig little girls.

I grabbed a condom off the table, working it open with my teeth, rolling it down my cock, edging myself, gripping and stroking my dick as she slipped closer as if she were a cat and I held a particularly tasty treat that she wanted – no – needed.

She stalked toward me, a sexy sway in her hips, placing her hands against my knees, curling her fingers under, dragging the tops of her nails against the tops of my thighs as she drew closer, closer, her mouth hovering over me, her breath tantalizing, her long straight hair sweeping over my skin, trailing her tongue against the underside of my cock. Fuck, her eyes locked on mine, the heat of that little pink tongue through the fucking latex almost too much as she kissed my stomach, a trail of sensation up my chest.

Her mouth met mine as she put first one knee to the bed, on the outside of my thigh. I put my hands on her hips to help hold her steady as she clambered up on the bed on the other side and I lay back, letting her have the control.

I was a big dude with a bigger dick and I wanted this to be good for her, so I was perfectly happy to take things at her pace.

She kissed me, and I threaded a big wad of that silken hair between my fingers, gripping it, holding her body close to mine.

"Take it slow, baby. One inch at a time if you have to," I murmured in her ear and she gasped.

"Help me," she replied breathily, and I delved my free hand down between our bodies, shoving my dick down at the root so it was out from my body and at a better angle for her to take me, to ride me, to fuck me at her leisure.

She moaned and slid her pussy against me a few more times before trying just the tip, groaning and gasping as it parted her pussy lips and plunged inside her waiting wet heat by just the first couple of inches. I just got wider from there, and she would need to work me in slowly.

"Oh, yeah, that's it, baby. So good, take that dick," I encouraged as she slowly inched her way down. She felt so good. Hot, slick, so slick, it was like being wrapped in satin. Hot, pulsating, satin, the grip of her cunt gentle and slight, edging me so carefully I dare not breathe or I'd come like some sloppy fuckin' teenager.

No way was I going to come first. She needed to get off at least twice before I came once. It was a personal rule.

She paused, panting, her breath hot and sexy against my neck and shoulder and I let her rest a moment as I felt her flutter, gripping and releasing me in a light irregular pattern that left me smiling both on the inside and the outside.

That's one. I thought to myself. Second one, I wanna hear her scream.

She rose up, arching back slightly, taking me in as far as I could go and I gasped. I said something, I can't remember what, as I was way too fucking busy trying to tear myself back from the brink.

Looking up at her while she looked down at me, her possessing all the power in that moment, me happy to serve it up on a silver fucking platter, my hands massaging the tops of her thighs as we both dragged ourselves back, getting our shit together so she could move.

And fuck, did she move.

She rode me, slow, sensual, and I felt it. Deep, like nothing I'd ever felt before, and I didn't even know her name.

"Tell me," I grunted, and she leaned forward. I pulled the cups of her bra down, freeing her tits, watching them bounce, dipping my head and capturing one of the stiff peaks with my mouth. She cried out, pussy tightening around me as I suckled at her tit, hands massaging her hips as she rolled them, the friction against my dick something I would die for.

"Tell me your name!" I demanded, her nipple popping free of the hold I had on it with my lips.

She pushed up, looking down at me with her lovely dark eyes.

"Bianca," she murmured…

Bianca…

It was a name that haunted me even now, months later as the shrill ring of my cell shattered the dream I'd had for a hundred nights and more since.

I sat up sharply and groped for my phone in the pocket of my headboard, squinting in the dark light of morning at the unknown number on the screen.

"Yeah? This better be good." I growled into it by way of greeting.

"Dump Truck?" The voice light, a feminine lilt, familiar but oh so far away, faint as the echo of my memory except when I dreamed.

"Bianca, that you?"

"You remember me…" The relief in those three words was palpable.

"Yeah, yeah, baby, I'm here, what's wrong?"

"Uh, I'm in Vegas, I hate to ask… but can you come get me?" she said, voice trilling with fear, fragile, nearly broken.

I sat up in bed and clicked on the light built into my headboard, grabbing for the pad and paper I kept there.

"What's the address?" I demanded tersely.

She gave it to me, her voice going hushed, the fear mounting. I wrote it down and asked, "Can you hang on for a couple of days?"

"I-I-I think s-s-s-o." I could taste her tears over the line.

"What happened?" I demanded and she gasped.

"I have to go!"

The line went dead silent, the tones sounded and the call had ended. I didn't dare try to ring her back.

I pushed myself up and looked at the clock on my phone, one-eighteen a.m. I frowned and shook my head sharply to clear it.

Bianca…

I hated that name for her. It was rich, preppy, and pretentious as shit. I didn't know what was going on, but I knew it was time to change it.

I got up and rubbed my face with both hands. I needed to go to the club. Maverick might still be there. I needed his permission to ride to the rescue. Might need to make him understand.

I picked my phone back up and shot him a text.

Where u at?

Barring anything else to do until I got my answer, I heaved myself up and into a shower. I would have a long, hard ride ahead of me.

An hour and a half later, I was packed, riding into Rat City and the club at the old boneyard on 15th SW. It was a front for the club, for the most part. A legal business, one of a few where we laundered some of the dirty money we got from running scripts down from the north. The club was actually across the street and up a quarter block from the motorcycle boneyard.

It used to be a Vietnamese billiard hall, but when it got raided in a combination RICO/ICE bust, either they scooped up the players or deported their asses, and we'd taken over when the property had come up for sale.

It'd taken some work to convert it, and there weren't a lot of people too happy about it… at first. Then, for the locals, the neighborhood miraculously started to clean itself up. The usual gangbanging activity slowed and some stopped altogether – it took a while for the little fuckers to learn their place on the food chain and the Sacred Hearts? Well, let's just say we were fat and happy.

"D.T., what's up, man?" Maverick, our president, asked as soon as I came in the back door. I turned sideways and slipped through his office door, shutting the door tight behind me.

"I got a favor to ask," I said.

His eyebrows went up and he swept back his hair, which was getting a little long in the front, back off his forehead.

"You, a favor? Must be big. What's going on?"

He leaned back in his desk chair and thrust his chin at the chair across from it. I grunted and lowered myself into it, straightening out my fucked-up leg as much as I could.

"I got a call tonight. A call for help. I need to ride to Vegas and pick her up."

"Vegas?" he echoed, and color him surprised.

"Yeah. I need a pin and your blessing. I ain't heading out to cause trouble, brother. I'm just lookin' to bring what's rightfully mine, home."

He frowned.

"You laying claim to this bitch? Oh, man… now I *gotta* know."

I could see the wheels in Mav's brain just a grinding away. There was a reason he was barely thirty and our president. He was smart as fuck, a real maverick with any situation we found ourselves in – especially when it came to the pigs. Hence his road name and his position as our fearless leader.

Hence, why I was here askin' instead of just taking off.

I respected Mav. We all did. I didn't want to bring any heat down on our heads from just haring off on my own fucking program. There were rules to the outlaw life, looser and fewer than citizen life, but the consequences for fucking up the few that we had were a lot bigger than just going to jail or prison for a few years.

I told him about Bianca, honest-like, as much as I could tell him. We'd only had the one night together. I'd woken up after some lazy post-fuck pillow talk and she had been gone. The only trace that she'd been, the open condom wrapper on my bedside table and the napkin from the coffee place I'd scribbled my address on.

Mav considered me and leaned forward in his seat, propping his elbows on the edge of his desk and steepling his fingers in front of him.

"Take Fenris with you," he said and I bowed my head and shook it, my long ponytail in its leather sheath to keep it from tangling in the wind, dragging across my three-piece patch on my back.

"No can do, man. This is something I need to do on my own,

just me."

"I don't like it," he declared, but he reached into the top center drawer of his desk and brought out a big ass safety pin and tapped it against the underside of his fingers on the opposite hand.

A single rider with one of them things pinned to his side meant he was just traveling solo through another club's territory. That he wasn't there to start shit with that club. I wasn't intending to. This was my own business to handle and handle it, I would.

"If there's anything we can do from here, you fucking call us," he said and tossed the pin closer to me, off the edge of the calendar blotter he had on the desktop.

"Yes, sir, that I *will* do," I agreed.

"You got my blessing and support, but only because it sounds like you ain't got nothing doing with the Sand Worms." I chuckled.

The Sand Snakes were an MC out of Vegas but they weren't shit. I would be riding through their territory, though, and some niceties were in order since I would be riding solo.

"Go on, git." Maverick thrust his chin behind me toward the door. "I'll make the necessary calls. Just get her and come back. We'll go from there."

"I don't know the situation," I said getting up with a grunt. "I just know she's scared and asked me to come get her."

"Like I said, you need us, you call us," he said, raising his eyebrows and I nodded.

"Thank you," I said and he nodded again, picking up his cell.

"Go on, now. I got some texts and calls to make."

I shot him a little salute, picked up the safety pin and left out, stopping just inside the back door to affix it to the side of my cut through the metal grommets the laces went through to either bring it in or let it out depending on how much size I lost or put on with any given time of year or situation.

I was looking at least an eighteen hour ride and a bad case of monkey butt if I tried to take the majority of it at once. I would likely have to break it up into two days. Find my ass a cheap roadside motel and catch a few hours of sleep - and that was only going one direction. Getting down to her.

I had no idea what to expect when I got down there, just that tremulous voice, fragile and somewhat broken over the line… *"I hate to ask, but can you come get me?"*

I limped across 15th to the front of the boneyard where I'd backed my bike against the corrugated metal building next to Mav's. It was off the street and safer for the bikes than parking around front of the club or on the street out back. It was also more secure parking them on the private property of the motorcycle wrecking yard because it was kept separate from the club and clubhouse on the books.

Meaning if the pigs came to shake us down at the club, they legally couldn't search the bikes without a separate search warrant for the boneyard's property if Mav had his math right – which he usually did. Of course, with us all arrested, which could be likely, it wouldn't stop 'em from getting a warrant after the fact. Still, it was always nice to be a pain in the ass where we could be, throwing in extra steps.

The one time we had been rounded up and tried on RICO, the whole thing had been thrown out on a technicality because their evidence had been attained illegally from searching our bikes which were outside the scope of the warrant. Gotta be specific. It'd blown up their whole case, and we'd been released from the King County Jail singing *sayonara motherfuckers.*

That'd been a thing of beauty, but it'd also been a close fucking call and one we hadn't wanted to repeat, so we'd definitely fine-tuned our operation to avoid making that mistake twice.

I hit I-5 South for around a hundred and fifty miles. It was around a two-and-a-half-hour ride, to 205 South across the bridge into Oregon. From there, I hit I-84 East, cruising at a good clip until I hit a spate of surface streets, riding to get to US 26 E for another hundred miles or so. I wound through a big chunk of Oregon, this part of the ride a solid seven hours. I watched the sun come up, rode under its inexorable march across the sky, and kept riding as it dipped lower in the sky, heading for the horizon and sleep.

I stopped then, finding a roadside motel in Burns, Oregon. I'd been riding a solid eight hours. I was cold. I was stiff, and I was damn sure fucking hungry, having not eaten all day. Hell, I'd only stopped to piss twice and only once had I put anything in me to drink and that was shitty rest stop coffee.

I couldn't abuse my body like that or I wasn't going to be worth a shit when I got to her. Truth be told, I still wasn't a hundred percent sure why I was even going to such lengths for a woman I didn't know and had only boned once… which was a damn lie.

Deep down inside, I knew. Connections like what we'd had that afternoon in my apartment only happened once in a lifetime. At thirty-six, I hadn't thought I was gonna be alive to make my connection. Figuring I would have done some stupid shit that had me knocked off before I was forty.

I pressed a hand to my aching thigh as I sat in a diner to feed my face and attempt to hydrate before I took my ass to bed.

I let my mind drift to the feel of her body pressed against mine, her gentle fingertips gliding over the seam of the surgical scar along the outside of my leg, hidden by the hair, but there. The long, long, slice, perfect dots on either side raised where they'd stitched me up after implementing the hardware in there to hold badly mangled bones together.

"What happened?" she'd whispered softly and had fallen silent, waiting for me to explain.

I'd told her. I was riding out past Raymond, Washington – running late, headed to the club's annual beach run. The highways out that way connected a bunch of forestry land owned by Weyerhaeuser, so there were usually a lot of logging trucks and dump trucks and the like that went along that way. The highways were usually one lane in either direction with passing zones dotted along the route. Sometimes, the highways widened to three or four lanes at a particularly steep hill to allow the big trucks with their heavy loads to switch to the outside to climb those bad boys.

I was riding up one such segment, minding my own, passing one of those big ass dump trucks with the double trailers, the long arm between 'em with the orange flashing light at the center to warn cages and keep 'em from smacking into 'em.

A truck was coming down my way the opposite direction, a pickup, one with the dualies on the back set of wheels and I wasn't thinkin' shit about it when suddenly, this motherfucking dump truck driver just comes right on over into my lane.

I didn't have anywhere to go, and that long arm between trailers swept into me, busted my fuckin' leg up *bad*. I don't even know where my bike went. I went up over that damn thing, thrown like a fuckin' rag doll and came down the other side of it.

Next thing I knew, I woke up, busted up, coughin' up blood and screamin' as we were flyin' on this rescue copter for the nearest trauma center.

I spent months in the hospital. Broken leg in traction, reconstructive surgeries trying to save it. Busted ribs, internal bleeding, broken cheekbone, no road rash thanks to my cool gear. My bike was *done*. Ended up under the front end of the pickup coming the other way.

I was lucky at the time. Had a good job. Good insurance, but I still ended up with a fuckton of medical bills. Never forgot the look on the guys' faces when I woke up and was lucid. I'd had some broken bones in my face, a busted arm that hadn't needed surgery… a hell of a concussion but my helmet had saved my fucking life.

I'd earned my broken wings patch ten times over with that one crash alone and I'd lived but it'd sucked ass.

She'd listened to me and it was only when a tear hit my chest, dripping off the end of her nose that I realized she'd wept for me.

I didn't know what I'd done to deserve her tears, but they'd touched me and touched me deep.

I sighed and came back to the present. Wondering about her. Worrying about her, as I sucked down the last of my water in my glass and hated that I couldn't just get back on the bike and ride some more. I needed rest. Badly. Or I wasn't going to be fit enough to handle whatever the fuck was going on.

I got up, wincing at the pull and the ache of tight muscles and limped my way to the front counter, settling up and heading back to the motel. I stopped to top off my tank so it was one less thing I would have to do tomorrow.

I didn't bother with a shower. The miles catching up to me. I just made sure my phone was plugged in and ready, fell into bed, and did a different kind of crash, but one that was just as hard.

CHAPTER THREE

$\mathcal{B}$ianca…

"You need to get up, work out. Do *something*, Jesus."

I cringed as Guy sat up behind me, expecting a blow. Grateful when none came. I sniffed and nodded, anything to keep him happy at this point. I sat up gingerly. Still sore from the monster that'd been in our bed beside me. I got up out of bed and made it carefully while he finished getting ready for work.

"Come do these cufflinks," he ordered testily, and I moved right away to comply.

My skin was crawling at the proximity as I carefully tried to suggest, "I could cover this up with makeup, maybe do a mile or two outside?"

I felt like I had only been trying to help, talking through the problem. I mean, I was the daughter of a real estate mogul in his own right, I *did* know a thing or two about the business… but that wasn't why I was here. That was only optics as far as he was concerned and any knowledge of the business I had to impart certainly wasn't why I was married to Guy. I was here because I was *pretty*. Arm candy, just another little lady meant to be seen and not heard and when I'd suggested he wasn't listening to me, that if he only heard what I was saying…

Well, he'd snapped. It was the first time he'd hit me, but it would damn sure be the last. We'd only been married six months, but the problems had started before the honeymoon had even been over. The little passive aggressive demeaning comments. The snide remarks. The belittling and finally, the night before last when he'd backhanded me into next week.

It'd gotten much worse than that. He had been on me with a savagery I had never hoped to know, and when he was through, he had left me broken, bleeding, and weeping on the bedroom floor.

I wanted out. Immediately. So while he was in the shower, I'd pulled on my satin robe, had gone to my little library, to my bookshelf, and had pulled down *Love In Purgatory*. I'd called Dump Truck, praying that he still had the same number… relieved beyond anything that he still remembered me when all this time I couldn't forget him. Even though I'd tried.

I'd been hiding in the little sitting room turned library, whispering into the phone, terrified Guy would find me and when he had called out my name, I had hung up. Hidden my phone on silent under the cushions of the settee and had taken myself to the credenza to pour a glass of brandy to fortify myself.

"What are you doing in here?" he demanded as though he hadn't just raped me. Although, I suppose, to him it hadn't been rape. I mean, he was the next generation of privileged good ol' boy. With his good looks, bank account bursting with cash thanks to the merger with my father's company. With their latest acquisitions in and around Vegas and an overinflated ego to match. Of the mindset so many of the other Chad's that had gone before him. Rich white male privilege in action.

Guy was fearless about what he'd just done to me because he knew he had the money and connections to, quite literally, bury me… and no one would ever be the wiser. A fact he had started insinuating before the honeymoon was even over. Before I'd even realized how isolated I was out here.

I'd swallowed hard and put on a nervous smile just for him and had said "Just getting a drink, you know, to calm my nerves."

He was still drunk. Probably the only thing to keep him from going beyond just eying me suspiciously. "Well come to bed," he'd demanded, like he hadn't just hit me. Like he hadn't just pinned me down and…

I took a swallow of brandy, afraid when he took a menacing step forward.

"No, I'll be right there," I'd said and he'd frowned as I'd pressed back against the credenza, the glasses jostling on the tray on its top.

"If you'd just know your place, I wouldn't have to resort to such drastic measures," he said finally. "Just get yourself together and come to bed."

I guess that was his version of an apology.

I wished I hadn't let my father talk me into this. It was supposed to be little more than a PR stunt… but Guy had been charming when I'd met him and I thought we had been getting along well enough. I even wondered for a while, *what if I was wrong? What if this actually became real?*

Well, now it was as real as it could get.

"I don't want you going out like that," he said, bringing me back to the here and now. I looked at him, he was shaking his head. "You never should have made me so angry as to hit you in the face. Really, Bianca. Just use the treadmill. A few more days and it'll be faded enough to cover with makeup. Right now, it's still too dark."

"Right," I said wondering to myself, *oh my fucking God, is this real life?* I mean, the way he just said that made it seem like he'd *done this before.* He pressed a thumb to the bruise he'd left, frowning at it – not because he'd done it but because he thought that somehow I'd *made him* the megalomaniac.

It was a pretty spectacular bruise with a matching vertical split in my lip. On the inside of my mouth, my teeth had cut into the inside of my bottom lip and I could still taste the copper tang of blood as it tried to heal. I had been lucky I hadn't lost any teeth.

"Don't look at me that way," he ordered and turned away. "I'll be back for dinner. Have Eloisa make that rancheros chicken dish I like."

"Of course," I uttered.

"Have her make you something a little leaner. I don't want married life making you fat."

Again with the belittling comments, he wasn't even trying to pretend anymore.

"I'll be back this evening."

"Sure. Um, have a good day at work." I tried to keep the sarcasm and bitterness out of my tone.

"Don't be smart, that's how you got into trouble in the first place," he said and smacked a kiss on my lips like some nineteen-fifties husband off to another day at the office while wifey stayed home to cook.

Thank fucking God, I had a five year implant. The last thing I wanted was to end up pregnant with his repugnant spawn. There was something seriously wrong with Guy Evans and I just wanted out.

I was terrified, though. He had connections all over this city. Hell, he had connections all over the world. I was even too afraid to depend on the cops. I'd been miserable, had wanted out for a while. I knew it was only a matter of time before he would become violent but had never expected the utter savagery, the depravity of his first full-blown violent episode.

I was not cut out for this.

All I knew was I didn't want to die by his hand and I was sure at this point that I would if I couldn't get out.

Except I had nowhere to go.

"Shit," I swore softly as soon as he was gone.

Dump Truck had said it would be a couple of days. I'd made it through one. I just had one to go… *but then what?* I asked myself.

I didn't know. I didn't exactly have a plan. I'd never been through anything like this and all I knew was I never wanted to go through anything like this again.

I didn't know what else to do, so I dressed in my athletic gear, went to the home gym and ran on the treadmill.

I knew Guy would check the cameras and I didn't want to do anything to upset the monster.

I didn't pray. I felt it was useless. There was no way God was watching. I ran until I quivered with exhaustion, my muscles twitching and fatigued. I stood under a hot shower for an hour or more and fought the temptation to retrieve my phone from the settee in my little library.

Guy would be watching the cameras. If I went for it now, he would know I'd made a call. I didn't want him to know a thing.

I didn't want him to hurt me again.

CHAPTER FOUR

*D*ump Truck…

Day two of this ride was just as brutal as the first.

I left Burns and went down 78 until it turned into 95 into Nevada. The ride continued for some hours until 95 turned to a hard left onto I-80 E which eventually dovetailed into Nevada State Highway 305. I followed NV-305 south, took a left on US 50 East, and got onto NV-376 South.

Somewhere in there, I stopped for food and water, putting a six-pack of bottles into one of my saddlebags. I was in the desert, had been in the desert since Eastern Oregon, and it was hot. Everything about it was hot, the sun beating down, the wind in my face, all of it. I kept my lid on, my sunglasses on my face, and a bandana around my nose. I had gloves on my hands and let my leather riding gear soak up the UV, preferring to keep my fuckin' hide unburnt.

Didn't keep me from sweating and it slowed me down stopping every hour or so to pound one of the bottles of water and to take the occasional piss.

Dehydration could be a killer, though, and I wasn't about it.

I started to feel like I was finally getting somewhere when I entered

Nye county, even though, realistically, I was somewhere between four and five hours from my destination, still.

When I hit US 95, I knew I was on the home stretch. According to my GPS, I only had around three hours and a few minutes to go. I stopped once I was outside Vegas itself to get a motel room – cash only from here on out.

I didn't waste much time after that. I refueled both my body and my bike, checked in with Mav, and headed out for a little recon.

Sunset was still quite a few hours away, and I wanted to get a load of this place. I plugged the address Bianca had given me into my GPS and despite how sore my ass was, got back on the bike.

I rode past casually and took stock. It was a gated property. The gates standing wide open. The rich fuck had a fountain in the center of the drive, the house a one story, no security detail that I could see but there were definitely cameras.

I headed away from the neighborhood, found a poorer one, and found a Starbucks. I went in, if only to take advantage of the air conditioning while I called Maverick.

"Hey, what's up?" he asked, picking up on the first ring. I could hear a commotion in the background as the boneyard was in full swing, bikes being disassembled, parts cleaned and put on shelves.

"I'm in Vegas," I declared.

"Trouble?" he asked.

"Nah, none yet. House is upscale. Rich. No security detail but definitely security cameras. Might be something you could do about that?"

"Uh-huh. Gimme a minute, I'll see what I can do. I'll call you back."

"Alright, I'll be waiting."

"Just sit tight."

He hung up with that and I went up and ordered a drink. It wasn't like back home. I didn't understand that. How an international chain with all the same fuckin' coffee, the same fuckin' recipes and the like, how it couldn't taste the same state to state, coast to coast… hell, even country to country. Of course, once we'd discovered Tim Horton's coffee over the border up in Canada, the Starbucks mermaid chick could spread those fins all she'd like – she could still go fuck herself.

My phone rang around twenty minutes later and I answered it.

"Called in a big fuckin' favor, my dude."

"Oh, yeah? How's that?" I asked, suddenly curious.

"Got that brother over in the mother chapter looking into it. Gave him your number. Might want to hustle, he's looking into things but says he can probably buy you a short window. You're going to want to get into a position where you can make the most of it."

"On it, thank you, Mav."

"Don't mention it," he said and in a more conspiratorial tone said, "Not many I would call in this kind of a favor for, but you're tried and true, brother. You call me and let me know if there's anything else."

"I sure do appreciate it, Mav. I will… and brother?"

"Yeah?" he asked.

"Never mind. It goes without saying. You already know," I told him.

"Now that, I surely do. Call me when you can."

It was better to keep it cryptic. You never knew who was on the line – even using pre-paid numbers like we did, I had still called on my personal one and we both knew that. Technology was creepin' data being traded, bought and sold. It was best to keep some shit low tech. For some reason, LEO's never seemed to expect that and that was a gas. Left us laughing all the way to the proverbial bank sometimes.

I went back out into the blistering heat and sun and mounted up, my ass thoroughly chapped from the ride, already putting me in a bad mood. Not knowing what I was about to find in that big house, souring it more with worry. Her tremulous voice, so full of hope – weepy, spirit crushed with fear playing on a loop in my head as I pulled back into her hood and set myself up as inconspicuously as possible, which wasn't saying much with this kind of rich. I stuck out like a sore thumb.

I didn't have long to wait, a text came through from an unknown number, 606 area code. Mother chapter – it had to be.

Green light. 15 minutes and counting. Better move.

That was a decent window, I'll tell you what. A lot of bad could go down in fifteen minutes. I started my bike, rode right down the block and through the open gate, parking my bike right out front but on the other side of the fountain, letting it block the view from the street.

I dismounted, went up to the door, and rang the bell, simple as that.

I was surprised when she answered, lip split, bruise spreading like a stain against her soft skin, discoloring her jaw. I scowled and pulled off my sunglasses.

"What are you *doing*?" she gasped, pretty dark eyes wide. Too much white surrounding them for my tastes. The sun kissing caramel in their depths where it shone over the fence, getting lower in the sky.

"Bianca! Who is it?"

I looked past her, jaw tightening at the living Ken doll walking up behind her.

"He do that?" I asked her, never taking my eyes off him.

She closed her mouth, her lips pursing into a grim line and she nodded.

"Excuse me? Who're you?" the man demanded and at the sound of his voice, she flinched.

"He do anything else to hurt you?" I asked, glancing back into the depths of her eyes and I saw it there, what he did. The shame, the fear, how she wilted like a flower left too long without water, left to the punishing rays of the sun to wilt and die.

I sniffed and nodded, clearing my throat of the rage blocking it, aware that the window was closing by the moment.

"Yeah." I pulled my piece while Ken was threating all sorts of shit, brought it up past Bianca whose eyes widened and before she could scream, I blew that fucker's head off in a welter of blood and bone.

Problem solved.

She turned and screamed, folding in on herself, tears pouring down her face and I grabbed her gently but firmly by the arm.

"Come on, baby. We've got to go."

I didn't expect her to take it well, I expected the screaming and the tears. It was a shock watching a man die the first time. It was awful. This wasn't my first time and it likely wouldn't be my last, but it was ranking high on the most righteous of kills I'd performed at the moment.

"Bianca, baby, *look at me*," I demanded and she tore her eyes off the dipshit's blood, leaking across his marble floor.

She brought her eyes around to mine and chest heaving, panting, locked onto my gaze.

"You with me?" I demanded. "You listening?"

"I-I-I'm listening."

"He ain't ever going to hurt you again. But we have to go now."

"Go?"

"The cameras are off, but only for a short while. We have to go before they come back on."

"Go where?" she asked. Lost.

"Home."

"They'll think I did this," she said sniffling, and I smiled a little sadly. Maybe. Maybe not, but that didn't matter now.

"Doesn't matter if they do. I've got you, now. You're safe and I'll fix it," I promised her.

"M-m-my documents, my passport –"

"I'll get you new ones. It's time to bounce. You called me, I came. You trust me?"

She looked up at me, broken, eyes glassy; her pain palpable.

"I don't know."

Good answer.

CHAPTER FIVE

*B*ianca...

I clung to him. He hadn't changed a bit in nine months. He was still a solid wall of muscle, he still walked with a limp, except now... now I was entirely unsure of my decision to call him.

He whisked me away on the back of his motorcycle in only the clothes that I wore and I was desperately afraid about what would happen to me.

What have I done? I asked myself over and over as the wind whipped my hair behind me, the hot air cutting through my thin athletic wear and we rode to – where, I don't know.

He stopped outside Vegas at this seedy roadside motel and pulled into a vacant parking space in front of the building, at the other end, away from the office. He leaned forward, shutting off the machine and folded his hands on the gas tank.

"Need you to get off first, this side, watch yourself on the pipes," he said gruffly, and I did as I was told. He sighed, and waited a mere moment before heaving himself up, dragging himself to his feet with a slight wince.

I stood still, or tried to. Hugging myself despite the oppressive desert heat, shaking on my feet. Desperate. Frightened. Hopeless.

In that moment, I felt better off dead.

"Easy," he said, putting hands to my shoulders, squaring himself up in front of me. My eyes climbed over the leather and patches on his chest. Over the faded Motörhead tee underneath, over the faded red bandana covering his chin, hanging loose around his neck, the dark beard bracketing his mouth set in a grim line.

Up the perfect, straight nose with the slight kink in the bridge just before his devastatingly deep dark eyes that were shrouded at the moment. Why, I didn't quite know.

"Don't fall apart on me, B. Not right now. Just a few more steps into that room," he took one hand off my shoulder and pointed at one of the doors, "and you can scream, cry; do whatever you need to do. But don't you *ever* fall apart where anyone but me can see it."

I stared up at him mutely, nodding dumbly and I think I even stopped shaking so badly.

"There's my girl," he murmured, and sliding fingertips over the cap of my shoulder and down my arm, he wrapped his large hand around mine and tugged gently.

I followed him the few steps to the door, jaw clenched tight, swallowing the endless screaming that wanted to crawl out of my throat. He rummaged in his pocket and unlocked the room's door and shoved it open, gesturing that I should go first. I did, and he slipped in behind me, closing the door on the outside world, the setting sun, and I think, with it, my old life.

"Do what you need to do," he muttered, tossing the room key on the little table with a clatter that spooked me and made me jump and all I could do was stand there, shake, and burst into sobs.

He shrugged out of his jacket and the leather vest layered over it, and with the creak of leather from his chaps, limped around my left to stand in front of me.

"What do you want me to do?" he whispered, holding his hands out, holding them up, a silent invitation for what, I didn't know. I put my hands in his, gasping for air as I cried and wept, sobbing brokenly, letting the panic seize me, without a clue as to how to stop any of it. He made soothing sounds and stood like a rock, just waiting on me – *me!* – to tell him what to do but I didn't know.

I didn't know what to do – and once again I found myself wishing for it all to stop. For the sweet oblivion of an eternal sleep.

"Okay," he murmured when there was no sign of my epic freak out abating. "Okay. Come on now, breathe, baby. Just breathe for me." He drew me in, my hands gripping his and I went – not knowing where else to go. Not knowing how else to deal, and even though I wasn't certain that I liked it, or wanted it, I let his massive arms go around me and leaned heavily on his giant, muscled chest.

Despite how his leg must have pained him, he held me up. He held me up until I was nothing left but a numb, empty withered husk of who I used to be.

CHAPTER SIX

*D*ump Truck…

She'd gone right over the high side. Lost all traction, her back tire spinning out, her entire being flung into the ether of chaos and discord. Her life truly altered. She'd been busted down to nothing and now it was clear, I was the only one left to build her back up.

Both of us needed some damn rest first.

I was surprised she let me hold her, with the state she was in. Eyes wild, hair wilder, face pale to the point her Vegas suntan was floating on the surface, artificial in its glow. The split in her lip looked bad, the bruise spreading out from it even worse and I knew my bruises. It had to be a couple of days old. I bet she'd called me, right after it'd happened.

I was glad she called me.

I was honestly amazed that she'd let me hold her. That she'd caved and had cuddled against my chest like a child afraid of the boogeyman. Except the boogeyman was dead. I'd slain the monster, but I bet she was trapped wondering what kind of monster I'd be. It was a legitimate question and the answer was a bigger monster than her man had been, just in a different kind of way.

She'd come and lain with me on the bed. Like once I had a hold on her, she hadn't wanted me to let go. So it was hella fucked up and disturbing when I woke to her broken weeping again. I sat up in the dark and froze. Her outline in the light from around the motel room's blinds put her on the floor, legs out to her side as she clutched something to her chest, rocking and softly keening.

I switched on the bedside lamp, squinting and froze all over again. She had my gun.

She looked up, tears streaming down her face.

"I'm so sorry," she said, brittle, broken. "I can't do this."

She put it to her head, pulled the trigger, fearless to the damn consequence but nothing happened. The fucking safety was on.

I lunged off the bed and ripped it from her hands, popping the mag, stripping back the slide and ejecting the round nestled in the chamber. I took it one step further, disassembling the thing and dropping the pieces to the carpet.

Let her figure that out.

Once it was done, I grabbed her, pulling her into my arms, holding her close, panting with the shot of adrenaline she'd given me.

I didn't know what to say, I wanted to curse her out – but I knew that was exactly the *wrong* thing to do.

"I got you, babe. You ain't going nowhere. It's *not* your time. I got you."

Except did I? I didn't know. This was certainly above my paygrade, but I was the only thing she got. I held her tight while she keened and whined, this wounded broken bird in my arms and *I* was afraid. Afraid I wouldn't do right by her, but that was the thing. You could never show fear, never show weakness. Showing those things was how you lost it all…

"I got you, B. Let it out, just let it out," I murmured beneath her wailing cries, until once again she exhausted herself into what I hoped was a dreamless sleep, curled against my chest as I sat there, not knowing what to fucking do.

I sat there for a long time, leg out straight, shaking a bit with exertion at keeping myself and Bianca upright with nothing supporting my back. With a great reluctance, I finally had to give in, murmuring, "C'mon, baby, help me get you up and back into bed, huh?"

I shook her gently and she sucked in a breath, raising her head.

"I don't know why you would want me after…"

"Shhh…" I soothed. "Not now. One thing at a time. Up you go." She got up, and I did too, with a lot more trepidation. It was a bitch getting off the floor when only one leg bent or worked right.

I couldn't get my right one up under me to leverage me into a standing position. Finally, after a few false starts, Bianca got in there and helped me, and I hated that. I can't tell you how much. She needed me, it shouldn't be the other way around. Not now, anyway.

"I'm sorry," she said finally, miserably, standing there hugging herself as though she were cold.

"Don't be," I said solemnly. "I get it."

She looked at me and I took a deep breath and let it out slow.

"Just stay with me, just for now. I'll get you home and I promise, shit'll get better."

She covered her mouth with her hand and I waved her to me. She took a false step forward, paused, and came to me and I sat her down on the edge of the bed.

"Lie down. Try to get some sleep. Things'll be clearer in the morning, I promise you."

She laid back down, and I laid down with her, she slept, I didn't. When I was sure she was out this time and wouldn't wake, I slipped out from behind her and got up, picking up the pieces of my weapon and putting them back together. I secured it in the back of my waistband, pulling my tee over the back of it. I picked up my phone and unplugged it from the charger and dialed up Mav, slipping out the motel room while she slumbered unawares.

I went over to my bike and dropped my big ass onto the seat with a wince as it rang through.

"Hey, what's going on?"

I told Mav what was up. He listened, silently, and let out a long controlled breath on the other end of the line.

"Shit, Bro. I'm sorry."

"Yeah, me too. I'm in over my head and I don't know what to do here."

"Honestly, every woman's different," he said quietly. "She's having a solid breakdown and who can blame her?"

"What's the chatter?" I asked.

"Home invasion robbery," he said, and I knew that he would know. "Right now, she's just 'missing' so you watch yourself coming home."

"Not even sure how I'm gonna get her home. She's just got this dumb shit women's workout gear on. I could use some kind of assist. She's not dressed for any kind of slide should we take one."

"There's the safety Nazi I know and love," my president said slyly. I chuckled, but it was bitter.

"Where you at right now?"

"Shitty little rathole motel outside and to the north of Vegas," I answered.

"Gimme the name."

I did.

"Know her size?" he asked.

"Fuck no."

"Find it out and text me, I'll see if I can't get a couple of the boys from Eastern Oregon to come down and bring you some leathers."

"Appreciate it. As much as I hate to say it, I need to get some distance between her and this hellhole. Maybe they can meet us half-way. I come north, they come south. Maybe hook up in the middle some kind of way."

"Not a bad idea, get me those sizes. I'll arrange something, then get your ass back to Rat City."

"Sir, yes, sir," I ground out and we ended the call. I threw my head back and stared at the stars for a long fuckin' minute and if ever I wished on one, I wished now - *let me do what needs doin' to make her whole.*

I sniffed, cleared my throat and stood up. If any of that were to happen, I had some work to do first.

I went back in the room, carefully checked her tags, and figured out her sizes – shooting a text to Mav with what I knew. Then I settled in to stare at the ceiling 'til sunrise.

CHAPTER SEVEN

 he lost girl...

"Mornin'."

I woke to D.T. holding down a cup of coffee in front of my nose. I pushed myself up to a sitting position and he took a step back, giving me some space, some room to breathe.

"What time is it?" I asked, automatically out of reflex. It didn't really matter what the time was. I guess it was just something *normal* to ask...

"Just after seven, maybe closer to eight, I think."

I took the offered cup and asked, "Where did you get this?"

"Hotel lobby. It's shitty, but I did what I could with the sugar and creamer they had available."

"Thanks," I whispered and took a drink. It wasn't the worst coffee I'd ever had, but it was definitely a close second. I swallowed it anyway and took another drink, hoping it might get better.

"So what's the plan for today?" I asked, as he moved around the room, gearing up to ride.

"I don't like it, but we ride north. We're meeting up with some of the guys from the Eastern Oregon chapter when we stop for the night. They're gonna bring you some proper riding gear."

"Why?" I asked.

"Excuse me?" He cocked his head and raised an eyebrow.

"I mean, why would they do that? They don't know me…"

"You're right, they don't, but they know *me* and the rest of my chapter. We all belong to the same club and that's what we do. Look out for each other."

I nodded. "Sorry, I didn't mean to offend you."

He raised a shoulder in a shrug and dropped it.

"You didn't. You're a citizen. I wouldn't expect you to understand our ways."

"It's um, scary," I said.

"What?"

"Going that fast with nothing between me and the road."

"Scary good, or scary bad?"

I thought about it.

"After what happened to you," I said gesturing to his bad leg, "a little bit of both, maybe more scary bad."

He nodded gravely and said, "Glad you were paying attention."

We were silent for a moment while I finished my coffee and he asked me, "How you feeling this morning?"

"Like a used Band-Aid," I said, making a face.

He chuckled, and I suppose it did sound sort of funny, but then he asked, "How's that?"

"Dirty, disgusting, and useless now that I've served my purpose, I guess."

He frowned.

"What purpose was that?" he asked.

I swallowed hard and murmured, "I'd rather not talk about it, if that's alright with you." I couldn't look at him, not directly. He stood still at the edge of my vision where I'd fixed it on my carpet and finally he shifted slightly on his feet and said, "Fine by me." His tone was gentle, almost sweet, and I looked back at him. Something was in his eyes, not pity, but close enough.

I stood, agitated, not knowing what to do and made the excuse, "I have to pee."

"We got time," he said and I set my half empty coffee aside and went into the bathroom, shutting the door behind me.

I let out a pent-up breath I hadn't realized I'd been holding and looked at myself in the mirror.

I didn't recognize the woman looking back at me.

The woman looking back at me was a bona fide mess of a human being. Hair wild and tangled, eyes too wide and red rimmed, face too pale, making the bruises stand out in sharp relief. The woman who stared at me was a wild animal, skittish, afraid, cheekbones standing out in sharp relief, the hollows beneath them sunken like I'd never seen before.

Her makeup was cried off, her light smattering of freckles showing and her heart, ragged on her sleeve.

I used the bar of hotel soap and scrubbed my face twice, wiping the tears and what was left of my careful mascara, meant to please Guy, away.

"He's dead," I whispered at the strange woman's reflection. "He can't and won't hurt you anymore."

But she was still afraid. *I* was still afraid.

"Hey, B. We gotta hit the road…"

I straightened and nodded, the lost girl in the mirror nodding with me and said, "Okay, I'm coming."

I used the bathroom, washed my hands, and left the bathroom. D.T. waiting patiently outside.

"Come here," he ordered gently and I went to him. He held out his jacket, the vest thing he wore over it already off and on his body. I turned and let him help me into it.

It was way too big, but definitely afforded more protection than the lightweight athletic jacket I used for running. I looked at it, laying on the bed and turned my head to look up at him.

"Won't you burn?" I asked quietly.

He held up a bottle of sunscreen and flipped it over in his hand.

"Motel had a gift shop. These are for you, too." He handed me a pair of ugly wraparound sunglasses, the lenses a reflective neon blue.

"Stylish," I said dryly and he chuckled.

"You'll be glad for them, trust me."

"Wind dries out your eyeballs, right?" I murmured. I remembered that from last night.

"Among other things. Nothing like a bug in your eye. At sixty, it could do some real damage."

"Eugh." I made a face and he smiled, a brittle thing and I knew the sentiment. I wasn't feeling much better.

"One more thing," he said, and held out a black bandana emblazoned with the famous Las Vegas sign in this god-awful repeating pattern.

"Over your nose and mouth. Keeps the bugs out of your teeth."

"Gross." I took it gratefully when he put it that way.

"Here, let me help you with it," he murmured and I turned away from him, letting him secure it behind my head, around my nose and mouth.

"Okay. Here's the deal. You need to take a leak, you tap my shoulder twice and give me this signal –" He flashed a signal with his hand. "Do it for me."

I repeated the motion until he was satisfied I had it.

"Food is this," he showed me. "Drink is this," he showed me another one. "Don't hesitate. As it is, we're gonna be stopping every hour to an hour and a half to hydrate. I've got bottled water at the bike."

"Okay."

He reached out a careful hand and paused, and when I didn't flinch or pull away, he cupped my cheek, running his thumb in a slow careful stroke along my cheek, beneath my eye, at the line cut by the bandana.

I closed my eyes and felt strange at that touch. Both quailing on the inside at it and desperate to lean into it. It was confusing and I eventually turned out of it, away from it, and swallowing hard said, "I thought we needed to go."

"Fair enough," he said with a careful nod and we went out to the bike.

It was not comfortable, or easy, but stopping every hour or so *did* help. He made me drink an entire bottle of water at each stop and never complained when I tapped him and indicated my need to pee when we approached a rest stop.

I don't know how long we rode, but despite his desire to get wherever it was we were headed for tonight, he refused to go more than five miles per hour above the speed limit. I asked him about that at one of the few rest stops we stopped at and he'd simply chuckled and said, "The last thing I need is another fast-riding award."

I'd frowned and asked what that was and he'd grinned and said, "A speeding ticket is what you citizens call it."

I'd laughed, probably for the first time in I didn't know how long and his smile had grown. It felt strange to do it, but it gave me hope, too. I was still scared. Still didn't know what was going to happen to me, but whatever it was… it couldn't possibly get any worse at this point than what I'd already gone through.

The second I thought it, was the second my heart sank. Right on the heels of that thought was *way to jinx it, you stupid woman.*

By the time we crossed into Oregon, I wanted to quit. It was still all ugly scrub and high desert, and I longed for the green of pine and humid air of the bay. For snowcapped mountains and air that wasn't so oppressive and hot.

I had hated every minute of Vegas and I longed to be home, even though I didn't technically have any home to go back to.

We stopped halfway, at some random Denny's for some food. He always paid for everything in cash. Had a great wad of bills in the top of one of his boots, secured with a rubber band that he would replenish what he wished to carry in his wallet from. All of them were smaller bills. Very few greater than a twenty.

He saw me looking at him curiously and smiled crookedly saying, "Explain later." I nodded and we were back on our way.

It was mind numbing, exhausting being buffeted by the wind with only my wretched thoughts for company, but hypnotizing and almost freeing at the same time.

I held onto D.T. as we took straightaways and leaned what felt like precariously into sweeping curves. There were points during the ride where we took exits and rode along regular town streets and along stretches of highways through towns.

Eventually, on one such stretch of highway, he slowed and thumbed a switch on his controls. I held on, preparing for the turn, and we swept off the road and into the parking lot for another rundown motel.

This time, two men in the same type of motorcycle gear, wearing the same type of vest that Dump Truck did, were waiting for us. The only difference that I could see was the bottom patch of the back of their vests read 'E. Oregon' instead of 'W. Washington' like Dump Truck's did.

They hailed Dump Truck and one of them put out his cigarette and I tried not to stiffen on the bike behind him. He said going stiff or ridged made it harder for him to drive, that I needed to relax and try my best to enjoy the ride.

I held onto him a little tighter and was relieved when he pulled into an empty parking stall by theirs. He tapped my knee twice, the signal to get down off the bike for him and I did, careful of the pipes like he'd told me to be.

"Whoa-ho! Good to see you, brother!" one of the men cried and Dump Truck sat up straighter, holding out his hand and grasping the man's forearm up near the elbow. They banged chests in an awkward hug as I worked the clasp on the chin strap of the spare helmet D.T. had brought with him for my use.

I watched warily as Dump Truck put down the stand to his motorcycle and leaned the bike onto it. He shut it off and said, "Preacher, good to see you, man."

"I'm Guano," the other guy said, eyes fixed unnervingly on me.

I raised a hand weakly and curled my fingers in a slight wave.

"You sure you want to stay here?" Preacher asked. "We got room at the club."

"Ah, yeah, here's fine man. It's not for me, it's for Wounded Bird. She needs some serious calm right now. A place to heal."

Both sets of eyes drifted in my direction and I pulled down the crappy bandana covering my nose and mouth. Something flashed in Preacher's eyes, something cold and unfathomable.

"Hope you served him up his balls on a plate," Guano said and spit on the ground.

"Blew his fucking head off," Dump Truck said matter-of-factly and I felt my eyes flare. *Was he crazy!?*

"Easy, darlin'. You're among friends, here. No secrets required." Preacher winked one of his bright blue eyes at me. He was a handsome man. Dark hair graying at the temples, another swath of gray dusting his stubble.

By comparison, Guano was small and dark. Mexican by the look of it, he had a scar that ran like a part through his super short black hair. His eyes, a warm, rich brown were cold as ice and there was something incredibly *off* about him.

"I'm going to get us a room, Wounded Bird," Dump Truck said. "See if I can't get you back to Little Bird with some rest. You want to stay out here or come with me?" he asked.

"Might draw unwanted attention if she goes into the office with you looking like that," Guano said and I swallowed hard.

"I'll be fine," I murmured.

"You sure?" D.T. asked me and he searched my face. I nodded and made sure to keep his motorcycle between me and the two men here to meet us.

"Just hurry… please?"

"You're alright with us," Preacher promised. He looked down to the shorter man and said a little more sternly, "Isn't that right?"

"Oh yeah," Guano agreed. "That's right."

"Back in a flash," D.T. promised and he made a point to lean down and kiss the top of my head. I closed my eyes and tried not to cringe away from the touch. I just knew he wouldn't do it if there weren't a reason.

"We'll be right here," Preacher assured him.

Guano tilted his head in this unnerving way and looked me over from head to my feet while I huddled in D.T.'s leather jacket.

"Guano…" Preacher said in warning.

I bit my lips together, afraid of making the observation that the way Guano looked at me was as though he wondered what I would look like without my skin. I honestly and truly didn't want to know.

"I know how Dump Truck got his name, he told me," I said softly. "How did you get yours?"

Preacher smiled kindly while Guano scowled at me.

"You're new to the life, I take it. That's not something you're supposed to ask one of us."

"Oh, I'm sorry, I didn't know… I was just trying to make conversation."

"It's alright, for now. Just know if you ask the wrong guy he could get kind of uppity." Preacher took a seat against what must have been his bike, a Harley like Dump Truck's only not quite as big. More sleek and a flat black with glossy red pinstripes along the tank.

Guano's bike was way flashier by comparison and had the stylized Mother Mary with the golden and pink halo all around her that was popular with Mexican culture. It was beautifully done on his tank and his bike had a lot more chrome than either Preacher or Dump Truck's.

"What's *your* name?" Guano asked, and I licked my lips that were suddenly dry.

"I… I don't know anymore," I said honestly. D.T. had taken great care not to use it, so I figured maybe I shouldn't.

Guano made a sound of detest and Preacher side-eyed him.

"I rest my case," Preacher said dryly and I nodded.

"I really am sorry," I said. "I didn't know it was a rule."

Guano nodded, but he didn't look happy about it.

"Everything okay out here?" Dump Truck leaned out of the office door and I nodded.

"I think so," I said gently.

"Preacher?" he asked.

"Just fine, brother."

"Just a few more seconds, babe. I'm just waiting on a key."

"Okay," I murmured.

We waited him out the rest of the time in silence. It just seemed safer that way.

CHAPTER EIGHT

*D*ump Truck...

An awkward silence had descended on the trio by the time I came back out with the key to our room. I'd ducked out one more time to ask my wounded bird if she'd wanted one bed or two, not wanting to take it for granted that she was cool sleeping with me another night.

"Two, if it's okay?" she'd asked and I'd ducked back in. The clerk had agreed and switched out my key for a different one. Second floor this time, and I was cool with that. Damn sure no one would be looking for Bianca in Burns, Oregon.

I went back out and the silence had only intensified, Guano on edge. I picked up rather quickly that B. must have said something or other to rub the little dude the wrong way. I just hoped he hadn't hit on her and was bristling at a rejection. She was mine as far as I was concerned, with all that entailed.

"You all set?" Preacher asked, getting into one of his saddlebags.

"Good to go." I nodded and got into mine, grabbing my duffel of clean clothes. It was high time for a change but I'd let Bianca go first.

I had her go in front of me, directing her with gentle low

comments, keeping myself between her and what to her were strange men. I handed her the key to our room outside the door and let her key us in. She moved in slowly at first, cautious, until her eyes adjusted to the gloom.

"What have you got for us, Preacher?"

"Just what you asked for," he said handing over a Walmart reusable shopping bag stuffed to the gills with black leather.

"Sweet," I grunted, accepting it from him. I went through it with Bianca while chatting with Preacher and Guano. There was a sturdy pair of leather pants, some chaps, a pair of jeans, and a Sacred Hearts' Eastern Oregon chapter ladies' cut tee. There was even a ladies' cut leather jacket someone's ol' lady might have out grown with a pregnancy or something.

What there wasn't was any socks or underthings. Nothing to sleep in, either, but we could make do with some of my shit for sleep. At least I hoped so.

I sighed and said, "Thank you, man. This'll get us home just fine."

"Not a problem, my brother. Anything else you might need?"

"Socks, underwear and a pair of boots. Think I can front you some cash and you could hit the local Wally World or Target for me?"

"Guano?" Preacher asked, eying him coolly.

"Yeah sure, I live to serve," the smaller dude said and I laughed a bit.

"Wounded Bird, you go on in and get a shower," I told her and held out one of my clean tees. She took it with a nod and a murmured 'thanks' slipping off into the bathroom, shutting and locking the door.

"She's in real bad shape, yeah?" Preacher asked softly once the water started. I nodded, peeling off some bills from the wad in my wallet.

"For the socks and undies, just get a pack of whatever's cheap," I told Guano. "She wears a size large in the tights or whatever she's got on. Shoe size nine and a half. Whatever you can get her, even if they're women's steel-toed work boots. It's a lot safer than the running shoes she's got on."

"You got it, but you owe me a beer – and please don't tell me she's on the rag and needs tampons or some shit."

I laughed, and Preacher told him, "Motherfucker, you're a Sacred Heart. Start acting like it. Ain't nobody gonna say shit, you buyin' ladies things."

Guano glared at us both and pushed off the wall he was leaning against by the door. "I'm buying some beer with what's left, homeboy. I'll bring it back with me," he said, and I opened up my wallet and handed him another twenty.

"Load up, brother. I could use a cold one."

"What d'you like?"

"None of that Mexican shit – other than Corona. That shit's alright as long as you got the limes to go with it."

"What, you a Bud Light drinking motherfucker?" he demanded, grabbing his crotch. I laughed.

"Naw, I like the microbrew and craft shit."

"Jesus Christ, one of those hipster beer junkies," Preacher ribbed.

"Damn right, I'm a beer snob. Get me an Irish Death if you can find it out this a way."

"Got it, anything else, Princess?"

"Nah, I think that's it," I said, ignoring the jibe.

He opened up the motel room door and went out, Preacher laughing and taking a seat at the small table in the corner of the room.

"What'd she say to piss him off?" I asked once I heard his bike fire up.

"Asked us how we got our names," he said and I nodded.

"She ain't in the life," I told him.

"I gathered," he said dryly. "A little behind on the curve."

"Other things have taken precedence. One crisis at a time."

"No, I hear you. You wanna campfire?" he asked. I sighed.

"The short version? We hooked up once a while back, then out of the blue she calls me but she don't sound the same… Asks me to come get her. So I went and got her." I shrugged my shoulders.

"She must have left quite the impression," he said smoothly, leaning back in his seat and crossing his arms. He looked me over, coolly appraising.

"Yeah," I agreed.

The shower cut and both of our heads turned. He raised his

eyebrows, and I turned my head with a look that plainly said, *I know. I got my work cut out for me.*

He nodded and said, "You guys hungry at all? I can have Guano pick up some food on his way back."

I laughed some and said, "Think I've pushed my luck enough already."

"Eh, you know how it goes."

"That I do."

"Needing some absolution?" he asked and I shook my head.

"Nah, I'm good. Thanks though, man."

Preacher was the East Oregon chapter's Chaplain. The closest thing to a Preacher or Priest us brothers had. He was the one to show up when a brother was drunk, fucked up, or on the brink. We had a chaplain ourselves. Deacon was our guy.

He'd been at the hospital every day while I'd been laid up. Had been prepared to give my ass last rites if it'd come to it. When one of us felt the need to confess our sins, it was our club chaplain to hear them.

"I may have killed the man, but the way I reckon, I didn't do anything evil by taking that fucker out. Just the opposite. I did the world some fuckin' good."

Preacher nodded gravely. He knew how it was, better than most of us. He was a Vet. Had served damn near twenty years overseas as a chaplain in the military. He'd seen it all.

The bathroom door opened and B. peeked out, her shoulders dropping with some relief when she realized it was just me and Preacher.

"It's all clear," I told her, and she pursed her lips and gave a nod.

"Sorry, I don't mean to be rude at all," she stammered and Preacher held up a hand.

"Guano got his name because he's a batshit crazy little fucker. I got mine because I was an Army chaplain going on almost twenty years. Now I'm club chaplain for the Sacred Hearts' Eastern Oregon chapter. I don't mind sharin' my story, but just like you probably don't want to share how you're 'Wounded Bird' right now, some of us don't want to advertise where we come from either."

She nodded, huddling in my shirt which was way too short with nothing else on under it. I went over and peeled back the blankets on the bed furthest from the window and door to the little room. I was happy to put my big ass between the outside and her. One more obstacle to go through.

"Come on, get in. You ain't gotta sleep yet, but let's get you covered up."

She got into the bed and I dropped the blankets over her long legs.

Preacher sighed and said, "You want I should step out while he takes his turn? I can if it'd make you more comfortable," he offered. She shook her head.

"No, it's alright."

He nodded and thrust his chin at the bathroom door.

"Hurry up and get your big ass in and out so she ain't gotta deal with Guano without you."

I gave a nod, grabbed some clean clothes and went in, showering quickly, skipping my hair and just washing my face and body. She'd used the little bottles of shampoo and conditioner anyway and I could deal with it at home just as easily.

When I got out, I dried off in record time, and got into a clean pair of jeans. I skipped the shirt, since she was wearing it and went back out into the room just as Guano opened the door and came in, a few Walmart bags in one hand and a six-pack of Shock Top in the other. I spied a couple of bottles of Irish Death in the bags, though.

"My man," I said with a nod and he grinned at me, a gold canine winking at me in the diffuse light of the room.

I went through the bags as soon as he set them on the table and pulled out the four-pack of cotton underwear he'd grabbed for Bianca, leaning over and tossing it to her when she was ready to catch it. She opened it immediately and swept the first pair under the sheets, working them up her legs and arching her hips to get them over her ass.

"Beer, honey?" Preacher asked her and she nodded, settling.

"Yes, please." He handed me one and I took it to her, my leg stiff and my gait uneven the few paces it took to get over to her.

She drank from the neck of the bottle greedily, and I couldn't tell if she was thirsty or if it was for the alcohol and the edges it might dull.

Preacher popped the top on one of my Irish Deaths with a fob on his keys and passed it over through Guano.

"Thanks, man."

Bianca settled in, lying on her side, hands tucked under her pillow listening to us as we swapped news and traded stories. We kept it mostly above board, talking about what was coming through the boneyard back on my side of the mountains and who was doing what with their bike restoration projects.

There was bitchin' about club bunnies and sweet butts, moaning and groaning over ol' ladies getting too big for their britches, and the usual talk of chicanery and fuckery on any given Saturday night.

All of it legal, all of it perfectly acceptable for Bianca to hear. The dead soldiers were clustered on the little table when Preacher sighed. It was getting pretty late.

"It was good seeing you, brother," he said finally, and we all stood, me from my bed and Preacher and Guano from the two chairs in the room.

"Likewise, man. Thanks so much for the assist – the both of you really helped my ass out."

"Don't mention it," Guano said and that was cool. We were square.

I shut them on the outside and turned. Bianca's gaze was tranquil for the first time since I'd picked her up, exhaustion playing into it, sure, but I think the two beers she'd drunk certainly helped. Whatever, though. Any port in a storm. I still took my damn gun apart again and dumped it in the drawer of the bedside table.

"I changed my mind, I think," she murmured and scooted aside.

I nodded and said, "You want to tell me why?"

"I feel safe with you, I guess," she said and shifted slightly uncomfortably as though she were being called out. That wasn't my intention.

"Cool," I grunted. "I was just curious."

She settled and I went over, dropping on top of the covers and raising an arm in invitation. She scooted closer and laid her head on my chest and I sighed.

"Anything you want to talk about, I'm here to listen," I told her.

"I don't want to talk," she said softly.

"That's okay, too."

I kissed her forehead and her eyes drifted shut.

"Sleep well," I told her and she drew in a slow but deep breath, letting it out a little shaky.

In with the good, out with the bad. At least, I hoped so.

CHAPTER NINE

$\mathcal{W}$ounded Bird...

"Bianca, wake up, baby. Come on, it's time to go."

I groaned, wincing, a big hand settling on my shoulder, shaking me gently, smoothing down my body to that dip, just before the swell of my hip. I froze and he kept it there, going no higher and no lower, an almost comforting weight once I realized it was Dump Truck and no one else.

"Come on, baby. It's time to get a move on."

"What time is it?" I muttered, stalling.

"After eight. We're on the home stretch. We'll be home by tonight."

I groaned and pushed myself up into a sitting position.

"Atta girl," he praised, the deep timbre of his voice holding the edge of a smile.

"I don't know if I can take anymore riding," I said with a yawn, stretching. "How much longer?"

"Around eight hours, I'm afraid and it's going to get dicey. It's raining up the way all through Western Washington."

"Grooooss," I whined and he chuckled.

"Still beats riding in a cage," he said and I frowned, pouting at him.

"Says you."

He chuckled again and sighed.

"Suppose a grocery getter is in my near future," he said ruefully.

"Why can't any of you call it what it is?" I asked.

"What's that?"

"A *car*."

"That's a citizen word, and you, my dear, are a citizen no more."

I frowned and eyed him as he laid out what I was expected to wear that day, not that I could complain. The clothes may not have been mine, but they were *clean* and offered way more protection than what I'd made my escape in. I groaned and scrubbed my face with my hands and said, "You must think I'm a total rich bitch prima donna."

"Why you say that?" he asked with a faint smile.

"I called, you came, even though I slipped out while you were sleeping. You take me out of that house of horrors and all I can seem to do is sit here and bitch about *everything*."

He chuckled and shook his head.

"You know what it takes to achieve the Iron Butt challenge?" he asked.

"No, what?"

"A thousand miles in twenty-four hours."

"Is that what we've done?" I asked and he laughed.

"No, but we'll have covered around eleven hundred miles over two days for you. That's a lot of miles in a very short time for a woman who's never ridden before. I got a serious case of monkey butt just coming to get you. I can't imagine you aren't feeling the same thing by now."

"Iron butt, monkey butt, are there any more 'butts' I need to know about?" I asked.

"Nah, monkey butt is essentially being really saddle sore. Chafed, like your ass is swollen like a monkey's butt."

"Now *that* I *am* feeling. Just promise me that after today, I can sleep for like a week uninterrupted and I *might* be able to make it." I dragged myself to my feet and into the bathroom, groaning. "Ugh, what I wouldn't give for a toothbrush and some toothpaste.

He dug into the side of his gym bag behind me while I drank wearily from the tap and when I straightened, he held out the items.

"You can use mine. I mean, we've kissed before so it's –"

I snatched the items cutting him off, "Oh, my God I don't even care! You have no idea!" I cried and he smiled nodding.

"I'll be right out, I promise."

"Better be, you got the shirt I need to wear on."

"Oh!"

I pursed my lips and took a deep breath. It wasn't anything he hadn't seen before. I pulled it off over my head, glad for the panties at least, and covered my breasts with one arm – holding it out to him.

He took it and gave a nod, and I shut the bathroom door.

A moment later after I'd peed, washed my hands, and had begun to brush my teeth he called through the door, "I got the key and everything else. I'll see you down by the bike. Give you some privacy to get dressed."

"Okay!" I called out, and he left me to it.

I stared in the mirror as I brushed my teeth and today was just a little better. I had more color and didn't quite look so lost. The hurt was there, but there was also hope and I could see why D.T. had started to call me 'Wounded Bird.'

I was hurt, incredibly so, but I also, incredibly, started to see some healing begin. My lip wasn't as swollen, the cut scabbed and not quite so fresh. I no longer could taste the copper tang of blood, but the cut on the inside of my lip stung horribly with the introduction of the minty toothpaste.

The shadow on the underside of my jaw had begun to retreat, the deepest, darkest part of the bruise beginning to turn that sickly green and yellow as it began to fade.

Four or so more days and there wouldn't be any more physical evidence of what I'd endured left.

I closed my eyes and breathed in slowly, letting it out measured and controlled. I didn't really care if I ever saw my father again after this. I was certainly glad that Guy was dead. That he wouldn't be able to do this ever again – certainly not to any other woman.

I opened my eyes and said to my reflection, "One more day. Come on. You can do it."

I wasn't just talking about the ride I was about to endure, either. I went out into the room and dressed, the leather pants a little tight, but doable. The boots were my size, functional and steel-toed. I had to hand it to Guano, he'd picked a pair that had purple accents at the inside of the padded ankle and on the laces. There weren't many 'pretty' work boots out there, but he'd certainly tried his best with these despite giving me every indication that I'd horribly offended him and had made him angry.

I pulled on a pair of the socks from the package and shoved my feet into the boots, laced them up and stood.

I *really* didn't want to put on the gross sports bra I had been sweating in and gross for the last two days, but I didn't really have anything else. I decided to forgo it and slipped the tee over my head. I huffed a breath, pulled on the jacket and stuffed my bra, the rest of the socks, my dirty pair of panties from last night; the panties that still remained in the pack – all of it into one of the Walmart sacks. The empty shoebox I left along with my panties and athletic leggings from Vegas for the trash.

With one last lingering look of disdain, I decided I didn't want anything from that place. Underdressed or not, and I left the bra too.

Fuck it. If I was going to start again from nothing, let it literally be *from nothing.*

As far as I was concerned, Bianca Evans was dead. She was no longer someone I wanted to know.

I went out onto the walkway and peered over. Dump Truck looked up at me and smiled, nodding.

"It's a good look for you, babe."

I cracked a smile and gave a nod in return and asked, "Got an extra hair tie?"

His smile grew and he nodded. "Toss me that bag and come on down here."

I dropped the bag over the railing and he caught it. By the time I reached the ground, traversing the parking lot to him and the bike, he had a brush out and an extra hair tie. I pulled his toothpaste and toothbrush from where I'd stuck it into the jacket pocket.

"Thanks," he said shoving them in his back pocket. "Turn around and have a seat."

I did as I was told, and he brushed the tangles out of my hair which was back to its natural waves before he twisted it into a braid, tying off the end. He whipped out a clean, stiff bandana, likely bought at the Walmart the day before and I looked up at him and smiled as he folded it into a triangle in front of my face. It was much better than the Vegas one. Black and edged in red roses, bordered in a sort of bike chain repeating pattern in white.

I let him affix it over my nose and mouth, tying it off. He already had my helmet down here and handed it to me.

"Wait until I back out before you get on," he said, starting it up.

I nodded and stepped back to give him room as I fixed my chin strap myself. He handed over a new pair of women's bug-eyed sunglasses and slipped his wraparounds on as I got on behind him.

"Let's go get some breakfast," he said and I nodded.

I settled behind him, held on, and away we went.

It was different today – less scary, more thrilling. The new, better protective gear did wonders for my sense of security, allowing me to relax and actually enjoy the ride today.

We put some miles between us and Burns before stopping. The brown was turning more from desert to hills full of scrub. It was still brown, but a different kind of brown that was beginning to give way to green. The further north we rode, the easier on the eyes the scenery became, and with less brown and more green, the knot in the center of my chest began to ease.

We stopped as much as I needed to, and like the day before, he never complained. We made it all the way to I-5 before we met the rain.

I closed my eyes and held on. Riding in the rain was certainly *not* my favorite thing. For one, the water seeped in *everywhere*, leaving me cold and clammy, and two, the spray kicked up by the other cars and trucks just felt *dirty* and *grimy* and the misery was just beginning.

For two-and-a-half hours, I clung to Dump Truck as he carefully steered us up the sopping interstate. My heart was most definitely in my throat the whole way. The fear and adrenaline keeping me from feeling the effects of the bone-chilling cold.

Riding in the rain in Western Washington in September was no joke, especially for the distance we had to go.

I nearly wept with relief when we reached the Highway 518 turn off to take us past the airport. It meant we were almost there. Any exposed skin I had felt raw with the cold and stinging rain that relentlessly hit it, and I was beginning to fear I would *never* know what it was to be warm again.

He took expediency over comfort and turned us onto 509 North to the 128th Street exit in Burien. A few scant blocks to 1st Avenue, he went right. I shivered against his back all the way to 117th and the turn to his apartment building.

By the time we turned off the street and under the covered parking, I felt the very chill of Death's bony hand along my spine.

"Ahhh, shit!" Dump Truck cried, straightening his bad leg as I clambered off the bike.

"You okay?" I called over the drum of the rain which had intensified.

"The cold and the damp is always a bitch, how are you?"

I pulled the bandana off of my face and said, "If that's what waterboarding feels like, then no, thank you!"

He laughed and shook his head and leveraged himself up onto his good leg, taking more than a couple attempts to get his bad one back over the bike's seat. I winced in sympathy.

He took me by the elbow and steered me in the direction of the stairwell to take us up to the front of the building giving us access to his apartment.

Like the first and only other time I had been here, I couldn't wait to get inside. I only wished it were for the same reason, but I was worried those days of carefree excitement were behind me.

I wasn't the same girl. Not by a long shot… nor would I ever be again.

CHAPTER TEN

*D*ump Truck…

Shit, she was fucking *freezing*. Dangerously so. I don't think she realized it, but her lips were tinged an alarming blue color when she pulled her bandana down. She was so cold that she couldn't stop shaking and her teeth chattered to an alarming degree. I wasn't in much better shape, and I wanted to fix things so bad, I sailed right into being a real pushy bastard which went at odds with keeping her boundaries intact.

"Come on, let's get you out of these wet clothes," I ordered as soon as we were through my front door.

I grasped the collar of her jacket and peeled her out of it. She didn't resist, simply unzipped it down the front and let me take it from her shoulders.

I hung both it and my own dripping jacket and cut on the coat-tree inside the door, sitting on the linoleum entryway so they could drip dry.

"This way." I took her hand and led her to my too small bathroom. She trailed along behind me and I went in, getting the shower running, looking behind me and ordering her to get out of her shoes.

She kneeled down and worked at the laces while I toed out of my motorcycle boots and kicked them into the alcove between the sink and the toilet out from underfoot. I ditched my piece in the empty bottom drawer of my bathroom sink's cabinet and kicked it shut. She stood, stripped of socks and boots and I grasped the hem of her soaked tee.

"Arms up," I said shortly and she hesitated. "Not trying to get fresh with you, just trying to get us both *warm*, baby."

She put her arms up and I peeled off the shirt and saw why the hesitation. No bra, just her perfect pair of tits, nipples tight buds, stiff enough to cut glass with the chill. *Fuck* that was hot, and I had to send my mind into overdrive to keep my cock shriveled in my pants. The cold helped, but not that damn much.

"Turn," I ordered, and she gave me her back, her arms covering her chest, as the bathroom began to warm and steam began to creep over the rail holding the shower curtain. I pulled my tee over my head and tossed it in the sink with hers. I reached around her, pressing my chest to her chilled back, and went for the fly of her leather pants. She leaned back against me and let me work, the involuntary trembling of her lithe body violent. I took down the leather jeans, panties and all, peeling them down her legs and she did her best to help. It still took a couple tries to step out of them all the way.

I kicked them on top of my boots to deal with them later and turned her, side-stepping to rotate us both in the direction of the shower.

"Get in, join you in a sec," I warned her.

"Okay," she murmured gently, her voice a bit lackluster, and I both felt bad and didn't – at war with myself over it. I just wanted her warm and I was sure desperate to get there myself. Still, I didn't want to set her back. She was doing better today it seemed, and I wanted her to continue to do better.

One crisis at a time, I reminded myself.

I got out of my chaps and peeled out of my jeans, stepping on the cuffs, dragging my bad leg out the rest of the way. It was paining me something awful with the cold and the struggle was getting tougher with the sounds coming from my shower, her moaning and groaning as the hot water worked its magic on both the chill and sore muscles.

"I'm coming in," I warned her, and I pulled back the curtain enough to step over the edge of the tub. It was awkward, but I managed without looking like a total dumbass. I fucking hated this leg of mine sometimes.

She looked back over her shoulder, my little wounded bird, her arms crossed in front of her chest as she huddled in the spray. The long, nude line of her back interrupted by healing bruises, fingerprints left on the outsides of her hips and thighs. I didn't let my gaze linger. I just silently took stock of what visible sign of her injuries remained and felt sick at the confirmation of my unspoken assumption that she'd been raped.

"Easy, just me. Just Dump Truck. I didn't get to do this before. Take care of you. Feel like I need to make up for lost time." I touched her elbow lightly and she turned slowly, keeping her arms over her chest, which was okay.

Her chin trembled, but her teeth weren't chattering anymore. Her expression crumbling as she shook with the beginnings of a sob and I merely opened my arms. She took a halting step forward and bowed her forehead to my chest and wept, and I let her. Holding her lightly, soaking up the warmth of her in my arms as the shower spray beat along her back.

"You're going to be okay, babe. I killed him for you. I killed him for you good. Ain't nobody gonna hurt you like that again," I whispered, and she broke down further and just cried.

She wept her broken heart out against my chest, and I don't think I'd ever held something so fragile, and so broken and in need of mending as I did this woman right here. This wasn't my wheelhouse. I didn't know what to do in this kind of situation and in some ways we were both lost right now.

All I could do was wait for the crying jag to pass and take care of her immediate needs with gentleness and as much kindness as a closed-off bastard like me could muster. Seems I had it in reserves I wasn't aware I possessed lately.

I sighed when she'd calmed after a minute or two and she pressed her hands to her face. Her voice shaky, she issued a muffled apology.

"Don't," I said tersely. "You've been really strong the last few days," I told her. "No one, not even me, could keep that shit up forever. You're doing really good, baby. Really good."

"You think so?" she asked dully.

"I know so. We're gonna get you through this. It's just gonna take some time. You believe me when I say that, right?"

She took a shaking breath and let it out in an explosive rush.

"Would you be mad at me if I said sometimes?" she asked and I smiled slightly. She went on, "Like, sometimes, yes I believe you, but other times it all seems so overwhelming and so hopeless."

I nodded slowly and said, "No. Wouldn't make me mad. Sounds perfectly reasonable and in synch with what you've just been through." I reached behind her and brought her lank braid over her shoulder, slipping the tie off the end, carefully working the strands apart so I could get at them with shampoo then conditioner.

She stood, self-conscious, arms still locked over her breasts, hands tucked into her armpits, one foot on top of the other, thighs pressed together. I paid none of it no never mind, figuring if I drew attention to it, I would just make it worse. I let her do her and when I got her hair free, slipped it back over her shoulder. I slid fingertips along either side of her graceful neck, catching her hair and dragging the stray bits back behind her and into the shower spray.

"Head back," I ordered and she closed her eyes and tipped her head back, wetting the already soaked strands with fresh hot water, letting it sluice through her locks and slick down her back. The water streaming from the ends behind her, running a slightly off-color with the road grime trapped in it.

I lifted down my bottle of shampoo and emptied a decent dollop into my palm, quickly setting it aside and asked her to turn and give me her back. She did so, slowly at first and I was hedging my bets that caring for her in the simplest of ways by washing her hair might help sooth some of her anxiety. I was hoping it would relax her rather than wind her up more. It was anybody's guess at this point.

I was way out of my depth, but I was trying and my intentions were pure even if my impact wasn't. It was a frustrating tightrope to walk, and none of it was my little wounded bird's fault.

I just felt so damn bad for her, and I didn't want to cause any more harm than what had already been done to her. I knew that only time and a steady pace would help her to heal and I wanted to do what I could in that regard. I knew I wasn't perfect, far from it, but I felt like I had to be and that was frustrating.

Mav was smart, and there were a couple of the guys that were way better with the ladies than me. As soon as I could, I needed to get with my club and get some ideas and suggestions on how to move forward. I know a big piece of the puzzle would be getting her a new identity. That was priority one in my book, but a new life and all the documentation that went with it? That shit wasn't cheap – especially in the age of technology.

My girl, she let out a soft whimper as I massaged the soap into her long tresses, her shoulders easing down incrementally, her arms following as I worked the suds all through her hair, piling it atop her head, a line of suds sweeping down her perfectly formed back. There was nothing sexier to me than the long line of a woman's nude back except for a perfectly formed pair of tits and B. had that going for her too.

I asked her to turn, softly, keeping my voice low and soothing and she did. Her eyes closed, lips half-parted, and even with the split and the ugly stain of bruising under her soft skin, she was heartbreakingly, devastatingly beautiful.

I didn't care about any of it. She would *always* be beautiful to me. The woman I couldn't stop dreaming about.

"Tip your head back for me," I breathed and guided it with my hands to either side, the shower spray sluicing through the dark strands; rinsing the suds away. The white foam held true, floating atop the gray water that swirled down the drain, taking the grime of the road and the rain and carrying it away.

I wished it carried the stain under her skin, the stain left on her soul, just as easily, but again, only time, patience, and understanding would do that I think.

"Turn again for me? Let me get the conditioner, get some of those tangles out while it's still wet."

She turned her back again, and I tried to banish the water and soap slicking over her breasts from my mind. I didn't have the cold working for me anymore on keeping my cock under control, and the heat that swirled through my veins didn't have anything to do with the water I had yet to take advantage of.

I pulled conditioner through her long, long hair with the comb I kept in here and let her hair hang along her back while it worked.

"Easy, you're good," I murmured when she jumped at my hands as I lightly rested them on her shoulders. I dug my thumbs between them, to either side of her spine and she gasped, relaxing, as if the gentle but persistent pressure reminded her to stop *guarding* all the time. Nobody was ever going to hurt her again. She didn't have to tense, but no matter how much I said it, it wasn't going to do a thing to make her *believe* it. I didn't know how to make that happen. That was above my paygrade, for sure.

She began to relax under my gentle ministrations and that was good. I asked her, "You want to wash up, or can I do that for you too?"

"What?" she asked, turning her head to the side to eye me over her shoulder. Her arms came back up to cover her chest and she licked her lips nervously.

"It's your choice, baby. I can keep going if you'd like or I can turn it over to you." I held up my hands in surrender but I ached to finish what I started – to soap my hands and a washcloth and run them gently over her soft skin.

She turned slowly, arms covering herself again, and looked up at me.

"I don't know what I want," she said sadly.

"That's okay, too," I replied. "Just talk to me. What's going on up there?" I caressed her wet hair and her eyes closed.

She turned her head into my touch slightly and said, "I feel like I shouldn't *want* to be touched," she murmured. "But this feels so good… I don't know. I'm confused."

"Let me ask you this, why do you feel like you shouldn't want it?"

"I mean, Guy really hurt me and I feel like… I don't know… dirty maybe, for wanting you to touch me after what he did."

"Nothing dirty about letting someone care for you," I said and slid my hands against her shoulders, fingers pressing lightly into her upper arms, thumbs caressing just below her collarbone, sweeping slowly back and forth.

"Ain't nothing past this has to happen, no matter what my dick says," I told her and her eyes flew back open and glanced down, immediately sweeping back up to meet my gaze. High spots of color raised on her cheeks and I said, "I'm a man, not an animal, and I have self-control. You ain't got shit to fear from me."

"Okay," she whispered, and it took a couple false starts for any sound to make it out of her throat.

"Okay, you get what I'm saying, or okay I can finish what I've started here and wash the rest of you clean?" I asked to be perfectly clear.

"Both?" she said hesitantly.

"You sure that's what you want?" I asked, giving her every opportunity to change her mind before I even got started.

"Yes, I'm sure," she whispered.

"At any point you change your mind, you tell me to stop and it stops," I said and I meant it.

"Okay," she said and nodded a bit too rapidly.

"Okay," I whispered and picked up the bar of skin-softening soap I kept in here. She seemed more comfortable turned away from me so I said, "Let me start with your back."

She nodded and I got my ass to work.

CHAPTER ELEVEN

Wounded Little Bird…

I turned away slowly and he moved my hair, only semi-rinsed and still slimy slick with conditioner over my shoulder. I moved it with my hands into the spray and ran my fingers through it, rinsing the ends as I waited with mingling emotions for his hands to fall against my body once more.

He slicked them with soap first, and started at my shoulders, massaging them carefully, easing the kinks and knots loose, utilizing the heat from the shower and gentle care and even pressure. His soap-slicked hands felt so good against my skin as he worked his way down my back to either side of my spine.

I winced and jumped when he hit a particularly tender spot where I still felt bruised and he immediately lightened up.

"You good?" he asked.

"Yeah," I replied, breathily. I mean, the breadth and depth of his kindness and care was astonishing to me. I was both in awe of it and desperate to warm myself against it; despite this constant low-key fear that the rug was about to come out from under me any second now. I'd grown so accustomed to walking on eggshells that it was like I couldn't turn it off now.

He ran his hands carefully over each arm, spreading the soap across my body, asking every so often if what he was doing was okay. I slowly began to unwind, with each little touch and every little ask, I started to feel… safe again.

"Turn," he said gently and I drew a deep breath, turning, the spray from the showerhead rinsing my back. I kept my arms down at my sides and met his gaze, smiling shyly in return to his slight smile.

He started at my shoulders again, washing my chest, high up and avoiding my breasts for the time being. I closed my eyes and swallowed the sudden lump in my throat at how desperately I wanted him to touch me, all of me. I was just too afraid to say it, to ask for anything, really.

"This okay?" he asked, misreading me and I nodded, not trusting my voice.

He skipped over my breasts and slicked soap over my stomach and a small noise of protest escaped my throat unbidden.

"Yeah?" he asked, his hands floating upward but stopping before he made any assumptions about the small noise.

"Yeah," I whispered and he cupped my breasts with his big hands, grunting in appreciation. I opened my eyes to find his fixed on mine and I reached up, tentatively, cupping his bearded cheeks with my hands and tugging gently, insistently in a silent expression of how I wanted him to come down to my level.

He bowed his head and leaned down, and I stood carefully on the balls of my feet to put my mouth against his, kissing him gently. He sighed out, arms traveling around me and pulling my body tight against his, caging me protectively in his arms, his erection hot where it pressed against my stomach.

I gasped against his mouth and he froze, growling against my mouth, "Too much?"

"No," I breathed. "Kiss me."

He kissed me back, tenderly, carefully, so strange in juxtaposition with how *large* and intimidating a man he could be and I felt like, somehow, I had a secret. That he shared that secret with me. Just how sweet, how gentle, and how caring he could be.

He backed me up against the shower wall and I sucked in a sharp and startled breath and again, he froze.

"Too much?" he asked and I licked my lips, savoring his taste and admitted my limitations.

"Yeah."

"Okay." And just like that, he eased off, slipping back just enough to give me the breathing room I needed, yet perfectly not going so far as to ruin the intimacy he'd created between us.

"Good?" he asked and I nodded. "Okay, water's going to get cold soon. Can you switch with me?"

I nodded again and we swapped places so that he could have the shower spray.

I hugged myself and stared at his powerful back as he ducked his head under the showerhead and scrubbed his face with his hands. Without being asked, I took up the soap and did for him what he'd done for me, soaping my hands, running them over his back gently, and feeling the corded muscles beneath them. I ran light fingertips over his skin, my palms pressed flat, and closed my eyes when on the one side of his ribs, I ran over a dip, another seam of scar tissue.

His body was a roadmap of hard living, of pain, and it hurt my heart, it really did. To know this giant of a man, so protective, so fierce, had the occasion to hurt for as long and as badly as he had did something to me. Tapped into something other than fear but so similar to my pain that it almost felt like I double downed into that part of me.

I tore myself from it and opened my eyes, tracing lines over his shoulder blades, up arching out against the broad planes of his wide shoulders, sweeping in, down his back, and back out against his hips, over and over until the lines I drew in the white froth of soap on his back resembled wings.

I smiled, as he leaned against the shower wall in front of him and groaned, gasping out a rough, "Oh, God," at the sensations.

I looked at my handy work, at the angel wings on his back and smiled to myself. They were perfect, and I had no desire whatsoever to tell him what I'd doodled.

"Can I rinse?" he asked after a moment, turning his head and peering at me with one eye beneath his upraised arm. I felt my lips twitch into an even greater smile and nodded once and his lips twitched into a smile of his own.

I'm afraid he was too tall for me to comfortably wash his hair for him like he had mine, but it was still a treat, standing there, watching the soap and water sluice over his skin, the soap running over the cobblestones of his serratus and his abs. His cock stood straight up, turgid and throbbing and I wished I were brave enough to reach out, to touch him, to jerk him off or blow him but I wasn't ready. I was afraid it would lead to something more and it was still hard to totally trust that he could or would stop if I asked him to.

Baby steps… I thought to myself and tried to quell the anxiety my thought had begun to raise.

"Hang on," he said, shutting off the tap, and I jumped at the sound the faucet and showerhead made. "Don't move, stay right there," he ordered, and he carefully got out of the tub, stepping out onto the bathmat.

"Just stay right there, I'll only be a second," he said again, even though I hadn't moved a muscle.

The cold was creeping in and I started to shiver again as he whisked the lone towel off the bar and wrapped it around his hips, tucking the corner.

He came limping back at this awkward but also kind of adorable trot with a fresh towel around his shoulders and another in his hands for me. He held out a hand and I unfurled one of my arms I had pressed to my body, not out of modesty, but for warmth. He steadied me as I stepped out of the tub and said, "You want to do it or can I?" and held up the towel.

"You can," I said and he held it open, wrapping me in the large bath sheet and rubbing me down briskly but carefully through the cloth.

"Thank you," I murmured and he smiled.

"It's nice taking care of you," he said.

I smiled a little wanly and he wrapped the towel around me, beneath my arms but over my breasts and let me take care of tucking the corner.

"Come here," he said gently and guided me to stand in front of him, facing the mirror. "Just stand for me."

"Okay."

He picked up his brush and brushed through my wet hair before opening one of the bathroom drawers and extracting a hair dryer.

"I am so glad you have one of those," I murmured and he chuckled.

"I'm pretty tired of being wet, too. Although it's real nice to be warm again."

"So true," I said as he plugged it into the outlet.

"I'm afraid you got the worst of it. I at least had the engine throwing a little bit of heat against my legs."

"I'm okay," I said with a smile and he grinned over my head and said, "Yeah, you are."

He switched on the hair dryer and I put a hand against my mouth to stifle my giggle as he whipped warm air across my back and shoulders and took the time to dry my hair.

I had never had a man do anything like it for me.

After a time, my hair warm, soft and dried, he shut off the dryer and pulled the brush through my hair a few more times, following it up by letting my hair slide through his fingers. I watched his reflection in the mirror and found myself transfixed by the soft smile on his lips, the light in his eyes as he watched the strands flow through his fingers.

He was in awe, the glow of the simple pleasure it brought him at the tactile sensation, at the light in his eyes as he watched my hair flow and sweep through his hand – well, it was mesmerizing.

"I'll grab you a tee, hang on." He went out the bathroom door once again, the smile never leaving his lips and his eyes never leaving the shining fall of my hair. I swore if it gave him that much pleasure, I would never cut it short again. If anything, I would grow it even longer if it made him happy.

He came back with a heather gray, logo free, soft cotton tee and rumpled it up. I chuckled lightly as he held out the ring of material and I ducked my head up into it, putting my arms through the sleeves. He tugged down the hem and I let the towel fall from beneath it, bending down and sweeping it up off the floor with my hands.

"I got it," he said and took it from me, hanging it up on the towel bar set in the wall.

He turned back to me and rested a hand along the side of my neck, caressing my jawline, his gaze weighted with some sort of emotion I couldn't define but that warmed me to my toes.

"I'm going to take a little time for myself in here," he said gently. "Jerk off, because you drive me crazy with how beautiful and sexy you are and then dry my own hair. You feel free to do what you want. Sleep, browse the bookshelves in the living room, watch a little Netflix or whatever." He swept his gaze over my face as though memorizing it and a faint smile graced his lips.

My face flamed at his bold proclamation about his planned activities, but by the same token, he'd given me serious food for thought.

"Okay," I whispered and he smiled.

"Can I get a kiss?" he asked, and I smiled and nodded carefully. He leaned down and brushed his lips across mine, his eyes closing and the concentration on his face like he was remembering, filing away this taste of me like it were a precious thing he would cherish.

I took a step back and with a last lingering look, he shut the bathroom door. I stood for several moments and stared at the faux-wood interior door, my heart aflutter.

Wow, I mouthed and took a step back, silently retreating to the living room.

His apartment was just as sparsely furnished as it had been nine months ago. A couch that was at least in decent shape, and a coffee table that looked like he'd found it out on the curb marked 'free.'

He had a television, flat screen, but it wasn't terribly big and sat on a little bookcase that was only half as tall as the two that flanked it.

There were five total in here. All mismatched. The short one was black, the two to either side of it particle board coated in wood-printed contact paper in a medium brown tone.

At the other end of the couch, there were two more tall white bookcases and all of them were chock full of books. Not just any books, but mostly romance books. He had everything alphabetized by author and no separation between genres, either. I smiled as I ran a finger over the ridges of spines and passed between books by Timber Philips onto motorcycle manuals.

There were books by Hunter S. Thompson and Sonny Barger as I wandered the shelves and any time I encountered one of those names, I pulled one of the titles so I could see what the books were about. Of course, they were about motorcycles, motorcycle clubs, or the outlaw life. I was curious and filed names and locations away for later exploration when I wasn't so tired.

The hair dryer kicked on, making me jump. After several moments and as I went back over the Timber Philips titles looking for *Love In Purgatory*, a deep bass thump against the front door caused me to come out of my skin a second time.

Whump! Whump! Whump! Whump! Whump!

"Dump Truck! I know you're in there, buddy! Rode by and saw your bike downstairs. Open up. I'm freezing my nuts off out here."

I stood mute. Not sure what to do. Frozen in place.

Whump! Whump! Whump!

"C'mon, man. I'll kick the fuckin' door in, you big bastard!"

Shit!

I didn't think he could hear over the hair dryer. I swallowed hard and went to the door and threw back the locks, backpedaling, moving toward the bedroom this time, standing well clear of the door.

It opened and a man nearly as big as Dump Truck came through.

"The fuck, man. Where the hell you – oh."

He froze inside the door and eyed me speculatively. His blonde hair shaved on the sides underneath; the mass of it braided in smaller braids and woven into a thick rope down his back. His beard was blond and had braids and silver cylindrical beads in it. A black bandana was tied around his head in a big triangle over his forehead and he honestly looked like Dump Truck's lighter cousin.

Like Dump Truck, he had on motorcycle gear and a vest. The same curved patch that proclaimed 'PNW' for Pacific Northwest up under his arm on the front, but where Dump Truck had a patch on his vest that said 'Dump Truck' this man's patch read 'Fenris.'

"Who're you?" he demanded and I tried to get my voice to work, my mouth opening and closing but no sound coming out.

He raised an eyebrow and tilted his head, eying me like I was stupid or something and said, "Come again?"

I didn't know how to answer him so I just rocked back slightly on my heels, relieved when the blow dryer cut and was set down with a clatter. The door to the bathroom behind me opened a second later as Fenris shut the front door behind him and instead of relieved, I honestly felt trapped in the middle all of a sudden... but I think that was just me.

"Whoa, hey..." D.T. said and Fenris turned back around.

"Same to you, fucker," he said, and I couldn't tell if he was angry or affable.

"Little Bird, come here," D.T. said and I went to him, wrapping my hands around his one where it rested loose at his side. He gave my hands a reassuring squeeze and looked from me to the man who'd come in.

"Gimme a sec, man," he said and tugged me lightly in the direction of his room. I went with him, casting a curious look back over my shoulder at the other man who walked further into the living room, shrugging out of his motorcycle jacket and vest, and hanging it up on the coat-tree like he was a frequent visitor.

His blue eyes never left mine and I could still feel the weight of his gaze after I passed through the doorway to Dump Truck's bedroom and out of Fenris's line of sight.

"Come here, babe. Best you stay in here while I have a word with Fenris out there. He can be a little... unpredictable like Guano yesterday only he's a lot less crazy."

"Good to know," I murmured. He pulled back the blankets on his bed and I got in and let him tuck me in.

"Just try to get a little rest."

I nodded and breathed a cleansing sigh.

"I'll be right out here."

"Okay."

He brushed a hand over my hair and kissed my forehead. I let my eyes drift shut beneath the brush of his lips and melted under the touch. When I opened them again, it was to the soft thump of him closing the door behind him as he moved back out of the room.

I turned my head and smiled slightly in the deepening gloom when I spotted *Love In Purgatory* on the bedside table.

CHAPTER TWELVE

*D*ump Truck…

"Who the fuck is that?" Fen demanded when I got back out in the living room. He moved over to the couch and dropped down on the near end, leaving me my usual side closer to the book-shelves so I could put my leg up.

"You want the answer to that before or after I put some fucking pants on?" I asked, holding up the pair of sweats I'd nicked off the top of my dresser on the way out of my bedroom.

"Shit, I go into the club and that's how I hear you've gone off to fuckin' Vegas on a lark without so much as a 'fuck you buddy'. What the hell's going on? You don't say you're goin', you don't call, you don't write, then you don't bother to let me know you're fuckin' back – that shit's not like you, bro."

I went around into the kitchen so I could lose the towel and get my pants on without losing sight of him in the living room but more importantly without flashing the dude my dick.

"More importantly," he added, "who's the bitch?"

"Don't call her that," I said, automatically coming to Bianca's defense and his eyebrows shot up under the bandana he had on his head.

"Start talking," he ordered and I knew when he was out of patience.

I came back around, decent, and limped to my customary end of the couch and dropped down, hauling my leg up onto it and straightening it out, leaning back against the arm.

I sighed and tried to decide where to begin and finally asked him, "Where do you want me to start?"

"The bitch. Who is she?"

"I told you not to call her that, man. I won't tell you again."

"Then put a name to her pretty, but fucked-up face," he ordered. I scowled. We didn't butt heads often but when we did, it could be pretty spectacular and a fight was brewing here.

"She doesn't have one anymore, but it used to be Bianca."

His head jerked back and his eyes went wide with surprise.

"That one-time hookup?" he asked. "The one from a while back? The one you keep dreaming about?"

I nodded and kept nodding through every subsequent question.

"You went all the way to Vegas to get her?"

"Yup."

"Start talking, bro. Why didn't you call me? I would have gone with you."

I sighed and filled him in on my almost week.

To his credit, he kept his mouth shut and listened.

Mine and Fenris's positions within the club dovetailed each other. There was a reason for that. While both of us were capable, he was just *more* capable than me and of the two of us, I was the more levelheaded. Thus, I was the club's sergeant-at-arms while he was the club's enforcer. I did more of the thinking and deciding, while he did more of the actual meting out whatever punishment or ass kicking that'd been handed down.

We were a team. A damn good one. A scary one. But the situation with my wounded little bird in there had been deeply personal for me and thus needed to be handled alone. Besides, it'd also been my business and not club business – and the last thing I'd needed to do was deprive the club of both of us while I'd hurried off to handle shit unrelated to the club.

One of us could handle both functions of SAA or Enforcer, but both of us gone at the same time would have left the club without and it was part of our job to serve as the wrecking crew for Mav. The president didn't travel anywhere by himself when there was a potential for any kind of hostile entities out there, and with as active as our chapter was running scripts and holding the Western Washington subsection of the Pacific Northwest territory? Naw. I couldn't have us both headed to Vegas. One of us needed to be here.

"I miss anything here?" I asked when I finished telling my story.

Fen sat silent, shaking his head as he wrapped it around everything I'd told him.

"Naw, man. It's been alright. Business as usual around here. So, what're you gonna do?" he asked.

"Honestly, one step at a time. One foot in front of the other, my brother. First thing, I'm gonna find her some things, some clothes of her own. Then I'll bring her in to meet Mav and see what I can do about getting her a new identity. Those are the top priorities right now."

"That's legit," he told me, nodding.

"I miss anything?" I asked.

"Shot the fucker in the head, rescued the girl, nope – I'd say you handled it perfectly. Just wish I could have been there."

"Yeah, me too."

Fenris had a sister. She'd been raped in college but hadn't told anyone. She'd just kept spiraling down and down inside of herself. She'd gotten lost in the dark to the point she'd done a suicide sundae – swallowed a bottle of pills, slashed her wrists in the bathtub and had duct taped a bag over her head.

She'd been determined. The pigs had been called in by her and Fen's mom. He'd found out about all of it in her journal and we'd gone hunting first, then he went on one hell of a bender. It was a dark time in his life and he held a special kind of hell in his heart for rapists as a result.

Consent was everything. You could be as rough as you wanted with a woman as long as she was on board with it first. There was no real reason to raise a hand on a bitch, even less to force yourself on one. We were *men* not *animals*. No matter what the citizenry thought of us. Fuck.

"Makes me wanna go in there and give her a hug."

"Dude, I'm working my ass off to make her feel safe. I think that'd freak her out like nobody's business."

He snorted and nodded. "Yeah. I know. Just a knee-jerk reaction. Forget I even said anything."

I chuckled and shook my head. "Consider it forgotten."

Whatever beef that'd been brewing was quashed, just like that.

He stood up and said, "Let me know when you bring her by the club. I'd like to be there to keep anyone from being dumb. I'll start by getting the word out – 'fragile handle with care.'" He gestured as though running a label or a line of text to stick on Bianca before she walked through the door.

"Yeah, 'preciate that. I'd rather keep strife from stirring."

He nodded and asked, "She talk about it yet?"

I shook my head and said, "Give it time. Too soon, I think."

"Yeah." He didn't sound happy about it. "Until we get her some I.D., we can't tap any citizen programs can we?"

"It's hit or miss on whether they would help or hurt, right now," I said and he nodded thoughtfully.

"Yeah, to be honest, I don't trust them either."

He pushed to his feet and waved me down but I just shook my head and got up anyway. I wasn't about to sit on the couch and leave my wounded bird in there by herself.

"Let me know if there's anything I can do," he said. I nodded.

"Will do. Thanks for understanding, brother."

"Always," he said and we hugged.

He went to the coat-tree and pulled down his jacket and cut, swinging into it. I went to the door and saw him out.

"Night, man."

"Night," I said and shut the door behind him. I locked it. Not for me, but for Bianca's peace of mind.

I bowed my head and sighed. I needed to come up with a new name for her. With any luck, her new I.D. would be something better than 'Bianca,' It was such a rich bitch pretentious as fuck name; and she was none of those things. It was right along the lines of Paris, or Muffy, or Buffy. I didn't honestly think anybody named their kid that kind of thing in real life. At least not outside the Hollywood elite.

Who's stereotyping now, jackass? I thought bitterly to myself.

I shut things down out here and left the light I always left on over the stove before stopping outside my own bedroom door. I rapped twice, not wanting to startle or scare her and was met by a soft, "Yes?"

I opened the door and left it wide and went into the room. She was sitting up in my bed, the blankets over her lap, the lamp on the bedside table on and my copy of *Love in Purgatory* open in her lap.

"You alright?" I asked, coming in and limping around to the side of the bed that was left unoccupied.

"Yes. I'm sorry."

"For what."

"Just letting him in like that – I didn't know what else to do. It was like I couldn't get my voice to work."

"Find anything good out there?" I asked, trying to change the subject and she smiled holding up the book in her lap.

"I was actually looking for this when he pounded on the door. I'm surprised you didn't hear it."

"I didn't hear shit," I told her and she smiled a little sadly. "I'm sorry if he scared you, but Fen is one of the good ones."

"That's good to know," she murmured.

She closed the book and set it aside, turning back to me.

"Hang on," I said and slid down under the blankets with her, raising my arm and inviting her to lie against me.

She fit against me so perfectly and I sighed, holding her close.

"This okay?" I asked.

"Yeah," she whispered.

We lapsed into a comfortable silence. One that was interrupted a short time later by her soft, "So what happens now?"

"Well, tomorrow I get you hooked up with some clothes of your own and we go in to meet Mav."

"Mav?"

"Maverick, my chapter's president."

"I don't understand how it all works," she murmured. "But I'd like to learn."

"Ask me some questions and I'll try to answer what I can," I told her.

"Can I?" she asked.

"You can ask *me* anything," I said. "If you want to know something and we're in mixed company, just wait until we're alone to ask. I should have told you that from the beginning but I had some other things on my mind. It was a lapse in judgment on my part and it won't happen again. I promise." I kissed her forehead and she cuddled a little closer and sighed.

"Where to begin?" she asked softly, chuckling a bit dispassionately.

"Wherever you'd like. There's a lot to learn about the life. We're our own culture, now. Separate. Other."

"Why?" she asked.

"Most of us are disenfranchised to be honest," I said.

"What's your story?" she asked.

"Same as any other man's, I guess." I hedged. I didn't tend to get deeply personal unless I was some kind of drunk.

"Obviously not," she said shifting against my side. "Not every man joins a motorcycle gang."

"Club," I corrected automatically and she stiffened slightly.

"I apologize," she said. "I didn't mean to offend –"

"You didn't. You're alright with me. Just might not be alright with some of the other guys, talkin' like that." I gave her a gentle squeeze and after a moment, she let out the breath she'd been unconsciously holding. It was warm and stirred the hairs on my chest, and I smiled in the deepening dark of the room.

"I'm scared about messing up again," she confessed.

"No one's gonna hurt you," I reminded her and she swallowed.

"I don't want to hurt anyone else, though. Not even by a little bit."

I chuckled and sighed out.

"Ain't nothing you could do to any one of us that ain't been done before, but I get you. I think that alone is what could make you one of us."

"How's that?" she asked softly.

"Any other citizen just wouldn't care."

"That's sad, isn't it?"

I nodded once and knew she felt it by the way my body shifted with the motion.

"Yeah. Yeah, it is."

"Does everyone who comes to 'the life' come from rough beginnings?" she asked.

"Not everyone, no, but a fair majority of us do."

"What are some of the things I should know?" she asked.

"School starts tomorrow," I joked.

"Okay," she readily agreed and cuddled into my side a little more. I thought about things, mind wandering a bit, and finally sighed. I couldn't expect to take without giving. I couldn't expect her to trust without trusting, so I cracked the vault door on my past and started talking.

"I grew up down south a bit, out in Yelm. My dad, he was an electrician by trade. My mom was a stay-at-home one for the most part, at least in the beginning. My dad was mean. Real mean. Used to beat on my mom. She put up with it, thinkin' that she couldn't provide for me – right up until he came at me when I was nine or so."

I was quiet for a second, reflecting.

"I think that was what did it. Some reason, she could tolerate him whoopin' her ass as long as his drunk one left me alone, but when that wasn't the status quo anymore? She found the will to leave him. We ended up in a shelter for a while. She got some job training, a divorce, and eventually we got our own place with some section eight housing assistance."

I looked down. She'd gone so still, I couldn't believe she was still listening. I needed to check and make sure she hadn't fallen asleep or something. She looked up at me, her deep brown eyes a window into her soul and all I could see was pain. Her pain. A mirror of my own. It was difficult to go on, what, with not wanting to add to what was already ravaging her soul but now that the vault door was open, it was gonna be hard to get it back shut again.

"Things were alright for a while," I lied. I mean, things *were* but by the same token, they were hard as fuck. "We were poor and moved up over near the eastside. We needed to put some distance between us and my father. He'd gone all obsessed and stalker status on my mom. So, we'd been relocated and things were okay except for one thing. The kids at my new school were fuckin' *mean*."

She nodded against my chest and said, "I can believe that. The eastside is full of people who are nice to your face but won't hesitate to stab you in the back and that's among what would be considered their peers. I can't imagine how they would treat someone they consider *below* them."

"Pretty fuckin' awful until I started gettin' mean right back," I said. "I started getting sent home a lot. Suspended for fighting – nearly expelled. Didn't seem to matter that I never started any of the shit. I just damn sure didn't have a problem finishing it."

"Sounds about right," she whispered.

"My mom tried everything, getting me into sports and whatnot. She was doing her best, but she was taking the shit the school had to say about me at face value rather than listening to *me*. It caused a pretty big rift. I was young. A dumb kid. Finally I started looking for acceptance anyplace I could find it, I guess."

"What happened?" she asked softly.

"Manny did, when I was around seventeen."

"Manny?" she asked.

"Yeah, shop class guy. Got me into fixing up this bike motor. The rest, as they say, was history."

"So that's where you got your love of motorcycles," she said and I chuckled.

"Rightly so."

"Then what happened?"

"I started prowling around online forums looking for a project bike of my own."

I could hear the slight frown in her voice when she asked, "Where did you come up with the money for that?"

I chuckled darkly and didn't answer. I didn't really think I needed to and her soft little '*oh*' proved me right.

"As for how I got into the MC? I've been in it for years. I got myself a bike that needed a lot of work. Manny let me bring it into the school's shop and work on it for junior and both my senior years for my senior project."

"Both your senior years?" she echoed.

"I missed a lot of school from fighting and shit. Didn't have enough credits to graduate on the first try."

"Oh," she whispered and hugged me a little tighter.

"So, I worked on that damn bike every day. Before school, after school, and even on the weekends if Manny was around to open up the shop for me. It was tough to find parts for and was majorly suffering from some *major* garage rot. I spent any minute I wasn't working on the bike either in class or stocking shelves at my mom's grocery store on the night shift. By then, she'd moved up from checker to manager but we were still barely making it. Didn't help that I didn't do a lot of pitching in. Every last red cent I earned was going into that bike."

"I can imagine," she said in a wistful soft tone that told me she was doing just that. Picturing it all.

"Eventually, I got it running, got my motorcycle endorsement and that was that."

"But how did you get involved with the club?" she asked.

"Finding parts for the bike. I would take the bus some weekends out to the boneyard, here in Rat City. A bunch of the old-school guys ran it. I was a hang-around before I even had my bike up and running."

"A hang-around?" she asked.

"First step of becoming a club member. You hang around long enough – express interest, eventually you become a prospect."

"And then what?" she asked, and she sounded utterly fascinated. I chuckled.

"You spend a year, sometimes more, doing everyone's bitch work, getting hazed, proving yourself and if you can manage to hang in there, eventually, they patch you in."

"Is that like a gang?" she asked softly. "Like how they beat you up and call it 'jumping you in?'"

"No, no… not at all. Patching you in means you get the center piece patch or colors part of your cut and your bottom rocker goes from 'prospect' to your chapter's location. That, and you get the top rocker, or the club's name."

"So the patches on your vest, each one of them means something?"

"They sure do. At least the ones you *earn*. Some are bought."

"What's the difference?" she asked.

"Difference is, if I go up to some RUB in a bar –"

"RUB?"

"Rich Urban Biker," I amended, "and ask them if the patches they got on their cut are bought or earned – the answer had better be 'bought' or we got a problem."

She got really quiet.

"I don't understand," she said.

"Okay, you saw the patch with the wings on my cut, right?"

"Yes."

"That one is *earned*. It means you've crashed your bike and you survived."

"Okay."

"There's a certain amount of respect that comes with that patch. So if someone were to tell me they *bought* that patch, without knowing what it means, well that fucker's a poser piece of shit."

"Okay!" she said catching on. "What about the diamond one, the one that has the one percent in it?"

"Now *that one* is a doozy," I explained. "If a guy in any other colors but Sacred Hearts' colors comes walkin' around town like he's cock of the walk with that one on, he's got a problem. The only men supposed to be wearing that are outlaw types. Now the Sacred Hearts? We own this territory."

"What, Western Washington?" she asked.

"No, that's just my chapter. We own the entire *Pacific Northwest,* hence the underarm rocker I got on there. My chapter is just the chapter that controls Western Washington. There are five different chapters holding down the Pacific Northwest territory," I said.

"Western Washington, which is us, Eastern Washington, Idaho, and then there's a Western Oregon and an Eastern Oregon chapter. Preacher and Guano, the guys you met are from the Eastern Oregon chapter."

"Right," she said and huffed out another breath.

"It's a lot to remember," she said.

"Yes, it is. One of the things to remember is that clubs like ours are inherently patriarchal in nature."

"Patriarchal or misogynistic?" she asked and I chuckled low with pride.

"Sometimes both. The SHMC has rules where women are concerned," I said. "I'd like to think we're a cut above. Wasn't always so, but in the last ten years or so we've undergone a sort of reorg on our priorities because reasons I can't get into. It's always been in our laws of conduct, though – no women, no children."

"What's that mean?" she asked.

"Means if we caught a brother doing his woman like your man did you, he'd have some real big fuckin' problems," I growled.

"You'd kill him, like you killed Guy?" she whispered softly, like she was afraid that if she said it too loudly the pigs would miraculously descend from the sky to lock us both up.

"Best not ever speak that aloud again," I said gently, "but to answer your question – it depends on what one of our own did. That's my job within the chapter. I keep the peace, deliver punishment decisions. Fen? The guy you met earlier tonight? He's our enforcer. He's the one to mete those punishments out."

"So you have an internal system?" she asked. "Like your own system of governing?"

"That's right."

She yawned and put the back of her hand to her mouth.

"Sorry," she whispered.

"Don't be," I told her. "Class dismissed for tonight. Get some sleep, baby. You had a big day."

"So did you," she murmured.

"Yeah, but I'm used to it. You ain't."

"You got me there," she said sleepily and I chuckled.

"I always got you," I whispered but she was already drifting, her body going lax against mine.

CHAPTER THIRTEEN

*W*ounded Little Bird...

I groaned and pushed off my stomach, turning around in bed and setting up some pillows at my back. It was kind of a fruitless endeavor, the one pillow basically stuffed itself into the cubby of his bed's headboard, while the other only provided marginal protection from the sharp edge of the top shelf.

I was alone in the room, but there was water running in the kitchen, so I knew Dump Truck was here.

I pressed fingertips into my eyes and rubbed them, drawing a cleansing breath to chase away the cobwebs from my deep sleep that refused to do anything but linger.

"Hey."

His voice was soft, the deep timbre soothing, and emanated from where he was stopped in the doorway. I dragged my hands down my face and smiled. He had a plate of gently steaming bacon and scrambled eggs in one hand and a steaming Harley-Davidson mug of fresh coffee in the other.

"Hey," I parroted back at him just as softly.

His lips crooked up into this sexy half-smile and he came into the room. He was dressed already, motorcycle boots scuffing over the worn tan carpet, frayed jeans that were *clean* but stained with grease and motor oil along the tops of his thighs, and a plain, heather gray tee that strained around his biceps and hugged his broad chest beautifully.

"Made you some breakfast," he said, handing down the plate. He set the coffee off to the side and just behind me on the bedside table.

"Thanks," I murmured and then, automatically, without thinking asked, "What time is it?" as though it mattered.

"After noon," he said.

"Seriously?" I asked, surprised.

"You slept hard. Can't really say I'm surprised. You still look exhausted."

"I feel it," I confessed. "Just sore all over and rundown."

"Hope you're not getting sick," he said and reached out, feeling my face, pressing the backs of his fingers gently against my forehead, lifting them, and gently doing the same to my cheek.

"You don't feel warm," he said.

"I'm just tired," I assured him and took a bite out of one of the three strips of bacon on my plate. It was perfect. Crispy, but still chewy. Just the way I liked it.

He lowered himself down onto the edge of the bed with a groan and stretched out his bad leg in front of him.

"Aren't you going to eat?" I asked. He smiled.

"Already did while I was cooking up yours."

"Oh."

"You remember anything we talked about last night?" he asked.

"Yeah, I remember," I said softly, putting one of my hands over his where it rested by his hip. He looked down at it and stared for a long moment before sweeping his gaze up to meet mine.

"There's a lot more, you ready to hear some of it?" he asked and I smiled gently, realizing that he was actually *eager* to tell me more about his world. Probably as eager as I was to hear it.

"Let me caffeinate," I said with a small laugh and he reached over and handed me my cup. I took a careful sip and closed my eyes in bliss. God, that was some good coffee. Rich and bold, sweetened just right and with the perfect amount of cream.

"Wow," I uttered and took a bigger mouthful.

"Nectar of the gods after some straight days of some truly awful shit," he agreed.

I smiled; I couldn't help it.

"Okay," I said, settling in for the long talk ahead. "What else should I know?"

"If a man in club colors ever tells you it's club business – drop it, right then and there. No more questions, no arguments. He won't say anymore and he shouldn't. It's as much for your safety as it is his."

"Okay," I said slowly.

"This life is intense, and there are just some things you don't need to know about."

I nodded slowly.

"Right. What happens in Vegas, stays in Vegas," I murmured.

"*Exactly*," he declared and it looked like he was, dare I say, relieved?

"Does violence… like that, happen often?" I asked carefully.

He shook his head. "No, but he had it comin' to him," he said and the look on his face said it all. How sorry he was. How sorry that'd it happened. How sorry he didn't get there sooner. How sorry he was that he didn't get to hurt the man that'd done it more.

That one soulful look was everything to me, and something inside of me… just ceased to hurt. Like this dull but sharp emotional ache that I'd been carrying around inside suddenly lifted and the air became somewhat breathable again.

"Thank you," I whispered.

He shook his head. He had half of his hair up today, the top half in a sort of half-knot, the ends trapped by the hair tie giving it a sort of clamshell bulge.

"Don't thank me," he said. "Not for that."

"Then thank you for this," I said pressing a hand over my heart.

His brow knit for a moment then smoothed out. He nodded and said gruffly, voice full of emotion, "Don't mention it."

He got back up to his feet with a grunt and said, "Hang on, I'll be right back."

He went out to the living room and I shoveled a forkful of eggs into my mouth.

Oh, my God, they were heavenly. Buttery and rich, they tasted just as golden as they looked, their texture fluffy and lighter than air. I closed my eyes and chewed slowly, relishing in texture and taste until he reappeared.

He stopped in the doorway, laughed lightly and asked, "Did I just give you an orgasm?"

"Hmm, no one ever has like you, and to answer your question – *yes,* I think so."

He laughed outright then and came back over and sat down. He handed over a paperback book.

"Hunter S. Thompson," I read aloud. "Isn't that the *Fear and Loathing In Las Vegas,* guy?" I asked.

"The very same, but before that, he wrote this. This was his first book."

I chewed the side of my bottom lip that didn't have any healing left to do. It was a book about a motorcycle gang – er, *club.*

"Thanks," I murmured gently and he smiled.

"Things have evolved quite a bit since '67," he said. "Best advice I can give you is to just sit back and observe. Don't repeat anything you overhear to anyone but me and only when we're alone and likewise for any questions. If it's one thing I've learned is if you're patient, and can wait long enough, most of your questions will be answered before you can get around to asking 'em anyway. Anything that gets by, most certainly, can wait until we're alone."

I looked up at him and asked, "Just what is it you *do,* anyway? I mean, outside of the club. You know. For work, or whatever."

He smiled and said, "There is no 'outside of the club' for me. It's my life. I live it and breathe it. To answer your question, I front as one of the parts pullers and mechanics at the boneyard."

"Oh. Is it owned by the club?"

"A shell corporation, but yes," he said and smiled. There was a tightness around his eyes as he said it.

"Am I supposed to know that?" I asked softly.

"Probably not," he said.

"Could you get into trouble for telling me?"

"Maybe, if anyone found out about it," he said.

"They won't," I vowed.

He smiled and held up a hand and I locked my pinky finger with his. His eyebrows went up and the expression on his face said that he found me utterly adorable. I smiled and he laughed a little.

"Eat your breakfast. Class dismissed for now. You gonna be alright if I have to go out for a little while?"

I held up the book and said, "Class may be dismissed, but I have homework."

He grinned and nodded and leaning carefully forward, asked with his eyes if he could kiss me. I smiled and met him halfway, kissing him back.

"Should only be a couple of hours," he said. "You need anything?"

"My own toothbrush," I said and he nodded.

"I'll grab some essentials for you. As much as I can, while I'm out."

"Thanks."

"You know, if you aren't up to being alone, I could always see if Fen is up to coming by. He could maybe sit with you for a while."

I bit my lips together and shook my head slowly.

"I think some alone time might do me some good," I said and he nodded.

"Was just a thought, I trust that dude with my life so…"

I nodded my understanding and he made to go.

"Dump Truck." I called after him and he took a bouncing step back and looked over in my direction.

"What happens to me now?" I asked and he gave me a crooked smile.

"Welcome to the first day of your new life, babe. I'm fixin' to get all that sorted."

"Oh," I swallowed hard, "okay."

"Be back as soon as I can," he said, "with some essentials and information."

I nodded and he disappeared from the doorway.

I looked down at my mostly cleaned plate and smiled, finishing every bite.

CHAPTER FOURTEEN

---

*D*ump Truck...

I headed for the club. I wanted to talk to Mav and fill the rest of the guys in on what was up with me. After Fen showed up last night, I was feelin' guilty. I figured Mav hadn't spilled the tea, figuring that I'd want my privacy. I mean, my main man wasn't wrong in that regard but he'd played it *super* close to the vest and I was afraid some of the club might be feelin' a little put out. Then again, the rest of the club, while close friends, weren't as close as Fen and I were.

Not only did our positions within the club's cabinet go hand in hand, we spent the most time together. If anyone was to be considered my *best* friend, then Fen was certainly *that guy*.

I pulled up on 15th SW and backed my bike into the heavy gravel outside the boneyard. A couple of the fellas were outside the back door of the club across the street, either smokin' a cigarette or a joint on the little wood back porch.

A rusted out old metal Folgers' can sat on the railing, a makeshift ashtray.

"D.T.!" one of 'em called. "What's up, man?"

I got up off my bike and sighed, throwing him some chin, but I didn't much feel like hollering across the road so Squatch could wait until I got there. I pulled my cane off my bike. I'd fashioned some tight metal clips that lined up under the seat to hold it.

A couple of the guys had made it for me. Fashioned the thing out of a length of copper pipe. They'd put a rubber foot on it, but the talking point was the knob on the top. A hand-cast and shaped nickel alloy skull that fit in my hand nicely, my fingertips in the eye sockets. It had a hood on, the grim reaper's head that fashioned into a hook to keep it comfortable in my palm. The hood had been carefully wrapped in black molded leather and some deep red garnet cabochons went in the sockets for eyes.

It'd been worked on for months while I'd been in the hospital and had been ready about the time in recovery that I'd needed a cane. I kept it handy for a few reasons. One, I still needed it from time to time when my leg pained me, which it was doing now after so many days of hard riding and two, it made one damned fine weapon.

More than one motherfucker had gotten a serious beatdown with it thinkin' somehow I was crippled. Naw, man, if anything my big ass was handi-*capable*, not handicapped and that was the way it was always gonna be or I would eat my fucking gun.

I checked both ways before stepping out onto the street because I was a badass and not *stupid* and crossed at a steady pace. 15th wasn't honestly that busy. We were one street to the east of the main drag through Rat City which was 16th SW.

"Where the fuck you been, man?" Squatch asked when I got to the bottom of the four or five stairs leading up. I switched hands and grabbed the railing, working my way up to him and Nine, clasping hands and bumping shoulders with first one then the other.

"Vegas," I answered.

"Naw, really, where you been?" Nine asked, laughing.

He'd gotten the road name 'Nine' because the motherfucker had nine lives. It was just too bad, that by my accounting, he was on something like his seventh one.

"Vegas, for real, bro."

Squatch laughed at Nine's expense. You could probably guess how Squatch got his name. It was because he was one *seriously* hairy son of a bitch. He had some middle eastern or Mediterranean or some shit in him with his dusky skin tone. He was something like five foot nine or ten so not a big guy but not a little one either, but he was covered in rich black hair. From long black hair that went past the middle of his back with its intense volume, to his thick black beard that hung to the middle of his chest. It was even worse when he took his jacket and cut off.

He favored tees, like I did, that had the sleeves ripped off which just showed off his ultra-hairy arms. I mean dude was covered. Chest, back, arms, legs. Being in the Pacific Northwest which was the origin of Sasquatch country, it hadn't been a hard pick.

What completed the look was when he walked. He kind of had this hunch-shouldered walk and every time he took a step, his hair and beard would move with the air currents generated so it sort of went whoosh-whoosh-whoosh.

That shit never got old.

"You seriously went to Vegas and didn't tell nobody?" Nine asked affronted.

"I told somebody," I said. "I told Mav."

"What was in Vegas?" Squatch asked curiously.

"A girl."

Both of them just stared at me for a solid second then both of them cut up laughing.

"Good one," Nine said doubled over.

"Why were you there, really?" Squatch asked, wiping tears out of the corners of his eyes. I pushed past them both and through the back door.

"I just told you. A woman."

They stared after me slack-jawed and I shut the door in their faces. I looked right, first into the open doorway of Mav's office. He was on the phone and threw me some chin in acknowledgement. I switched my cane back into my right hand and leaned heavily on it, limping my way into the office.

"Mm-hmm," he said into the line and listened to whatever the guy on the other end had to say while I reached around to my flank and squeezed the big ass safety pin together. It sprang open, and I wrestled with it sight unseen for a couple of seconds to disentangle it from the side of my cut.

"No, yeah, I hear you, man. I'm pretty confident we can help you out," he said.

I squeezed the pin back together so it was closed and handed it over. Mav cradled the phone between his shoulder and neck and took it from me, sliding open the center drawer on his old writing desk and dropping it into the plastic tray inside.

I gave him a nod in thanks and he gave me another chin lift.

"Let me take it to the table and I'll get right back with you," he said into the line and I backed out of the office.

Across from Mav's office was the closed chapel door. Further up the hall, the men's room was on the left and the ladies room on the right.

We didn't have a lot of steady ol' ladies, just a legacy who kept coming around. A legacy was a woman that'd belonged to a brother who'd passed. The one that still came around was Momma Kat, and acted almost like a den mother to the rest of us. She was a sweet, older lady who tended the bar and smoked like a fuckin' chimney. She was good to talk to when Deacon wasn't around, though. Got more than one of us through girl troubles on more than one occasion and never hesitated to let one of us know when we were bein' a fuckin' moron.

That being said, we had *plenty* of steady pussy on parade through here.

The front room, or great room as we called it, had the bar along the left wall as you came in through the back. Fenris was sitting at it, beer in hand while Momma Kat stood behind it, polishing a glass.

"How you doin' Ms. Momma Kat?" I asked, parking it on the nearest barstool.

"Aw, I'm alright, honey. Where you been at?"

"Vegas," I said.

"Club business or personal?" she asked.

"Personal, but I'm not quite up to sharing just yet," I told her.

"Say no more, baby. What can I get you?"

"Just gimme a Coke."

"Jack and Coke?" she asked.

"Naw, just a Coke."

"Comin' right up," she said.

"Doesn't anyone work around here no more?" I asked and Fen leaned back eyeing my ass sideways.

"Dude, it's Saturday. Prospect is minding the boneyard and the rest of the guys'll be over in a minute. Mav just sent out the mass text for a church meeting."

"Shit, did he?" I pulled my cell outta my jacket pocket and frowned. "Son of a *fucking* bitch." It wouldn't turn on and was slick with moisture. Fen was cracking up.

Momma Kat twisted her lips and her shoulders dropped. "What the hell you do? Ride through the Sound?" she asked, referencing the Puget Sound, the largest nearest body of water.

"Fuck no, try three hours of hard freeway riding up I-5 to get back last night."

"Huh," she said and I could see the wheels turning. "Well, Momma to the rescue." She brought a big freezer bag full of rice out from under the bar and dropped it with a thump in front of me. Fen damn near fell off his stool; he was howling.

"What's going on in here?" Mav asked curiously, coming in from the back and his office. I dropped my phone into the rice and sealed up the bag. "Oh," he said and scratched the back of his head.

I sighed and Momma whisked the bag back out of sight behind the bar saying, "Give it a day, maybe two. Either it'll work or it won't."

"I'll get you a burner to use in the meantime," Mav said.

"Thanks."

"Good thing you were already here," he said.

I grunted noncommittally. I wanted to be home, with my wounded little bird but that wasn't gonna get shit handled.

"You got a minute?" I asked Mav and he nodded.

"Sure, come on back."

I followed him back down the way to his office and shut the door behind me.

"How's your girl?" he asked.

"Hangin' in there," I answered. "Touch and go the first night but getting stronger."

"Oh, yeah? Somethin' go down?" he asked.

I told him about how she got a hold of my piece and he looked somewhere between sorry and disgusted.

"Wish you could'a made him suffer," he said.

"That makes two of us," I said, lowering myself into the seat across from him. A knock came at the office door.

"Yeah!" Mav called out.

"Forgot your Coke, baby." Momma Kat handed it to me and I gave her a nod.

"Quit your snooping, woman," Mav said grumpily, running a hand back through the thick top of his hair which looked like he'd been at it more than a time or two. His GQ messy look erring on the side of just messy.

Momma Kat just waved him off and shut the door behind her. I took a drink out of my glass and he fixed me with a baleful look between his fingers as he palmed his face.

"That don't look good," I commented dryly.

"Heavy is the head that wears the crown," he said and I could sympathize. I had my own pressures at the moment and I was sure I would find out what was up, and there was *definitely* something up. Mav had one hell of a poker face when he needed it, but when it was just him with us around the clubhouse, he didn't bother.

We sat in a comfortable silence for a minute and he huffed a cleansing breath and shook whatever was bothering him off.

"Back to your woman," he said and I nodded, sucking down some more soda.

"She's gonna need a new identity," I said and he nodded slowly.

"Yeah, she definitely needs that to go along with her new life," he said staring off into space. His brain was going a mile a minute. I could see the processor whirring and clicking away, just behind his eyes and I heaved a sigh.

"How much that gonna run me?" I asked and he raised his eyebrows.

"Let me make some calls, but it ain't gonna come cheap."

I swore softly. "I got some put away, but it probably ain't near enough."

"I'll get it figured out," he said. "Let me get a baseline and if you're cool, I'll let you know when church is in session. I gotta make these calls *now*, though."

"Say no more, Big Cheese." I got to my feet, a little bit of a struggle but I managed.

"Go sit your big ass down across the hall," he said. "Have one of the boys or the prospect come get me when everyone's here."

"Copy that," I said and left him scrolling through the contacts in his phone as I slipped out and awkwardly pulled the door shut behind me between having to balance my drink and cane.

I sighed and went across and opened up the door to the chapel as Squatch and Nine came through the back door.

"Oh, shit. We starting?" Nine asked.

"Nah, I just need to sit down, put up my leg. Send Fen on back here for me, would ya?"

"Sure thing, man."

"Once everyone's here, come on back. Mav's making some calls for me, so once we're all assembled, he said to come get him."

"You got it, Boss," Squatch said.

"Fuck you," I said and he laughed.

Boss wasn't a term of endearment. It started down in one of the Texas state penitentiaries way back in the day. They started calling the COs or Corrections Officers, B.O.S.S. The COs didn't know any better at first, but the inmates knew. B.O.S.S. was Sorry Son of a Bitch backwards.

It was a tight ass fit in the chapel. The table and chairs took up most of the long, narrow ass room. You kind of had to walk sideways along the wall, edging your way around to get to your seat.

Mine was two seats down from the head of the table, to the left of the president between our secretary, Cipher, and Fenris as the enforcer. Cipher wasn't here yet, unless he'd snuck in while I was in with Mav.

"What 'cha doing in here?" Fen asked, coming around the door.

"Sitting my ass down," I replied and he worked his way around the table to his seat. I used Cipher's empty chair to prop up my bad leg and sighed.

"Paining you bad, huh?"

"Just the rapid changes in temperature, altitude, barometric pressure – all that science bullshit."

His head bounced and he smiled in one of those silent laugh chuckle things, then he spun around in his plush leather office chair and set his beer on the coaster which sat on the table. The table was a seriously impressive piece. A thick slab of live edge wood, the heart of it scored by a lightning strike and filled with a shimmering resin. Looked like we had a blood red river flowing down the middle of the fuckin' table, the edges blackened from the lightning strike that'd taken down the tree.

There were no windows in here. The only light provided by this round cut steel light fixture. Hanging from it were cutouts of motorcycle pistons and when the light was lit like it was now, it cast the shadow of a bike on the ceiling.

The walls in here were painted black, the ceiling a gunmetal gray, and the floor was a polished concrete. Behind the president's seat, on the shorter end wall, was a mural of the club's colors.

"How's she doing?" he asked me and I shrugged, shaking my head, propping my cane against the table and massaging the thigh that was paining me.

"Too soon to really tell. She got a good night's sleep last night and seemed pretty okay this morning, but I don't want to take anything for granted."

"She safe to be at your place alone?" he asked, and I would be lying if I said I wasn't worried.

"I don't know, bro, but what choice do I have?"

"Right," he nodded.

"She likes to read," I said. "I gave her Thompson's first book."

"Think that was a good idea?" he asked.

I shrugged a shoulder.

"If anything, it'll hopefully get her so full of questions she'll be dying to get 'em all asked and wait for me to get home."

He laughed and I sighed.

"Hey, we getting started?"

Glass Jaw, our VP ducked his head around the corner.

"Waiting on you and a few others," I said.

"Well I'm here," he said, sliding in around the table, taking up his spot at the president's right hand.

"I'll go drag the others back here. See who we're missing," Fen said and got up.

A second later, Squatch, Nine, Cipher, and our road captain, Tic-Tac came in. That meant we were missing our tail gunner, Blackjack, and our chaplain, Deacon, as well as one general member, Major.

"Want me to grab Mav?" Nine asked.

"Does it look like everybody's here yet?" I asked.

Nine nodded, conceding my point, and dropped into his seat. We had some empty ones. Plenty of room to grow – which with any luck, we would by Sauley. He was pretty fuckin' promising.

Wasn't ten or fifteen minutes more when the rest of the chapter showed up.

"Sauley here?" Glass Jaw asked.

"Yeah, he's out front with Momma Kat," Squatch answered.

"Prospect!" Glass Jaw shouted.

A second later, Sauley poked his head around the corner.

"Yeah, Boss?" He was still a young kid, early twenties, so he didn't know the story behind Boss and why I didn't like it. He just knew not to call *me* Boss.

"Go get Maverick and let him know we're ready," Glass Jaw ordered. "Just open the door and stick your head in." We all tried to keep a straight face. We didn't want to snigger and ruin it.

"You got it."

He went across the hall and opened up the office door and said, "Yo, Mav. They're ready."

"Don't you fucking *knock first*?" Mav demanded, giving the kid a ration of shit to a track of our laughter from the next room.

"Never mind, get your ass out front and don't let any bitches come back here. *Especially* Momma Kat."

"Copy that," the kid said and we listened to his footsteps recede.

Mav came in and shut the door, edging behind seats and finally taking his own.

"Y'all get rid of your fucking phones?" he demanded as Cipher opened up the ledger he kept our minutes in. He had a knack for codes and dead languages. He was also a massive conspiracy theorist, but it was his knack for codes and ciphers that made him the perfect candidate to take our minutes. That and he was a stellar fuckin' bookkeeper. He kept our books – both sets. The ones above board and the ones below written in codes that would keep any law enforcement types in the dark.

There were grunts of assent and agreement around the table and Fen started busting up when he looked at me. I shifted in my seat and growled, "Fuck you, man."

"What's up?"

"Mine's in a bag of rice behind the bar," I griped and grins split faces around the table. Good to know I wasn't the only one.

"To order?" Mav asked, raising his gavel and when everyone kept their mouths shut, he cracked it against the raised disc meant for the purpose.

He heaved a big sigh. "Got a call from Skeeter's Ol' Lady," he started with. "Until further notice, we gotta pick up the slack on the Yakima runs. Half his club got themselves arrested without bail."

"What?" someone cried, voice cracking.

"That's some good news for *you*," he said, giving me a sharp look. "That is if you're serious about raising those extra funds."

"Extra funds for what?" Glass Jaw asked.

Mav raised his eyebrows and I gave a tight nod. "Dump Truck has the floor," he declared.

"I left out of here four or five days back on a personal thing," I said, and cleared my throat. I didn't much like being the center of attention.

"What's up, man? You okay?" Blackjack asked. I looked down and across the table at him, sitting next to Tic-Tac and nodded.

"There's this woman I met a while back… we had a one-night thing and she called me up. She needed some help and I got Mav's blessing and went and got her. She's in a real bad way and at my place now. Had to do a little violence and she just needs a new start… a new life and as we all know that kind of shit don't come cheap."

"And *you're* footing the bill?" Tic-Tac asked with a scowl.

"Didn't give her much of a choice on starting over," I said and again had to clear my throat. "I'm not sure how much of it is really my story to tell, but the long and short of it is I killed her husband – *with good cause* – and brought her back here with me."

"Well he done fucked up if it made *you* pull the trigger," Blackjack declared.

I nodded.

They knew. They all knew. I was the *last* motherfucker to go off half-cocked.

"You gonna bring her around here?" Glass Jaw asked.

I nodded slowly. "As soon as I can get her straight. Clothes, some of the other essentials – and as soon as she's up to it."

"She's a citizen," Fen said. "He's got to school her some."

"You meet her?" Squatch asked curiously.

Fen nodded. "Briefly, last night."

"Okay," Mav said with a wicked grin. "I gotta know."

Fen smiled and nodded, chuckling.

"She's hot," he said.

I scowled.

"Dude, I'm having a hard time wrapping my brain around this one," Tic-Tac said, lacing his fingers together on top of his head, peering down his nose at me. "You ain't *ever* gone to this kind of length for no pussy before."

"She's different," I said with a shrug.

"Can't wait to meet her, brother." Glass Jaw looked impressed.

"Hope I can get her to a place where that's possible, sooner rather than later," I said. I looked at Mav and asked, "How much am I lookin' at for the papers she's gonna need?"

"Birth certificate, SSN, driver's license, and passport good enough to fool any government type is gonna run *steep*," he said.

"Fuck," I muttered.

"What's her name?" Nine asked.

"New one or old one?" Fen cracked.

"No old name. That woman's dead and I don't want it slipping out and fucking with her head, like *ever*." I was adamant.

"What the fuck happened to her?" Tic-Tac demanded frowning hard.

"Let's put it this way," Mav said. "It's really too bad you can't kill a son of a bitch twice."

We let that shit sink in.

"Right, so what do *we* call her? You know, when we get to meet her?" Nine asked, and he was way too curious for my taste but that was just the way he was. He didn't mean anything by it.

"For the price tag, she should get to pick her new name," Mav said and I smiled to myself and chuckled.

"That's not how *the* life works," I declared. "For now, in my head, she's my 'wounded little bird.' Hopefully, sooner rather than later she'll be just my 'little bird,' all better and ready to fly."

Silence crept around the chapel and Deacon said, "That's really beautiful, man."

"Right, so how much *is* it for a new life?" Squatch asked.

Maverick named the figure and Blackjack let out a low whistle.

"Fuck me," Glass Jaw declared.

"Count me in. I'd like to help," Deacon said with a shrug.

"Yeah, me too. Let's get this done," Fenris said.

"I'd like to at least meet her first, but yeah. I'm in too. I think if we all pitched in something like two shares from the next two runs we do, it should be square," Cipher said and his eye twitched as he did the math.

"I can't ask you guys to do that," I declared. I have at least a quarter of it saved up already.

There were noised of dissent around the table.

"How you boys feel about dipping into the coffers and getting the ball rolling on this shit?" Maverick asked. "We all pitch in; we could have this shit done in two runs. Cipher, correct me if I'm wrong but we got it in reserve, don't we?"

"We got it. Not much left over, but yeah. Adding in Yakima and the grower's route, we could have it back in around six months' time," Cipher confirmed.

"From a curse comes a blessing," Glass Jaw declared.

"Eastern Washington chapter reach out for funds for their situation?" I asked.

"No, and if we have to, we'll borrow from outside the region, but I don't think it'll come to that."

"It might," Cipher declared. "We'll be riding the razor's edge for the tail end of the fourth quarter coming up here, but it shouldn't be as bad as all that."

"So long as we don't slide down a razor blade and land our ass in an alcohol river, I'm game," Major declared. Barely suppressed laughs went around the table. That was Major. A major smartass, and at times, a major pain in the ass.

Mav put it to a vote and unanimously, the boys voted to help me with my wounded little bird. It was pretty intense, and I'd be lying if I said I didn't choke up some.

"Thank you. Really. You don't know what this will mean to her and you damn sure don't know what it means for me."

"Need to have a name if I put this through today," he said. "At least a first name."

"Shit, what sounds pretty?" I asked.

"Something *free* sounds appropriate, given her circumstances," Fenris said and I nodded.

"What's she look like?" Major asked.

"Long dark hair, big dark eyes, tall and sexy as hell with the cutest freckles across her nose and cheeks," I answered and when I refocused, a bunch of the guys were exchanging looks and grinning.

"Man, you got it *bad*," Blackjack declared.

I nodded. No reason to deny it.

"What about Robin?" Squatch asked and I frowned and shook my head. "Sorry, thought it work, I mean, it's also a bird's name."

"Naw, I think you're on to something there," Deacon declared good-naturedly.

"Shit, this is one of those times a phone would be handy for a fuckin' Google search," Glass Jaw said.

"We're in session," Mav reminded him unnecessarily.

The guys started calling out random fuckin' bird names around the table and were cuttin' up about it.

"What about Kestrel?" I said.

They shut up.

"That's pretty," Mav declared.

"Yeah, that's real nice," Glass Jaw agreed.

"What's a Kestrel? That some type of bird?" Blackjack asked.

"It is," Fenris declared. "It's a type of hawk."

"Real graceful flyer," I said.

"It's a good name for your little bird, man." My best friend nodded and I looked to Mav.

"Let's do it."

CHAPTER FIFTEEN

ounded Little Bird...

When Dump Truck came back home, he found me curled on the couch, the blanket from the back of it tucked over my lap, my nose buried in a romance book. I had read a little out of the Hunter Thompson book but it had stirred questions and fears, and I had to set it aside for the time being.

"Hey," he said as he came through the door, one arm loaded with grocery bags, the other gripping a cane. I stood in one fluid motion and set my book on the coffee table.

"Come sit down," I demanded and he smiled over at me. He held out the bags.

"As soon as you take these."

I took them from him, setting them aside on the coffee table. He leaned heavily on his cane, limping in my direction. I got out of the way and he folded himself onto the couch and lifted his leg with his hands to stretch it out.

"Ahhhh," he complained loudly and hissed.

"What can I do?" I asked.

"Gimme a whiskey. Some in the freezer, you can find the glasses."

I went into the kitchen, found the glasses, and took the bottle of whiskey out of the freezer. I poured two, thought about it and made his a double. I replaced the bottle and took the glasses back to the living room holding his out to him.

"Thank you," he said. He took a healthy sip and sighed. "You should go through your spoils," he said and leaned back against the arm of the couch.

I took a small sip from my own glass and grinned impishly at him over the rim.

"It's just like Christmas," I joked and he laughed.

Toothbrush, toothpaste, deodorant, pads *and* tampons which made me laugh, bodywash which made me groan happily – bar soap murdered my skin – and finally shampoo and conditioner. The good kind. *My* kind. I frowned and looked up at him.

"How did you know?" I asked.

"The smell," he answered with a blasé little shrug, like he hadn't just gone to a salon and literally *smelled* everything on their shelf.

"This isn't sold in grocery stores," I said.

"Nah, but there was a cheap salon next door and when I described it, the girl knew and told me where to go."

I sank down to sit on the edge of the coffee table and stared at him.

"Lilacs, right?" he asked.

"Right," I said softly.

He smiled faintly and nodded and took another sip from his glass.

I was speechless, frozen; just staring…

"You cool?" he asked, and I nodded dumbly and tried to close my mouth.

He cocked an eyebrow and asked, "So what'd you think of the book?"

"Oh, I, uh… I couldn't read very much of it. It was – I mean, you aren't like that – with women I mean, but what about the rest of your club?"

"Shit, I forgot about that, and no – we *aren't* like that. We have a rule. No women, no children. We're *men*, not animals."

I swallowed hard and he sighed.

"One day at a time, baby," he murmured and polished off what was in his glass and set it aside on the other end of the table from me.

"Come here," he said softly and opened his arms. I set my new things aside and went to him and he got me situated, nestled in the cradle of his arms.

He let out a big sigh and said, "I didn't mean to upset you. I just thought it might be nice to have *something*, however small, that was part of your normal."

"I'm not upset," I said, voice quavering.

"Then why you crying?"

"I don't know," I warbled and he chuckled slightly and held me tighter.

We cuddled like that, for a while and he said, "I ordered a fuckin' pizza. I couldn't be sure you'd eat something while I was gone, and I figured this would be faster. Truth be told, easier on me than cooking."

I sniffed and nodded. "Sounds good," I said.

"Hope you're not allergic. Anything you don't like, I figured this time around you could just pick it off, and I'd know for next time."

"Um, there's nothing that I can think of off the top of my head except pineapple. Pineapple does *not* belong on pizza."

"Hey, you're a woman after my own heart, there."

A knock fell at the door and I got up, self-conscious over my lack of pants. I opened the front door and peeked around and smiled at the delivery guy. I figured the least I could do was keep D.T. off his bad leg.

"Hi," I said quietly.

"That'll be thirty-four eighty-nine," he said and I nodded.

"One sec."

Dump Truck reached past me with two twenties and a five and said gruffly, "Keep the change."

The guy snatched the money, slid the pizza box out of the protective sleeve thing to keep it warm, and I took it from him.

"Thanks," I murmured.

"No problem, you all have a nice night now."

Dump Truck shut the door, but he lingered in my personal space just that little extra moment and I couldn't say it was unpleasant. Quite the opposite, in fact. The attraction we'd shared in the beginning just as bright as it had ever been despite the shadow of what'd happened to me looming over me like some damning specter.

"What's wrong, babe?" he asked me, limping into the kitchen. I followed a little more slowly with the pizza box in my hands.

He took it from me and slid it onto one of the counters beside the stovetop, flipping open the lid.

"I don't know how to explain it," I said.

He watched me, slowly opening up the cupboard that I'd discovered earlier, which held the plates.

"You know you can talk to me, right?" he asked. "Tell me anything. I won't judge."

He brought down two plates and slid two slices onto the top plate. He held it out to me, and I took it wordlessly and nodded. "No, I know," I said softly and couldn't meet his eyes. Every time I did, I felt this nameless rush, this tingling energy that made me yearn, made me *burn* and I felt so *lost* from it. This sense of wrongness, like if anybody *knew*... It made me feel so dirty on the inside but every time he was near, I also felt so *cleansed,* so *validated* somehow and it was so confusing and difficult to wrap my mind around. It was as if my heart and my head were at war and it was so *exhausting.* Reconciling who I was and who I wanted to be.

His heavy frustrated sigh brought me back to the here and now. I glanced up and he looked down at me, but not *down on me.* Never that. His jaw tightened nearly imperceptibly beneath his dark beard and he considered me.

"You're just getting yourself all tied up in knots," he declared. "The more you think whatever you're thinkin', the more upset you seem to get. I hate that for you, so now I'm not askin', I'm tellin' you – tell me what's wrong, Little Bird."

"I don't know how I'm supposed to feel," I blurted.

His scowl deepened and he asked, "About what?"

He gestured I should move back to the living room, both of our plates laden with food, and I turned moving before him yet keeping out of his way so that he could sit first. I was worried about his leg. He seemed to be in some real pain today and I didn't know if that was his normal or not... at least not yet.

I didn't know what was going to happen to me. If he intended for me to stay… any of it.

I huffed out a breath and sat down once he was situated to his liking. I knew he wanted to hear it, but I was still so self-conscious about putting anything I was feeling into words.

I nibbled on one of the slices of pizza on my plate to buy me some time and he seemed satisfied with that. At least, with the fact that I was eating something. I had been careful of how much I ate since he'd come to get me – an ingrained habit now, I suppose.

"I guess, I'm just not sure how I'm supposed to feel or how I'm supposed to act given what's happened to me," I said finally.

"What do you mean?" he asked, scowling.

"I don't know," I said. "I guess I'm just confused."

"Let me ask you something," he said, finishing a bite and I waited, curious as to what he was about to say. That was the thing about Dump Truck. He never said or did anything that I honestly expected, but whatever he did say or do had hardly been what you would call unpleasant.

Surprising, unexpected maybe, but never mean or cruel and never unpleasant.

"You keep using a word in there and I want to know why. Why do you keep saying *supposed?* Baby, you ain't *supposed* to think or feel any kind of way other than what you think or feel. There's no universal guidebook for surviving a man forcing himself on you. There's nothing that says you gotta act a certain type of way or that says you gotta be afraid of all men or be afraid of being touched ever again. There's no hard and fast rule that says you're gonna have nightmares or that you'll never be able to let a man touch you ever again."

He gave me a hard look and said, "There's nothing that says you can't be attracted to me or that you shouldn't want me to touch you… if that's what you want, I'm all for it. You just have to let me know – but that's the crux of it. It's what *you* want. How *you* feel in the moment. Those thoughts, those feelings, they're *your own*. Ain't nobody here going to fault you for having 'em. Ain't nobody here gonna tell you you're wrong. There are wrong ways of dealing with what happened to you – hardcore drugs, alcohol, things that straight up hurt you like bottling those feelings up or hurting yourself – other than that you deal with them however you need to deal with them. I'm here for it."

"I don't know what to do," I said in a moment of raw naked honesty. "It's like I want to cry or to scream. Part of me wants to fuck just to get the feel of him out of my head, but I don't know what's okay or what's not okay."

"That last part is you thinkin' like a citizen," he said. "Truth is, it's *all* okay. Whatever you need to do to get to feeling like you. There's no right or wrong way to grieve what you've lost. You just get to grieve. Get through it. Do whatever you need to do."

I chewed thoughtfully, both figuratively and literally as I ate my slice of pizza. I set my plate aside and stared at the second piece longingly for a moment, but I knew if I didn't want to get fat, I should just stick to the one.

"Eat another slice," he said gently and I smiled.

"Oh, no, it's okay," I said and he raised his eyebrows.

"Eat another slice," he said again gently but a little more firmly. "What are you afraid of?" he asked after the silence dragged for a moment or two longer than was comfortable.

"Getting fat?" I asked meekly.

He lifted one shoulder in a shrug. "Just more cushion for the pushin'," he said. "Gotta have something to grab onto when you get to feelin' like I can rail that sweet ass again."

Something low in my pussy gave a pulsating throb of need at the image. Even so, I couldn't help but giggle at the thought.

He smiled, genuinely pleased he could make me laugh and said, "There's some of the girl I remember."

"I think about that afternoon a lot," I confessed, picking up my plate and nibbling at the peak of the second slice on it.

"Yeah?" he asked curiously.

"By far the *best* sex of my life, so it's kind of hard not to." I was surprised the admission came so easily.

"Well, thank you kindly," he said and smiled, well pleased with himself. He'd earned it, to be fair. "You're definitely at the top of my list too," he said, reaching out and depositing his empty plate on the coffee table. He'd inhaled three slices to my one in less than half the time.

"Yeah?" I asked, expecting that he was just shining me on.

"Baby, I've dreamed about you every night since that day."

I stared at him wide-eyed. Not only was I not expecting an admission of that caliber, I also wasn't expecting the fervency with which he'd said it.

"I want that feeling again," I whispered and he smiled.

"You just let me know when you're up to it, when you're ready, and I'd be happy to make that happen."

"Why?" I asked, suddenly curious.

He gave a blasé little one-shouldered shrug.

"Because I want that feeling again, too. I've missed you, as strange as that probably sounds. I mean, why else would I ride over a thousand miles in two days just to come get you?"

"I wondered about that," I said, voice breathy simply because he'd stolen it.

He reached out and cupped my cheek, thumb playing back and forth along my jaw and I don't know for how long we sat like that, enveloped in silence, simply drinking each other in. The sheer intimacy of that moment etching itself in my heart, or maybe it was stitching the ragged pieces of it back together.

"You have no idea how bad I want to kiss you." The timbre of his voice was enough to make my eyes slip closed, the comfort radiating from him enough to make me turn my cheek further into his touch.

"I want you to," I whispered.

"Yeah?" he asked softly yet made no move.

"I think I need you to."

"Consider it done," he said, voice a deep purr of satisfaction as he leaned forward, hand sliding along my jaw, strong fingers kneading the back of my head and neck, seeking out that spot where my spine met my skull and where the fine muscles there seemed to hold all the tension in my body.

I blindly set my plate with its nibbled slice of pizza aside on the coffee table with a clatter, reaching for him as he drew me closer. He leaned back slowly, his warm breath fanning across my lips; the carrot on a stick that left me practically climbing his body like a tree, or, well, in his semi-prone state on the couch, it was still like climbing a tree just more like a fallen one. He was so solid and strong beneath me as I eased up the length of his body, putting my mouth against his.

One of his big hands twined in the back of my hair, cradling my head, pressing my mouth to his while the other slid up the back of my bare thigh, gripping my ass, urging me on as I rocked my hips uninhibited against the bulge in the front of his jeans.

"Here or in the bedroom?" I murmured and he chuckled, the sound rich and sinfully dark like gourmet chocolate with a fine whiskey chaser. That sound sent my senses to thrumming in all the right ways. My pussy growing wet, my need for this and for him increasing exponentially.

"I'm not fucking you on my couch," he said. "You deserve better than that." With a light little smack on my bottom he grated out, "Bedroom."

Yes, sir!

I pushed up off the couch, Dump Truck's hands guiding me, helping me to stand from the awkward position. He waved me off when I tried to help him up after me and leveraged himself up on his own, his leg held out somewhat stiff and not fully cooperating with him. I suddenly couldn't wait to get him stripped and into his bed where he could rest it for a time.

He followed close behind me, his hands on my shoulders, lightly resting, the warmth from his palms and fingertips leeching through the thin cotton as he limped behind me, guiding me to his bedroom door.

God, it was so not right how excited I was. My body low-key tingling in a wash of eagerness. I wanted his hands on me. I wanted his cock inside me, and I wanted to drape myself over his body and feel his warmth and the solidness of him beneath me.

He stopped me, just beside the bed, and turned me in his grasp.

"You're sure, now?" he asked, looking down at me and that was one of the things that I loved about being with him like this. There wasn't much that made a girl who was five foot ten feel small and like some kind of a fairy princess, but Dump Truck, for all of his rough language and gruff demeanor, did. He towered over me, but it wasn't intimidating in the slightest. I smiled up at him and felt a serenity that I hadn't known in some time and nodded carefully.

"I'm sure," I whispered and he smiled down at me, lifting his black tee off over his head, dragging it from the back of his neck, discarding it on the floor.

I giggled and went for the hem of the tee I wore, but he stopped me with gentle hands over my own.

"Stop, slow down," he murmured. "I'll get to it."

I let it go and went for his belt instead. He moaned and closed his eyes briefly and I realized how much it got to him. How much he loved the sight of me undressing him, sliding the strip of leather out from its buckle, my fingers slipping the button at the top of his fly through its denim eye.

He stood there and watched me, head bowed, fixated on my hand as it dipped into the front of his jeans and I wrapped light fingers around his shaft.

"Fuck yes, baby…" he whispered and drew a sharp breath between clenched teeth, letting it out slowly in an appreciative hiss as I worked him with my hand, pressing my body up against his, raising my face for a kiss. He slid his thick fingers into my hair, holding it back from our faces and kissed me as though he were ravenous for it.

I worked the velvet, hard length of him with one hand and pushed his jeans out of the way with my other as he wrapped an arm around me and crushed me to him, his mouth hot, lips insistent; the intensity between us scorching and causing me to melt against him.

He tried kicking off his boots so I could get his jeans off the rest of the way and things turned into a bit of a comedy of errors – the boots uncooperative and his jeans putting up a fight. Finally, he sat down on the edge of the bed and let me get him the rest of the way undressed.

I went back to him, straddling his lap, nothing but the borrowed tee I wore between us, which wasn't much of a barrier at all in the grand scheme of things. His hands delving beneath the hem, rough against my skin in a tantalizing way I couldn't even begin to describe.

He touched me gently, firmly, the need telegraphing from him to me by way of tight muscles and careful intention behind each one of his movements. He was tightly controlled, careful of me in a way he hadn't been our first time.

It sort of broke my heart.

I wrapped his ponytail around my hand and jerked his head back, taking his mouth from mine and stared down into the deep dark well of his eyes.

"I won't break," I murmured and a dark light ignited in the depths of those eyes.

"What're you asking?" He arched one eyebrow, an almost challenge.

"I'm asking you to love me," I whispered, slightly unsure of myself all of a sudden with just *how* he looked at me; the intensity of his gaze.

"Just give me some direction if you need to," he said and lifted the hem of my tee with purpose. I relinquished my hold on his hair and held up my arms, allowing him to strip me bare and once I was exposed? He didn't waste any time being overly gentle. His arms went around me, pulling me to his mouth which he used to ravish my throat and the side of my neck, trailing kisses and little love bites over my collarbone as he held me fast, allowing me to arch back over his big arms so that his bearded lips could reach more of my skin.

He licked, nipped, and sucked at my chest, lips and teeth playing with my nipples, tongue teasing them, hot and wet as I rocked in his lap.

It felt so incredibly good, his mouth on me, the hard, hot length of him pressed against my pussy lips. I shamelessly humped him, hips rocking back and forth, wishing and impatient with not having him inside me.

He was even bigger than I'd remembered, but I also knew how amazing it had been to have him entrenched deep in my body. How it'd felt to have him so incredibly close. How it'd felt powerful and at the same time how fragile, how delicate I'd felt by comparison to his big frame. It was a type of invincibility I didn't think I would ever feel again and yet here it was, here *I* was, and he was giving me my heart's desire because I'd only *asked*.

"You good with me on top for a bit?" he asked.

"Yeah," I said back, breathily, wanting every bit of him that he was willing to give me.

"Hold on to me, baby." He breathed into the side of my neck, and I did. In an amazing display of strength, he rolled us both, laid me across the bed, and lightly hip checked my inner thigh, keeping my legs spread around him as he reached between us.

"Not letting another thing come between us," he said softly, then asked, "You okay with that?"

I was more than okay with that and I said so, arching back as he guided his long, thick cock to my entrance and lying over the top of me, caging me in an embrace that was both possessive and protective, he began to work his way inside. Easing himself in inch by inch, withdrawing just a bit when I made a slight noise of protest. Dump Truck carefully molded our bodies together until I wasn't quite sure where I left off and he began and vice versa.

"Hold on to me, baby," he said again, his voice constrained as he fought to hold back, and I could have wept at how wonderfully considerate he was being.

I held onto him, arms around his shoulders, fingers buried in the back of his long hair, feeling cheated by the stupid hair tie getting in the way. The thought was fleeting as he drove himself deeper and I had to arch to keep it from becoming too intense.

I didn't ask him to slow down. I didn't ask him to stop. I wanted him to unmake me, to break me, and to remake me. I wanted him to make me whole again.

CHAPTER SIXTEEN

---

*D*ump Truck...

I held her close and didn't hold back. I knew she could take it. Hell, she could take more than she ever gave herself credit for. She was beauty, she was grace, and if she'd had the gun, I was damn sure she would have shot him in the face – but instead it was me. I was good with that. She was *too good* for that kind of a thing and the only regret I had was that she'd had to endure what'd been done to her in order for me to get her back.

She arched underneath me as I drove myself mercilessly deep inside of her and I can't tell you how good she felt wrapped around my cock. Hot as hell, slick with her arousal and her desire, she felt phenomenal and the way she *moved* was so sexy, so *free*, like the flight of the bird I'd named her after.

She'd asked me to love her; I guess she didn't understand that I already did. I never would have gone to get her otherwise. I'd never felt such a deep connection with anyone else before. There was chemistry, for sure, but there was something deeper than that at play here.

I kissed her chin lightly, her head thrown back as she moaned beneath me, writhing, her legs going around my hips, my leg screaming and on fire, the pain a distant dull roar, riding tail gunner to the pleasure that was mounting.

I couldn't hold off, but I would be damned if I would go before her. I wanted things I could never speak out loud, not without risk of damaging her already fragile heart further. Like how I desperately wanted my touch to erase his. How I wanted to keep her under me like this forever. How I wanted her to come out the other side of this fiercer than the poor little rich girl I'd met in that bookstore, who I'd underestimated in that café.

I wanted the woman who'd shown up on my doorstep, bold as brass, in nothing but an overcoat and some sexy lingerie.

I was afraid if I said any of those things right now, I would risk losing her a bit more than she was already lost inside of herself.

Still, none of it stopped me from going looking for that woman. None of it stopped me from deep-dicking her in my bed, None of it stopped me from kissing her like she'd never been kissed. None of it slowed me down one bit from making her come all over my dick, from holding her tight as she shuddered in pleasure against me. None of it even slowed me down.

She'd come for me, and there wasn't anything that stopped me from coming with her, from spilling my seed hot inside her, from claiming her as mine and mine alone and I'd kill ten more just like the son of a bitch back in Vegas if any so much as looked at her sideways.

She was mine as long as she wanted to be and I whispered in her ear, "That's my girl," my voice dripping with approval. She did come so beautifully, after all. She never needed to know there was any double entendre to it.

"Promise me," she said breathlessly.

"Anything you'd like," I assured her, kissing across her chest, slipping out from her body.

"Promise me I *am*," she murmured, her palms pressed to my shoulders, fingernails digging slightly. I glanced up her body to where she stared at me between the valley of her perfect tits and I smiled.

"I just did," I declared and resumed my way, languidly kissing down her supple skin just for the hell of it, just for the feel of her underneath my lips.

She sighed out and I glanced back up, her eyes closed, her body relaxing into the cloud of my bedcovers and I smiled to myself.

I think it was the first time I'd seen her truly relax since I'd picked her up.

"You're all good, baby," I murmured against her skin. "You're all mine."

"As long as you'll have me," she said and I smiled to myself.

"You really want to put that decision off on me?" I asked, chuckling.

"It only seems fair," she said softly. "You killed a man for me. Came and got me simply because I called and I asked you to… I owe you my life."

"You don't owe me shit," I told her succinctly. "I didn't do anything I didn't want to do."

"Why then? Why did you do it? Why'd you come get me?"

I kissed my way back up her body, lips lingering a little longer against her skin as I thought about what she'd just asked me. Carefully, as I drew nearer those questioning big brown eyes, as I vaulted her leg carefully and settled on my side beside her, propping my head in my hand to look her beautiful face over, I gave her the only answer I could. I gave her the truth.

"I wanted to see if what I was feeling was real. If the vibe I got from you the evening you were here, was real, too, or if it was just all in my head," I said.

Her eyes widened slightly and she turned on her side, mirroring me, her fingertips playing lightly over my chest as she walked them in an idle touch across my skin and I loved that about her. That she seemed just as desperate to maintain contact with me as I was about maintaining contact with her. Even the simplest of touches – light, gentle, fingertips against her cheek, lips against her hair… I don't know. It was almost *energizing* somehow. Made me feel good. Wasn't about sex in those idle touches but it was definitely something else… the word intimate or intimacy came to mind.

It wasn't something I'd ever really allowed myself with anyone. Anyone but her, and it felt so fuckin' natural, so good, so *right* with my wounded little bird here that I had no desire to ever go back to the hard-ass motherfucking dick I was before.

Not that I'd ever change for anyone else. I had no desire to be anything else to anyone else.

I just had this deep desire to be everything to *her,* and I couldn't tell you why that was except for chemistry. I mean, we damn sure had plenty of that in spades.

"So, you rode over a thousand miles just to see me, to see if it was all in your head?" she asked softly.

"Think I'm crazy?" I asked with a half-smile.

"A little crazy, maybe," she said. "Honestly, though… that's really crazy *romantic,* God!" She drew a deep, deep breath that seemingly went on forever before letting it out in an explosive sigh.

"Maybe I've been reading too many of those damn books," I said and she smiled and scooted closer to me, pressing her mouth to mine, and I captured the side of her face in the palm of my hand, stroking my thumb over her beautiful cheek, keeping my head propped as we lazily made out amidst our mutual afterglow.

Afterglow that glimmered like the coals in a forge, the renewed contact the oxygen, the catalyst, to stoke the flames of our desire once more. She scooted carefully closer and closer still. Her arm sliding over my flank, palm pressing to my back so she could draw herself nearer still.

I groaned into her mouth as her tongue stroked hot against mine and my dick started to stir between us.

She moaned softly against my mouth, writhing in her slight agitation, and I thanked my lucky stars that she was ready for more so soon because I was damn sure ready to go all night. It'd been one hell of a dry spell. I'd quit fucking bitches probably around five or six months back when I couldn't come anywhere close to what I'd had with my little bird who'd up and flown away on me.

"Again?" I murmured into her mouth.

"Please," she begged and who the fuck was I to argue?

"You're on top this time, baby," I said and turned onto my back for her.

"I like it on top," she whispered with a smile and straddled me, teasing me with her hot little pussy, sliding it up and down my growing erection when fuck, I'd kill again just to be inside her. I liked this, though. Her coy smile, her shy movements picking up speed along with her bravery.

She was so beautiful above me like this and I could spend all night watching her, tasting her, feeling her…

"Time for you to love me back, babe," I growled in my aroused state and she smiled, put her hands against my chest and raised herself up. I was all too happy to help get myself situated to be inside her again.

~

"ALRIGHT, ALRIGHT!" I shouted. The insistent knocking on my front door seriously starting to piss me off. Especially considering it had roused me out of my warm bed and had forced me to unwrap myself from around my little bird and leave her to find out what dipshit couldn't get the fucking hint and just *fuck off.*

I threw back the locks and jerked open my front door to look down at Ms. Dahlia Darling, one of the girls that frequented the club. She was this Burlesque performer at this little place down in the bowels of Pike's Place Market.

"Just *what* the fuck are you doin'?" I demanded.

She raised one of her perfectly arched black eyebrows at me, her equally perfectly painted matte red lips quirking in a smirk. Dahlia was something else. She didn't need a man, didn't *want* a man, but she sure liked to fuck and thus had a sort of symbiotic relationship with the club as a result. Truth was, she was handy in a pinch, had provided alibis in the past, and had an outlaw's spirit. I still couldn't exactly decide if she was fearless or stupid, though. Not with her banging on my door at – *what the fuck time was it, anyway?*

"Mav sent me over, said you had a lost chick in dire need of a fashionista of my caliber. That and he needs your ass back to work at Ironheart."

Ironheart Salvage was the official name of our old boneyard and bike shop. The one I was supposedly gainfully employed at, all on the up and up – and shit, yeah, I needed to get back to work or shit was gonna start lookin' suspicious to anyone who might be keepin' tabs.

"What the fuck time is it?" I growled, scowling at her but stepping aside so she could come in.

She rolled her deep brown eyes and with a sway of her hips walked past me into my living room.

She was undeniably hot with her own sense of retro forties and fifties pinup style, but the tattoos ruined it a little for me. I didn't really dig them either on me or on a woman and Dahlia had some fuckin' tattoos.

She was in this white fitted off-the-shoulder shirt with these black polka dots on it, her bosom thrust up and together but the chest plate tattoo she was rockin' took center stage today.

It was a purple casket, open, a human heart in it, surrounded by deeper purple roses and deep green foliage. Truth be told, it fit right in line with the club and the joke between her and Mav was that it was a mark from the universe that she belonged.

She and Mav were thick as thieves, the best of friends, but I don't think they'd ever banged. She fucked her way through a few of the guys, though. Maybe someday one would get around to taming her.

She turned in her light pink pedal pusher pants that were skintight, standing on her wedge heels, white with black polka dots, the twist in them matching the center of the retro top she wore, and she shouldered her light pink handbag.

That woman was always put together.

She crossed her arms, her red nails a perfect match for her lipstick, slightly digging into her tattooed arm as she looked at me nonplussed.

"It's after eight. Honeymoon is sadly over, big guy. Don't you worry about a thing. I'll look after your wounded little bird today. Get her some new, nice things, some makeup. Make her all pretty and help her feel good."

"Mighty altruistic of you," I said waiting for the catch.

"It is, though, isn't it?" she asked with an enthusiastic grin and I couldn't help it. I broke first and chuckled.

"How much you need for this little venture?" I asked.

She looked under her arm where the little purse was tucked and reached into it, pulling out a rubber banded wad of cash.

"I think Mav has it covered," she said with a wink.

"Dump Truck?" My little bird's voice came lilting from the bedroom.

I sighed and murmured, "Fine, but be careful with her. Anything comes up, anything at all, you *call* me. I mean it, Dahlia."

"I hear you, loud and clear," she murmured back and smiled at me completely unfazed.

That was Dahlia, cool as a cucumber and didn't take shit off nobody.

"Gimmee a minute."

"Take your time, not like I don't have anything else to do today!" she called after me, flipping her ponytail. She had her hair perfectly coifed to match the outfit, of course. A real June Cleaver, short ponytail with one of them poof things in the front. Hell if I knew what it was called.

"Well, go on! What are you looking at me for?" she demanded.

Truth was, I didn't have a fuckin' clue how I was going to explain this to my wounded little bird. If she was gonna be cool going out with Dahlia for the day or not. She needed the clothes, and I sure as fuck didn't want to go shopping with her – except for at the Harley store. That I was totally on board with. I wanted her in the *proper* gear that fit her like a dream.

"Who is it?" my girl asked, apprehension written all over her face as she clutched the sheets to her chest.

"Mav sent one of the girls from the club on by to take you shopping," I said. "You need some clothes. I don't really want you to be alone, and I gotta get my ass in to my day job today so..."

"Oh." She looked vaguely disappointed.

"It'll be all good. Dahlia will get you all hooked up." I sat down on the edge of the bed and pulled the pad of paper and pen I kept either in the headboard or on the bedside table to me. My little bird watched me, twitching, flinching off to the side as I reached past her. I didn't pay it no mind.

She was uncomfortable, her anxiety clear, and to take it personally would just make her double down on feeling worse and that wasn't where I was trying to get her to go. I figured given enough time, enough security, the flinching would stop. It'd be a miracle if after one night of sex, she were suddenly cured of almost a year of trauma. To expect that would make me a damn fool, and my momma didn't raise no fool.

I scribbled down my phone number. It'd been a gamble on if the sim card had been okay. We'd just switched housings and it'd worked, thank God.

"Here's my number –"

"I already have it," she said and tapped her temple with her two fingers.

I smiled and nodded. "Good. You keep it up there."

She took the written number anyway, folding it in quarters, holding onto it like a talisman.

"I'll run down to the bike and get you the rest of your hand-me-downs. It'll be nice to get you some of your own clothes, won't it?"

She took a deep breath, and I tried to keep the smile off my face as she nodded bravely. Wouldn't do to appear condescending. That was the last thing she needed.

"Hang on right here." I got up and bent, kissing her on the fore-head. Her eyes slipped shut, her hand came up, and she hooked me around the back of my neck, bringing her mouth to mine.

I kissed her back, gladly, and whispered, "I'll be right back."

"Hi."

We both looked over to Dahlia standing in the bedroom doorway.

"Um, hi," my girl said back, a little timidly as she let her eyes rove Dahlia from head to her peep toe shoes.

"I'll let you two get acquainted," I said. "Dahlia, this is Little Bird. Little Bird, meet Dahlia."

"It's nice to meet you," Dahlia said, and she walked forward with that effortless sway to her hips and dropped down onto the corner of the foot of the bed.

"It's nice to meet you, too," my little bird said, huddling beneath the blankets, blushing furiously.

"I'll be right back," I told them.

"Take your time," Dahlia said, waving me off without looking at me. Lord, I could already see the wheels turning in that pretty head of hers.

I went down to the bike and hustled doing it. I didn't want to leave my little bird in any more of a predicament than she already was without any clothes.

By the time I got back upstairs, the two of them were giggling over something or other.

"Alright, get out, let my lady get herself dressed," I ordered and set the bag of clothes I had for her on the end of the bed.

"Feel free to grab one of my tees," I told Little Bird, knowing all she really had left by way of scrounged ladies' things were a pair of jeans, the socks I'd bought her, and the rest of the pack of ladies' undies.

Truth be told, a weight was off of me and Dahlia was helping me out. God bless Mav for reading my situation and knowin' just what to do when my dumb ass was too proud to ask for help.

I owed him a beer or six.

I'd been worried about leaving my girl alone after what'd happened in that first hotel outside Vegas. I'd taken all the guns with me yesterday, and it hadn't exactly been a mistake that the rest of her clothes hadn't made it up here before now. I felt shitty and manipulative doin' it, when she'd damn sure had enough of that – but I wanted her *safe*.

I shut the bedroom door behind me and Dahlia turned from where she'd been just ahead of me.

"Little Bird?" she asked, arching a brow.

"Yup. That's the way it's gonna stay for now, too," I said and she gave a sage nod.

"Her protection, my protection, or both?"

"Both," I said. "Listen up and listen good, if *anyone* out there recognizes y'all – get out of there immediately. Come straight to the boneyard. We'll get things handled. I don't care where you take her shopping, just avoid the eastside. No Bellevue, no Kirkland, no Redmond. Am I clear?"

"Loud and," she said nodding. "Like you would catch me dead over in yuppie central anyway."

"Just have to be sure."

"Well, by the time we're done today I'll have your baby feeling like a million dollars. You just wait."

"She's had it rough, D."

"I know," she said softly. "Mav told me."

I nodded slowly. If Mav saw fit to trust Dahlia with that information, I had no problem. I trusted Mav implicitly to have my back.

I grunted and said gruffly, "Just look out for her, she's new to the life."

Dahlia nodded slowly and said, "Momma bear in the house."

"Thanks."

"Don't mention it." She stared at me for emphasis. "Seriously, don't go ruining my reputation as the bitch with no fucks to give – I'll make sure it ends badly for you. I'm talking *all* the drama."

I cracked a grin and nodded.

"I'ma get ready for work," I declared.

"You do that."

I slipped back into my bedroom to find my wounded little bird sitting on the edge of the bed, underwear on, a fresh one of my tees on, socks bundled in her hands and jeans still laid out at her side. She looked up at me.

"You doin' alright?" I asked.

"A little nervous," she answered softly.

"How come?"

"I mean, isn't it a little weird going shopping, having my nails done, buying *makeup*?"

"Thought girls dug shit like that."

She snorted and put a hand over her mouth to keep from laughing. I sat down next to her and leaned toward her, bumping my shoulder lightly into hers.

"Life goes on," I said. "With or without you, the earth keeps spinning, the days pass and ain't none of us getting any younger while it does. You can't sit here waiting for your life to start again, baby. You gotta grab it and wring everything out of it bare-handed if you truly want to *live*."

She stared at me, face open with wonder. "Profound," she murmured.

"Yeah, well, I have my moments," I declared and smiled down at her. "Dahlia's a little intense, but she's good people," I said and Little Bird nodded.

"She seems nice," she said and I barked a laugh.

"When she wants to be, which truth be told is more often than not."

She smiled and leaned her head on my shoulder with a heavy sigh.

"Look, I know you don't want to go, but humor me. You need the things and you probably need the girl time, too. I'll have D. bring you to the boneyard and to the club when you're through." I got up and went over to my dresser and the glass bowl I had on top. I fished through the myriad of change, hair ties, and other miscellaneous junk in it and came up with my spare apartment key.

"Here. Bring your shit back here before you come to the club. Make my life a little easier, would yah?"

"Yeah," she murmured. "And thank you. I don't think I say 'thank you' enough."

"You ain't gotta thank me," I said. "You survived, now put it in their eye and thrive."

I raised my eyebrows and held out the key. She took it from my fingers in a light grasp and smiled murmuring, "I'll do my best."

"That's all anyone around these parts can ask for, love. Not one iota more."

With that, I set about getting my shit together and headed across the hall to grab a quick shower.

"We're leaving!" Dahlia called through the bathroom door a minute or two later.

"Babe! Come in here!" I hollered out. A second later the bathroom door opened, and I pulled back the curtain and puckered my lips. She smiled at me and it lit up her whole face. She came over to me and kissed me 'see you later' and that was a damn promise I had every intention of keepin'.

I'd see her forever and always if I had my way about it.

CHAPTER SEVENTEEN

---

*L*ittle Bird...

"Aww, you two are adorable!" Dahlia declared when I shut the bathroom door behind me.

I blushed and tried to minimize it by saying, "I'm sure he's like that with all of his girlfriends."

Dahlia looked amused and shook her head slowly.

"Well, Dump Truck has never had a *girlfriend*, really. At least not that I can remember. He's always been a hit-it-and-quit-it kind of a guy. Never had anything going on longer than a few weeks. You, my darling girl, are special and that's awesome. Come on, let's make your outside look as fabulous as what you must have going on inside to tame that absolute beast of a man."

She came over, hooked an arm in mine, and escorted me to the front door. I locked it behind us once we were out on the landing. The key worked, although the wood of the door was swollen and as such, you had to sort of lift up on the handle to get the lock to slide home and engage.

"Tricky," I commented and she smiled at me.

We went down to Dump Truck's parking space where she had half-assed parked in what remained of his spot with her car, the ass end hanging out in the driveway some. I hadn't known what to expect, the light blue Toyota Matrix hadn't been it.

She disengaged the locks and I opened up the passenger door, sliding into the seat. She had a frilly garter hanging from her rearview mirror, change in one of the cup holders, and aside from some dust, her car was really clean.

"I am so happy to be your personal shopper today," she said, starting up her car and reaching for her seatbelt at the same time. I clicked mine into place across my body. It honestly felt a little *weird* being in a car after all that time spent on the back of Dump Truck's bike.

"I honestly have no idea what to even buy," I said. "I mean…" I trailed off. Just what was I supposed to get to match this whole new life?

Dahlia read my mind. "Well, you have a whole new life in front of you. I guess the first step is to decide, what do you want to look like? I mean, the world is your oyster at this point."

I hadn't thought of it like that. I mean, I felt like I was in a cage. Not as bad as *before*, gilded though that cage had been. Except now, I was somehow a fugitive. On the lam – whatever that meant. I mean, how much of myself should I change?

"Maybe it's less about what you should *change* and more about what you want to be? Girl, you are a *phoenix*, rising from the *ashes*. You are probably the *freest* you have ever been in your life. *Carpe diem!* Seize the day!"

She grinned over at me and said, "You know what? I think we should start with the grass roots. Let's do something with your hair, get your nails done – you've just been through the mother of *all* breakups. It's totally time for a new you. What do you say?"

"How… how do you know?" I asked stunned. She rolled her eyes and gave me a crooked smile, blinking at me until I got that *that part* wasn't something we were supposed to talk about. I took a deep breath and ignored the elephant in the car and said, "Honestly, I like my hair the way it is, but a slight trim wouldn't be bad."

"How about a trim and a tint? Not like outright *dying* it but maybe a streak or a light wash of red color over the dark so that when the light catches it you see it?" She raised an eyebrow and I smiled.

"Maybe, yeah." I nodded slowly.

"We'll go see Trinny – she's not club so mum's the word, but she *is* a good friend of mine and does fabulous hair."

"Okay," I said. "Will she have any openings?" I asked.

"Only one way to find out," Dahlia declared, and that's how we found ourselves right down First Avenue in Burien at the Union Jack Salon.

"Just remember," Dahlia declared, throwing her car into park, "the best lies and stories you can tell about your situation are rooted in truth. If anybody has anything to say or asks about that – he hit you, you called an old friend, and you left him. Keep it simple."

I nodded, hanging on her every word, realizing now that she was partially here to coach me.

"Got it," I said, suddenly relieved, grateful to have the guidance.

"You're welcome," she said and smiled and with a nod full of assurance. "We're going to get you through all this. One step at a time. It's going to be a big day today – exhausting – but I promise, it'll be worth it."

I nodded and she opened her door. I opened mine, following her lead.

I was really apprehensive about doing anything with my hair. I genuinely liked it the way it was but agreed some form of change was definitely warranted. Trinny *did* have an opening available and agreed it was long, healthy, and beautiful and she would hate to do anything to it too drastic either.

In the end, we forwent tinting it in favor of a wash, a deep conditioning treatment, a light trim just to get any dead or split ends off and a blowout. She finished things off with straightening it just as her first appointment of the day arrived.

It was just the thing, the three of us laughing, talking, discussing fashion and what styles may or may not suit me since I was going the route of overhauling my wardrobe.

By the time my hair was done, I felt fresh, almost brand new, and ready to take on the rest of the day.

Dahlia smiled at me over my head in the mirror and asked, "Clothes or makeup next?"

"Makeup," I answered without hesitation.

She smiled. "Ulta, Mac, Sephora, or Bare Minerals?" she asked and I reeled slightly in my seat before pushing to my feet. I was deliciously sore between my legs and smiled faintly on the inside over it. A sense of satisfaction at knowing I was still desirable to D.T. crept through me. It seems it was the day for ego boosts.

"Sephora?" I answered hesitantly.

"Good choice!" Dahlia declared. "To Southcenter we go!"

Southcenter Mall was in Tukwila, just past the airport as you headed east on 516. It was a big shopping mall; however, it didn't have the best reputation. Several times a year, it was in the news for gang activity in the mall – a fight or a shooting. It wasn't somewhere I would have chosen to go willingly in my previous life. Instead, I would have found myself in the heart of downtown Seattle at Westlake Mall or Pacific Place – which were right next to each other and were practically the same place.

Either that, or I would have gone to Bellevue Square on the eastside of Lake Washington – which would have been closer to home anyway. Of course, it wasn't home… not anymore, and I couldn't exactly say I was sorry about that. My bitterness, my hurt, rising to choke me with its acid burn of bile.

Now, Southcenter was the 'closest to home,' I guess. Especially now that 'home' was with Dump Truck.

Funny, that.

It surprisingly felt more like 'home' than any other place I had lived before. The more we moved through the day today, the freer I began to feel. Like these invisible shackles or bonds were being unlocked or falling away with every purchase made, with every store we went to.

Every time we stepped foot in a place, I asked, "What's my budget?" and every time Dahlia said, "Will you stop it? It's on Mav and the guys, you don't really *have* a budget right now. We run out of cash, I call Mav, we go pick up more. That's how this works."

"I don't understand," I said as she led me from Sephora, laden with a shopping bag full of makeup. I mean everything I could need, too. From foundation, concealer, and finishing powder, to three different eyeshadow pallets, mascara, eyeliners, sharpeners, lipsticks and lip glosses – just everything you could think of. Dahlia didn't even blink at the price tag, simply peeled off some bills and handed over the cash. We easily cleared over five hundred dollars in makeup alone.

We had dropped close to three hundred dollars more at Lucky Seven Jeans where we had stopped first, and had only came out with three pair. Now we were crossing into a real danger zone, at least for me… Victoria's Secret was the bane of my existence.

"Girl, relax." Dahlia stood in front of me, her hands on my shoulders giving me a little shake. "I seriously expected less resistance from a rich girl. Oh, my God!"

I rolled my eyes and said, "I had no problem spending my daddy's money – it's true. I didn't have any trouble spending what Guy gave me by way of allowance. This is different," I said defensively.

"Guy? Really? That was dude's name?" Dahlia made a face. "How douchey."

I laughed and shook my head, stopped and then nodded. "Accurate," I said with a sigh, glad that I was made up and the bruising was covered from our foray into Sephora. One of the girls had taken one look at me and had sat me down to make me up.

"Hey, sorry I brought it up," she said and hugged me unexpectedly. I guess my face had changed, my expression going dour as the image of Guy, laying on our entryway floor, blood seeping across the expensive stone flitted through my head.

It'd been horrifying. Not the imagery, not the scent of copper and brimstone hanging in the air – but the pure, unadulterated *relief* I'd felt as his body had hit the stone.

God, I felt so *awful* about that. I mean, how horrible was I that I could be so *relieved* at the taking of a human life? What did that say about me? I mean, what would I do if we were ever *caught?* I certainly couldn't or wouldn't testify against Dump Truck and I didn't understand at all how he could be so… so… *unconcerned.*

"You need a bra," she said, snapping me out of it. "Oversized tees do nothing for you and I bet you have an amazing set of girls." She gave me a keen, sharp-eyed look. "And if you got it, flaunt it, has *always* been my motto."

I laughed slightly and dashed at the waterline of my eyes with a fingertip, determined not to ruin my careful makeup that the kind girl in Sephora had spent so much time on.

"Right, so bras, panties, and whatever other kind of trouble we can get into," she said and smiled big.

I laughed again, an uncomfortable chuckle, but I went with it. Dahlia was a force to be reckoned with so it seemed and was more than a little intimidating. It wasn't as though she'd said anything untoward. It was more that she did this thing where she would say something and would stare at you, smiling, until you made the right decision. It was somewhere between creepy and comedic but had left me shifting on my feet with a discomfort a time or two. I mean, I didn't know how to handle it – or her, but I imagine that was the way she liked things.

I stopped at the rack of matching bra and panty sets and plucked a white set from the rack.

"Honey, you don't have to go straight for the clearance rack!" she chided and I shook my head.

"No, it's not that..." I said trailing off as memory took over. Of course, it was a memory I would happily get lost in. "I like these," I declared with no further explanation. She looked me up and over, searching my face and finally nodded.

"They have your size?" she asked and I smiled, relieved there was no argument coming.

"I don't know, let me look." I got lucky and found one last set in my size, the memory of Dump Truck pulling down the cup to the bra to take my nipple into his mouth strong as I went back with the set and an armload of other bras and matching panties to the fitting room. No – I wasn't going to try the panties, but I did need to make sure the bras would fit and as comfortably as any bra *could*.

We walked the whole mall, *twice*. Flitting from store to store, sometimes making more than one trip into a given store all so I could find things I would be satisfied wearing. Dahlia only shot down a couple of items. Still, by the end, even with as much money as we had spent, I didn't feel like we had garnered a lot.

"Never fear," Dahlia declared. "We aren't done yet."

I groaned and she laughed at me. "Shoes, girl. We need shoes to go along with some of this and we also could stand to get you a few skirts or dresses. You won't be on the back of the bike *all* the time."

By the time we were done with the mall itself, we'd had to packrat our haul out to the back of her car and we *still* weren't done! Apparently, there was a whole *other* wad of hundred-dollar bills to be spent at the Harley-Davidson store in Renton, which was our next stop.

She called up Dump Truck to let him know we were on our last stop and it sounded like she was arguing with him.

She rolled her eyes as she turned into the lot and said, "Fine, fine, fine, fine, fine! We'll just look. Jesus! You're acting like a child. Like I told you 'no' to going into your favorite toy store."

I couldn't make out what he said, but it made Dahlia laugh. She nodded and handed over the phone.

"Hey, baby. How are you doing?"

"Okay," I said softly, a bit self-conscious in front of Dahlia who was pretending awfully hard that she was minding her own business.

"Dahlia getting to be a bit too much?" he asked.

"Oh, no. It's fine," I said and I meant it. It was.

"Cool, cool. You go on into the toy shop, see what you like and we'll go down together to pick some things that you liked. Deal?"

"Sure, I'd like that," I said.

"Okay. See you in a while. You girls take your time, now."

"Okay. We'll see you when we're done."

There was a slight pregnant pause where it was like he wanted to say more but he didn't. Instead, he just said, "Bye now," and the call ended. I smiled and thought deeply, *I love you, too* as I handed Dahlia her phone back.

She smiled affectionately at me and took it.

"Let's go see what we can see," she said and I smiled nodding.

CHAPTER EIGHTEEN

*D*ump Truck...

I was sitting at the bar in the main room of the club, waitin' on Dahlia to bring me my little bird. Momma Kat was moseying around the other side of the polished wood, drying glasses and putting them up, her mind on other things keeping her silent for the most part. I could dig it. It'd been a long day. A total drag. Anything that could've gone wrong had gone wrong with my rebuild project and I couldn't get my mind or my worry off my girl.

Tic-Tac was sitting next to me, fucking around on his phone, nursing a beer of his own, his mind on his own business which was typical of the dude. I was grateful for no one bothering me. I was tired. I didn't have it in me for small talk, and all I wanted was to see my girl walk through the front door.

I think my current state of nervousness had a lot more to do with how she would deal with coming up in here and meeting the rest of the guys than anything. Honestly, I was just as nervous for them meeting her. I mean, she was such a fucking *citizen* which automatically put her at a real disadvantage.

Some of the other guys were behind me, clustered in a knot on and around one of the leather couches back there with the coffee table in front of it. The little nook took up most of the corner to the left of the front door as you came in, right before the dart boards and the pool tables started.

It was just supposed to be a comfortable spot to get high or to fuck the odd club bunny that happened to be on hand for such a purpose. We didn't have none around now – at least not yet. Night was young and it bein' a weeknight never stopped one of us.

The guys there were cuttin' up, clustered up around Nine's cellphone, dying laughing over something and the noise was starting to piss me off. All I wanted was to drink my ice-cold beer and have a minute of some fuckin' peace after a long ass day and these knuckleheads were all sorts of pissing on my parade.

The laughter reached a crescendo, and Tic-Tac fuckin' beat me to it demanding, "What in the good goddamn is so fuckin' funny over there?"

Nine pushed to his feet, Fen wiping tears from his eyes and Blackjack nearly falling on his ass he was laughing so hard, Cipher reached out to support him. I shook my head, my curiosity good and piqued.

"Okay, I'ma set the stage here," Nine said. "Mav comes 'round and tells the prospect his bike is dirty, right? Tells him to take it to the Elephant Car Wash on First Avenue there in Burien."

"Oh, Lord," I said shaking my head, already knowing where this was going.

"Tells me to go along with him to make sure he does things right. I bring you…" Nine cue's up the video on his phone and holds it out between me and Tic-Tac and sure as shit, it's a view through the fuckin' car wash tunnel of the Elephant Car Wash. The prospect's on his bike cursing up and down a blue streak, lowering a set of neon green goggles over his face, shoving a snorkel in his mouth. These dipshits had even put fuckin' water wings on his damn arms.

I couldn't help it. My mood was pretty much instantly elevated.

The dudes manning the place looked dubious as fuck as they started pressure washing Sauley and his bike down, and he started duck walking it forward, slow but sure.

It was a hoot watching him struggle like a motherfucker against the brush action and man, they went with the works. The pink and blue foam, the blow dryer, I mean *everything*. They even made him sit out the end of the tunnel, goggles all fogged up as the dudes wiped him and the bike down with those useless hand towels.

Tic-Tac and I grinned at each other.

"Now I bet that was cold as fuck riding back to the boneyard," Tic-Tac said.

"Bet his balls crawled right into his booty hole for warmth," Nine said cackling with glee, and I helped myself to a laugh.

"How'd you get the car wash to agree to that shit?" I demanded.

"Tipped the attendant on duty a hundred bucks." Nine gave a shrug.

"Jesus Christ," I chuckled, just as the door off to my right and behind me opened and Ms. Dahlia herself stepped on through, leading the way.

I stood and Tic-Tac, unsure of what was up at my swift movement, stood with me, just as my little bird appeared through the door behind Dahlia.

She looked apprehensive until her eyes landed on me, then her shoulders relaxed and the tension eased out of her some. She made a beeline for me and I didn't hesitate to open up my arms and fold her into them.

"Hey, baby," I murmured.

"Hi," she whispered back softly. She felt good and smelled even better. She was in her hand-me-down leather jacket, a long-sleeved, form-fitting black top with a cut out to show off her cleavage, which I definitely could appreciate.

It paired nice with her new, boot-cut jeans with the rhinestone embellishments on the pockets in the form of angel wings. Lucky Seven's if I weren't mistaken.

She looked every inch the carefree badass biker bitch. If only I could buy her the attitude to match… *time,* I thought to myself. *Just give it time. Things like that'll evolve naturally.*

"You have a good day?" I asked and she looked up at me, her makeup careful and understated – the remnants of her healing bruise concealed perfectly. Her lipstick a pale nude with a touch of gloss made her lips look perfectly fucking kissable, and I didn't bother to resist the urge after she said, "It was okay. A bit overwhelming." I smiled at her furtive glances around us and touched my lips to hers.

It was worth it to feel even more of the tension riding her narrow frame drain out of her as she melted into me in relief.

I kept things chaste, the guys were watching, and while normally I wouldn't give a fuck if it were some random hookup I was looking for – something about having *her* here with me – I don't know, I just felt like keeping my private business private. It was new, a little weird for me, but felt right and good.

"What's going on?"

I jerked my head up and turned us slightly so Mav could see what was up. He was standing at the back, at the mouth of the hallway leading back to the chapel and his office. His expression went from hawk-eyed and sharp, softening up as I turned my little bird in my arms so she could face my president, my hands on her shoulders, thumbs kneading slightly between her shoulder blades letting her know I had her and it was all good.

Mav strode over to us, stopping in front of my little bird. He reached up, hands descending onto the crown of her hair as she flinched slightly. He smoothed his hands over her straightened silky locks and I gritted my teeth. He leaned forward and kissed her forehead gently before leaning back with a wink and saying, "Welcome home, darlin'."

He let her go and a rowdy cheer went up from the rest of the guys and I chuckled and couldn't help but grin. Dahlia stepped forward and hugged Mav and stepped to his side, leaning on one of his shoulders while he kept an arm around her waist. He swept my girl from head to toe with his eyes and nodded appreciatively.

"Money well spent; you did good D."

"Aw, why thank you!" she declared and handed him a fold of bills. "I even stayed in budget."

Mav snorted and took the money from her.

"First time for everything," he declared then crowed, "Let's get this party started!" at the top of his lungs. A loud cheer went up, and some guys filtered our way while others went for the bar to work on getting liquored up.

"What was *that* all about?" Little Bird asked me softly, carefully making sure she wasn't being overheard. I smiled and put my lips near her ear.

"My guess is Mav is rollin' on some E," I said. "It's his drug of choice to unwind when he's stressed out."

"Oh," she said, jumping slightly when I kissed the shell of her ear.

"Curious?" I asked softly when her gaze lingered in Mav and Dahlia's direction, where they'd disappeared up the hall – likely to his office.

"Yes and no," she said.

"How's that?" I asked, picking up my beer from over on the bar and guiding her over toward the couches and love seats.

"I think I'm more curious about Mav and Dahlia – like I didn't know they were together; she didn't say anything the whole day about it."

I chuckled and we sat down together. I propped a booted heel up on the coffee table, just as the jukebox blared to life with some Type O Negative. My little bird jumped at the onslaught of thumping bass.

"They aren't," I said raising my voice above the music. "Just friends, have been since they were kids. What about that other thing?" I asked. "Curious about that?"

"What? The MDMA?" she asked, using the more technical term for the drug.

"The E," I agreed, correcting her. She bit her lips together and blushed. She looked curious and I could see her weighing the pros and cons, watched her thoughts sliding back and forth just behind her beautiful brown eyes and she finally quit biting her lips and shook her head.

"You ever change your mind, you just gotta let me know," I told her.

She craned her delicate neck to put her lips near my ear and asked, "Do you guys use a lot of illegal drugs?"

I shook my head. "Weed mostly, though that's perfectly legal nowadays. Other than that, maybe some E from time to time. A couple of guys drop some acid. Nothing super serious."

"Is that a rule?" she asked. "Or just a preference or a choice?"

"A little of both," I warned her, "but that's for later."

She immediately clammed up and nodded her understanding and I smiled and kissed her temple, lingering a moment to breathe her in. I was just happy she was here, finally with me.

It wasn't just us for long, though.

CHAPTER NINETEEN

*L*ittle Bird...

Things were a bit overwhelming. It was like we had just enough time to settle on the nearby couch, to chat for like thirty seconds and then the music started and it was like every one of his friends or brothers or whatever came up to us at once.

My mind drifted back to Mav and his being touchy-feely. As awkward as it had been, it hadn't been *awful*. Not that it made a bit of difference to the strangeness of his actions, but he had been attractive enough.

Slender in build, tall, with thick brown hair in a shorter cut. He'd been clean shaven unlike several of the other men here. His jaw chiseled, his cheekbones high, and his eyes expressive – framed in thick dark lashes any woman would kill for. He was almost too pretty to match the rest of his men and that left me curious.

I pushed my questions about him to the background as a club member that went by the name of Nine came up to introduce himself.

He favored unrelieved black, from his tee, to his jeans, to his boots. His haircut didn't seem like it was a choice so much as indifference or indecision. His medium brown hair shaggy, flopping over his forehead into his light green eyes which seemed to always be laughing. There was something vivacious about him. As if he were so full of life, it seemed to bleed out around the edges.

Tic-Tac had chin-length blond hair that he had pulled up at least halfway into a bit of a man bun, though with the constant dour look on his face, I don't think anyone would be willing to yank his chain over it. He seemed like he lived with a perpetual chip on his shoulder and that he was angry all the time. I got the impression that he was less than thrilled at my being here. Like he'd already made up his mind about me despite this having been the first time he'd ever laid his intense blue eyes on me.

I felt myself tuck into Dump Truck's side a bit tighter while we spoke with him and I was honestly relieved when he went his own way, off with his beer.

Another man dropped onto the couch across from ours and took a drink out of his bottle of Budweiser.

"Glass Jaw, nice to meet you," he said with a wink.

I raised an eyebrow. "I know I'm not supposed to ask…" I trailed off, but I had to know. He laughed and nodded.

"Happened *one* time," he said shaking his head.

"One time is all it takes." Dump Truck grinned.

I knew the term; I just wasn't sure if its typical application was the one made here. It would seem as though it was. Glass jaw was an old boxing term. My father was a boxing fan, which is how I knew. It was a vulnerability some boxers had to being knocked out cold with one punch to the jaw or the chin and wasn't something I would think a man in Glass Jaw's position would want to advertise. Then again… he said it had only ever happened once. Perhaps now it was a misdirection.

Glass Jaw, unlike the rest of the club I had met so far, kept his dark hair buzzed short, close to his scalp. He had a deep five o'clock shadow that was bordering on just plain scruff and a notch out of one of his eyebrows that declared he could very well be a man who enjoyed fighting.

Unlike Tic-Tac, he seemed pretty chill with me, a borderline harmless flirt. At least, I hoped it was harmless. My judge of character was pretty much deeply called into question at this point.

After Glass Jaw, a man called Blackjack came over with another they called Cipher. Blackjack was a fairly attractive and unassuming guy. His light brown hair shoulder length, his beard trim. He was cleaner and more kept than some of the other guys, with a hidden depth to his sparkling hazel eyes.

Cipher was of a rarer combination for coloring. So white it hurt, his thick red hair was shaved down on the sides and slicked back with product where it remained longer on top. Still, he kept it short enough that it didn't go into or belong in a ponytail. His beard was well-kept, slightly longer than most but not overly so, and where he was a rare one was his light green eyes. I think I read somewhere that something like one percent or less of redheads also had light-colored eyes. Typically, the genetic normal was brown eyes to the red hair.

It was a small point of laughter for the guys when I stumbled over myself and commented on it.

"Ay! He's a one percent of a one-percenter!" one of the men crowed and they all laughed. The joke was lost on me. I knew they all wore a diamond patch on their vests with a 1% in them, but I had no idea what it meant. Still, it was yet another thing to file away and ask Dump Truck about later.

"She's a little lost, I can tell," Glass Jaw said with a wink and I felt myself blush.

"Sorry, I just don't know why one percent is a thing or what it means," I said.

"That one's easy," Cipher declared.

"Back in the 60s," Dump Truck said, "the AMA or American Motorcycle Association, tried to disavow the rough and tumble clubs. Somebody made this bullshit comment to the press that 99% of motorcycle riders were law-abiding citizens and it was just the 1% left over that were making the whole institution look bad. They went on –"

"Like just about every other motherfucker in existence to that point," Tic-Tac chimed in from over near the dartboard, throwing a shot.

"– to say," Dump Truck glared at Tic-Tac's back for the interruption, "that the 1% didn't have anything to do with the AMA and what was supposed to be a dis to a lot of the clubs turned into a point of pride."

"Because fuck riding with those RUB pieces of shit anyhow. Buncha fuckin' weekend road warrior types." Blackjack grinned from behind the joint he was licking along the seam of the rolling paper to seal.

"RUB?" I echoed.

"Rich Urban Biker," Cipher supplied.

Oh. Right. I'd forgotten.

"What's up, what's up!" someone called from the back hall where Mav and Dahlia had disappeared to.

A man appeared and Great Scott! Once someone called out his road name, he pretty much was the only one I *didn't* need to ask Dump Truck later how he got it.

"Yo, Squatch! Come meet, Dump Truck's ol' lady!"

"Oh, shit! She here?"

Squatch lumbered around one of the pool tables. It was the only word I had for it even though he wasn't overly big or imposing in stature. His semi-hunched walk in combination with that wafting nimbus of black hair around his head lent to the description.

"Hey, hey, hey, what's going down?" he asked, sidling up to our little cluster and dropping into one of the love seats on either end around the coffee table, propping a booted foot on the scarred wood.

"Squatch! Whataya havin', honey?" the woman behind the bar called out. She was older, like probably sixties? Her hair was long and straight, a good two to three inches of gray roots at her part, the rest of it a really good highlighted brunette, salon-quality dye job. She was heavyset, but you couldn't tell how much or exactly where she carried it aside from her stomach which pushed out pronounced against the billowing satin kaftan she wore in a loud orange-gold and black tiger's stripe pattern.

"Gimme whatever's on draught, Ms. Momma Kat!"

"And Dump Truck, how about your girl, you damn animal? You even stop to think she might like some liquid courage walkin' on up into this zoo?"

"Shit," he swore under his breath.

"I doubt you guys have anything fruity or girly behind that bar anyway," I said with a giggle, not wanting him to feel bad.

"She said fruity and girly, Momma Kat!"

"Fruity and girly is my specialty!" she called back scooping ice into a shaker bottle.

"Thank you!" I called back.

She winked at me, a cigarette pressed between her lips, bobbing as she said, "No problem, honey!"

It was about then I realized someone had turned the music down so that talking was easier. I just hadn't noticed right away. I was of mixed feelings about that considering I was the central topic of conversation.

"So, you got it all picked out what you wanna be when you grow up?" Glass Jaw asked me, taking a hit off the joint that Blackjack had handed him.

"Sorry?" I didn't quite follow.

"He's asking if you know what you want to do for work or whatever once you get your new secret identity," Cipher said.

"Oh! Um, no… I hadn't really had a chance to stop and think about it," I said, a slight panic rising within me.

"World is her oyster." Dump Truck slid into the topic smoothly and like in all things lately, put himself in front of me, shielding me from anything that might be considered unpleasant. While it was an innocuous question, and I *should* be thinking about it, I honestly had no idea and it was a bit much to contend with… knowing I had this big amorphous *future* that was wholly undecided was anxiety inducing.

"I know, that… but what is she good at?"

"Nothing," I murmured and I think Dump Truck was the only one to hear me because his arm tightened around me and he kissed my temple.

"She can decide on all of that later. She's had a big day. Give her some breathing room, huh, fellas?"

"She's here, huh?" I looked up to, at first glance, an older man coming through the front door. Gray beard to just above mid-chest, he had a haircut like Cipher, though instead of slicked back, it was sort of brought forward and off to one side. His hair, while generous with the silver of his beard, still held more of the dishwater blond that was the original color of his youth. Blue eyes twinkled in my direction from his wizened face – although truth be told it was more *weathered* than *old*.

My initial estimation of late sixties was pared *way* back to forties, maybe fifties?

"Deacon," he said coming forward and holding out his hand. I reached up and shook it faintly and he smiled.

"Nice to meet you K –"

"Hey!"

"Whoa!"

"No, man, you gonna spoil the surprise!"

I was taken aback by the shouts and jeers from the other men around us and Dump Truck chuckled.

"Little Bird will do for now," he said.

"Ah, well, it's nice to meet you, Little Bird," Deacon amended.

"What was that all about?" I asked as he moved to the bar, looking slightly embarrassed.

"Almost gave up your new name. We ain't got the documents yet, so ain't nothing official."

"Oh, I don't get to pick?" I asked smiling vaguely, a mix of disappointed and oddly grateful.

"Nah, that's not how it goes," Dump Truck said.

"Who picked? You, I hope." He smiled and nodded and I instantly felt better about it.

"As long as it wasn't something generic like Crystal or Kristina," I said and he chuckled.

"Nope. I promise, it's unique like you, and no, you'll never guess so quit while you're ahead. That's all you're getting." I pouted but it was interrupted by Deacon coming back over, setting a tray of our drink orders on the scarred coffee table in our little makeshift circle.

"I presume this is yours," he said, handing over a pint glass layered in pretty colors. I took it and smiled.

"Yes, thank you."

"So who we missin'?" Deacon asked as the guys reached out for whatever drink they'd asked for off of the tray he'd brought over.

"Just Major and the prospect," Dump Truck said.

"Oh, shit! Deac, Squatch, you gotta see this!" Nine pulled out his cellphone and came over kneeling next to me and angling it so we all could see. Deacon and Squatch came over and hovered behind the couch to look over our shoulders.

"Oh, my God!" I felt my jaw drop at the man on the motorcycle at the carwash tunnel, affixing a diving mask over his face and fitting a snorkel into his mouth.

The screen shook as he made his way through the tunnel and the brushes whirred to life. I laughed at the absurdity of it. I couldn't help it, but at the same time I had to declare, "You guys are so *mean!*" which of course made the men gathered around the phone howl harder, laughing so hard I was afraid their sides would split.

"It's a rite of passage, baby. We all went through it."

"You all went through a carwash on your bikes like that?"

Dump Truck laughed.

"No, we all went through the hazing in some form or another," Deacon declared.

"Wow." I took a fortifying swallow of whatever was in my glass. It was strong. Strong, but good.

"You eat yet?" D.T. asked me, eyeing me after the slight cough I let out after my first swallow out of my glass.

"No, not yet. You?"

"Nah, was waiting on you. So, what's for dinner?"

"Could order us some pizza," Squatch suggested.

"Had that last night," Dump Truck informed him.

"Pizza's *always* good," Nine said standing, messing around on the screen of his phone.

"What do you feel like, babe? You're a guest, it should be guest's choice."

"Uhhh." I closed my mouth, feeling quite put on the spot. My brain scrambled for the answer in a mad panic as my cheeks flamed scarlet but I couldn't for the life of me come up with one.

"Food?" I said, trying for humor. "Food is good."

Dump Truck chuckled and said, "You want to get out of here, just you and me?" he asked.

"Only if that's what you want," I said, not wanting to make the decision.

Dump Truck smiled down at me and took my drink from my hands gently and set it aside on the coffee table.

"Come on and help your ol' man up. I'll take you home," he said and I smiled and pushed to my feet, which were aching by quite a bit from all the walking and shopping I'd done today. I held a hand down and he shifted and said, "Plant your feet, lean back a bit, put all your weight on that back foot."

I did as he told me and he grasped my hand and leveraged himself up out of his seat.

"There you go! Good job," he praised and I know it was simple, a silly little thing, but I couldn't help but glow from it a little.

He put his arm around my shoulders and tucked me into his side calling out, "See you around, fellas," to a track of groans.

"Shut the fuck up!" Fenris cried from over by the pool table, giving me a nod. I had vaguely been aware of him being here but had missed out on saying hello. I smiled and gave a nod back, feeling self-conscious, more than a little overwhelmed.

Dump Truck led us toward the back and we stopped by Fen.

"Come take a ride with us, grab some grub," Dump Truck said and Fen lifted his chin.

"Let's roll," he said, and I smiled but my nerves seemingly reactivated. My relief at going back to D.T.'s little fortress of solitude entirely too short lived.

Fenris put up his cue and followed us out the back door. Across the street, there were a line of bikes in front of a corrugated metal building painted a tan color with a reddish corrugated metal awning above the front door. The old wood door had seen better days. The window in it busted out and replaced by a piece of sheet metal. Above the awning was a big, hand painted sign – *Ironheart Salvage* with a motorcycle painted on it, the words arching above and curving below in a throw-back to the motorcycle club patches on Fen and D.T.'s backs. There was a closed pen to the left of the door and out front? Bikes backed to the building in a long swath of chrome and glossy tanks and saddlebags.

The building had a white garage door on the far right, next to a closed gate that led around back. The chain-link fence surrounding the place had reddish privacy strapping threaded through it that matched the awning roof over the door.

It seemed deserted out here in the gathering dark but the front door opened up to reveal a couple of men I hadn't met yet.

"Major, Sauley, what's happenin'?" Dump Truck asked.

"Just finishing up in here, Boss," Sauley declared, holding open the door for us. "Hi, how you doin' miss?" he asked me. I smiled and recognized the lanky man from the video in the car wash tunnel.

"I could ask you the same thing," I said with a light laugh.

"Nine showin' everybody, then?" he asked with a rueful grin.

Sauley was cute. Younger than the rest but still probably mid-twenties, I would hazard. He was a brunette, too. Lighter, with short cropped hair and a beard that was trying but was still this side of just scruff that didn't look like it would get much fuller.

Major, on the other hand, was the exact opposite. While he too was young, his complexion was as dark as Sauley's was light. Pencil thin dreadlocks sprouted from his head and swung to brush the tops of his leather-clad shoulders. He grinned and his teeth were very white, set in all that dark skin which was honestly lovely to the eye. A rich deep brown that reminded me of good soil that was full of life and nutrients. Likewise was Major, his smile full of life and mischief as he winked in my direction.

Inside the front door I could get a better look at the place. There was a short, half-wall to the right with chairs in front of it, a sort of waiting area. Behind it was the bay the garage door led into. A motorcycle on a lift, in the midst of being rebuilt.

To the left, was an 'L' shaped metal counter. This shorter end meant to ring up prospective customers, the long end separating the cash wrap area from the racks and racks of parts that took up the rest of the room.

Behind the counter, where Major stood was another door and drywall enclosing it, the ceiling to whatever room was there a loft of more storage, with dusty bins and boxes up there. The door was shut, so there was no telling if it was an office or a restroom or what.

I couldn't see down the hall leading between the counter and the racks of parts to the back there, but straight back from the front door was a metal back door to the outside.

"What do you think?" Dump Truck asked, and I realized they were all staring at me as I took it all in.

"It's nice for a motorcycle wrecking yard and repair shop," I said.

Chuckles were traded.

"You two assholes good to lock up?" Fenris demanded. "We're goin' to get something to eat."

"You comin' back later?" Major asked.

"Nah, brah, been a long day," Fenris answered for all of us.

"Awright, cool." Major bobbed his head and stopped stacking bolts and nuts on the metal counter.

"It was nice to meet you both," I said softly.

"Likewise," Sauley said with a smile.

Dump Truck put a light hand to my lower back, guiding me with gentle pressure around, his hand slipping slightly to cop a feel of my ass once his big frame was between us and everyone else as we went out the door. I giggled slightly and glowed from the contact as we walked over the loose rocks out front to the slab of concrete where his bike was parked in line with the others.

"We going to Huck's?" Fenris asked and Dump Truck grunted and checked the big watch on his wrist.

"Yeah, sounds good," he said.

Huck's was Huckleberry Finn's, a diner up past 128th street long past where 16th Street SW turned into Ambaum Boulevard. In fact, it was far enough past 128th that it was *almost* to 148th and Burien's other main drag which turned into the 518 Freeway going past SeaTac airport.

At this time of the evening, the parking lot of Huckleberry's was almost deserted, the restaurant only a few hours from closing time. We were seated almost as soon as we stepped up to the hosting station. The man seating us younger and in his twenties, wearing a nice button-down shirt and a pair of Dockers with a professional and sensible pair of shoes. He looked us over slightly nervous and I tried to soften the guys' rough appearance with a genuine smile meant to be comforting.

The fear in his eyes lessened slightly, and he gave me a quick, small, timid smile in return – which was a start.

We were seated all the way in the back, near the restrooms. The restaurant's aesthetics unique, very tribal with lots of Native American art and natural wood stained a warm golden brown. The material of the booth backing a woven native blanket pattern, although instead of the traditional black, red, and white common to the area, the scenes depicting salmon jumping from rivers and streams on their spawning migration were picked out in maroon, navy blue, and a taupe.

The vinyl seats of the booths were likewise maroon, and an entire birch wood skin, one-person, shallow canoe hung from the ceiling back here, complete with oars. I'd never had the occasion to come into this particular diner, but it was cozy, clean, and with plenty of seating.

"Missed the rush," Fen grunted.

"Yeah," Dump Truck agreed as he stood by to allow me to slide into the booth first.

I slid in and he sat beside me, stretching his bad leg out straight into the aisle and absently massaged the muscle through his work-stained jeans.

"Is this place usually busy?" I asked.

"Usually, it's packed all day long," Fenris said.

"Older clientele," Dump Truck explained. "The retiree's come breakfast, lunch, and dinner. The place has good food, is cheap, and appeals a lot to the older crowd. Most come get their three meals a day here something like seven days a week."

"Oh, how'd you find out about it?" I asked.

"Ride by a place with a packed parking lot and see that it's packed often enough, you get the hint that somethin' is drawing 'em here. That something is usually some damn good grub," Fenris said with a wink.

I smiled and nodded and picked up the single sheet of the two menus we'd been provided. It was the list of the daily specials – breakfast, lunch, and dinner – the times they were served, the two soups of the day, and other little pieces of information such as what beer or wine was on tap or on sale.

"Careful of the specials," Dump Truck warned. "Especially if they sound like they're someplace exotic."

"Yeah, if it looks like they got Chinese or Mexican or something as a special, it could be a trap," Fen agreed.

"How so?" I asked.

"The food here is straight up American, so shit like sweet and sour chicken is never what you actually expect it to be. It sounds good on paper, but what hits the plate is sometimes like a school lunch facsimile of what's written down." Dump Truck didn't look at me while he explained, he just perused the menu.

"Ew, um, okay, so what's safe?"

"Their soups are always good," Fen said. "The sandwiches are awesome. The burgers are pretty safe. The steaks are good but if you order it a type of way, I would take it down a notch – they almost always overcook them, so if you're a medium-rare girl, order it rare."

"Yeah, even then it can be kind of hit or miss and you might get well done," Dump Truck warned.

"I thought you said this place was *good*," I said, laughing to myself.

"It *is*, you just gotta learn the ropes."

I smiled to myself and closed my mouth as the waitress approached and asked after a cheerful greeting, "You know what you're drinkin'?"

The guys ordered coffee; I ordered an iced tea. The place served breakfast all day and the guys swore the omelets were to die for, even so, I was eying their dinner menu and the turkey and mashed potatoes.

"Are their dinners good?" I asked. "Like the pot roast or the roast turkey?"

"Hell yeah," Fen said. "You may have just changed my mind." His eyes roved over his menu to the page I was on.

In the end, I *did* go with the turkey dinner. Fen ended up sticking to his British Bacon Burger, which just sounded like it was a cheeseburger with bacon added to it, and Dump Truck went with the surf and turf on offer as special for the dinner tonight. A steak he ordered rare with golden fried shrimp and mashed potatoes and brown gravy on the side.

"You look tired," Fen said after they finished doctoring their coffee while I added sugar to my iced tea. They didn't have sweet tea this far up north which was a real tragedy if you asked me. Just plain, unsweetened iced tea you had to make do with sugar packets. It didn't even come close. It was the one thing I wished I could have brought home with me after my travels in the south from my old life.

"It was a *very* long day," I said. "Dahlia drug me *everywhere*."

"If it's one thing that girl loves more than dick, it's shopping," Dump Truck said ruefully.

Fen laughed.

"She told me it was makeup," I said with a straight face and it caught D.T. off guard, making him chuckle spontaneously which in turn made me smile.

"So, what'd you think about the club and the rest of us rag-tag bunch of guys?" Fen asked, and there was a sharpness to his keen blue eyes as he searched my face.

"Jury is still out," I said softly. "It was barely an introduction."

"Yeah, that's my fault," D.T. said. "There'll be plenty of time. I just was worried you were maybe too tired and were gettin' overwhelmed."

"Accurate," I said succinctly.

"Doesn't help you didn't eat all day," he said.

"Well, no, we had a smoothie at the mall –" I tried to defend Dahlia.

"That ain't food," Fen countered flatly and I smiled at their protective instincts. It was nice to be thought of and looked after for right now. I could get used to it and I didn't find it at all overbearing coming from them for some reason. Wasn't that strange?

The waitress came back with our starter soups and salads we'd ordered that seemed to come standard with every meal on the menu. Well, except for with the sandwiches or burgers if you ordered fries or chips to go with them.

"There you go," she said breezily, setting things in front of each of us. "You fellas good on coffee?" she asked, pushing some of her blonde bangs off her forehead with the back of her hand. She was likely in her fifties, slightly overweight and maybe had bad hips or something because she swayed back and forth when she walked in this pronounced way that was otherwise inexplicable. It wasn't quite a limp, but I didn't know how else to describe it… God, my mind was shot. I was tired, and I needed to eat.

I tasted the vegetable soup I ordered and found it to be quite good.

"A little more coffee would be good, thanks," Dump Truck said softly.

"Okay, I'll be right back with that."

She did her strange little waddle-walk and disappeared up the aisle behind us.

Quiet ensued as Dump Truck and I ate our soup and salad, respectively. Fen had ordered a cup of soup in addition to his burger and slurped quietly across from us.

I let the comfort slide out from the middle of me at the warm soup and the coziness of our little gathering wrap me up and meet it halfway. I was too tired by this point to let my anxiety keep me wound tight and it felt nice to just be.

The guys didn't pepper me with questions or try to make me engage in conversation and I was grateful for that.

They were right, I was *tired*. It really had been a long day. Suddenly, all I longed for was the bed and to curl up against D.T. like a sleepy kitten, warm and safe.

God. That sounded so good.

CHAPTER TWENTY

*D*ump Truck...

She went quiet and simply ate her soup. She looked dog tired, and I figured a lot of it had to be emotional exhaustion more than anything. Fen and I traded a look and chatted some, but we let her be. She'd done more than enough today and didn't need to keep us entertained.

She ate in silence and seemed to be attentive as Fen and I talked some shop about bikes, and I talked about some of the irritating dumbass customers that came through the boneyard's front door that day.

It was pretty fuckin' low key and kind of a nice way to end the day. Poor Little Bird, though. By the time Fen and I ordered some pie, for dessert – she passed – she looked completely wiped out, and I couldn't say I blamed her. She looked like she was up past her bedtime and it was kind of adorable.

"Hey." I gave the waitress a chin lift and she paused. "Can I get one of them cinnamon rolls to go, please?"

She smiled at me. "Sure thing, I'll be right back." I peeled off a fifty and a ten and handed it to her.

"Thanks, keep the change."

Her eyes lit up. This place was so on the cheap, I doubt our bill came in over forty bucks, even with dessert and the cinnamon roll. It's one of the reasons why this place was so popular with the locals. Aside from the breakfast food being so good, it kept getting local awards and shit with that one evening news station.

She came back with a brown paper bag, the top folded over and a receipt, sliding both onto the edge of our table.

"You all have a nice night now," she said with a smile that held more of a sparkle to it than it had the minute before.

Popular, yes… with the silent generation. The last of the folks who'd survived the Great Depression, and who just plain didn't understand the value of a good tip and how waitstaff nowadays depended on that shit for basic survival.

Fenris sighed and sat back in his seat, putting a hand to his stomach. I was right there with him. Stuffed.

"Girl, you look like you turned into a pumpkin right about an hour ago," Fen commented dryly. I looked over and down at my little bird where she cracked a faint smile and just as faintly nodded and said, "I'm tired."

"Right, let's get you home," I said gently. "Fen, you crashing on my couch?" I asked. He nodded.

"Yeah, I don't feel like goin' all the way home."

Fen lived all the way out on the Auburn/Black Diamond border. He had a solid house out that way with some land – a decent piece of property. Idyllic with an outbuilding that housed his forge. His pops also lived with him and sometimes his gettin' home late led to some awkward.

"Cool."

"Um, there's *a lot* of shopping in the living room," my little bird said quietly and shifted uncomfortably like she thought it might get her in trouble.

"It's no worries," I said dismissively. "I can move it."

We got up, and I waited for her to slide out to me. When she got to her feet, I pulled her into a hug. Fen stood by, relaxed, patient, and let us go for a minute. Finally, he put a gentle hand to my girl's back and with a smile when she startled said, "Let's get you home and to bed."

"Think you can hang onto this?" I asked, handing her the cinnamon roll I'd bought for her breakfast in the morning.

"Sure," she said with a smile that radiated so many things, a deep tired chief among them but also a comfort and trust, with us both, I think.

We left and stepped outside, breath fogging lightly in the damp cool air. It'd sprinkled while we'd been inside and Fenris made the joke, "Never go anywhere without your towel." I chuckled, and we both went for the compartments where we kept ours, respectively, to wipe off the seats of our bikes.

I put my girl's lid on for her, wanting to make sure it was done right. Nothing made you a safety Nazi faster than earning your broken wings, let me tell you. I felt my broken wing patch damn near was burning a hole in my side, the tingle in my ribs over where it'd been affixed to my vest giving a very real warm tingle.

"Watch yourself, Fen," I told him. "Keep the shiny side up."

"I ain't wiped out yet," he reminded me and I chuckled. It wasn't a dig, just a sort of 'knock it off, you're not my dad' reminder. He was right.

"Just be glad I care, asshole."

He fired up his bike. "You care about my asshole?" he called over the thrum of his bike, the rumble of his pipe.

I gave him the finger and got onto my own bike and fired it up. Little Bird got on behind me and wrapped her arms around me once I'd backed out of the parking space.

The ride home was a short one, back the way we'd come, make a right onto my street, head down close to a mile and right into my underground spot. It was one of the reasons I liked Huck's. It was close to home.

We went up to my apartment, Little Bird unconsciously hanging back some, or trying to, and I got it when I opened up the front door.

"Jesus Christ, that's a lot of shopping bags," Fen said. I chuckled. It was a lot. The couch and the coffee table covered – there were even a few perched on the end of the dining room table.

"I'm sorry," she said slightly mournfully. "We got back here and

Dahlia was in such a hurry to get me changed, makeup freshened up, and back out the door to meet you all."

"It's no worries. It's gonna take more than a few shopping bags to start a new life, babe. You buy anything to sleep in?"

"Yeah," she said softly.

"Grab that one first. Fen, grab a beer or something and put this in the fridge. I'm gonna put my woman to bed, tuck her in, then I'll come out here and move this shit for you."

"Pfft, take your fuckin' time. I know how to clear off a couch," he said.

"I figured." I handed him the cinnamon roll from my girl's hands and he went for the kitchen. I went for her helmet which she still wore, hung it on the coat-tree before taking off my own. She shrugged out of her leather jacket and I took it from her hands, hanging it up then followed it with my jacket and cut.

The fridge door had shut in that time and there was a hiss and metallic click as Fen divested the bottle of its cap.

"Be right back, man," I said after pulling off my boots and setting them up at the base of the rack. I didn't give my little bird time to do the same, giving her a gentle little push toward the shopping explosion in my living room.

She picked up a Victoria's Secret bag and came back to me, and I marched her sweet ass ahead of me into the bedroom and swung the door shut without actually closing it all the way.

"Sit," I ordered gently and kneeled on the floor in front of her. Finally, I got to do what I'd been itching to do all day.

I started with her boots, untying the laces, loosening them up, sliding them off her feet and easing off her socks. She sat on the edge of the bed, leaned back onto her hands, eyes closed as she started to drift already.

She was taxed to death from her day but the slight smile at the edges of her lips told me it'd been a good one. I knew it wasn't possible for no bad days, but every good one felt like a hell of a victory right now, so I would take it.

"Stand up for me, baby," I whispered and she did, pushing to her feet with some effort.

I took her jeans next, kissing lightly her stomach, above the band of her simple cotton bikini panties. Her hands touched my head and I looked up sharply at her eyes fixed on me, gazing down her body at me.

"Your friend is just in the other room," she whispered aghast.

"Not trying to fuck you, babe. Just couldn't resist. I love making you feel good. It makes *me* feel good."

"Oh," she said softly, her expression softening, losing its anxiety, turning gently bewildered.

Ah, she was so tired. Took me a couple tries, but I clambered to my feet. Taking the hem of her soft, long-sleeved top in my hands and peeling it up off her even softer skin, it took some reserves not to press my hands to her body as I lifted it. I felt the missed opportunity to feel her beneath my hands keenly, but she'd already said no in her own way; *and no meant no.* She was uncomfortable with Fen just in the next room and I wasn't here to push her boundaries. Not tonight. Not so soon.

She let me undress her, raising her arms to help me as I slipped her shirt off over her head.

"Get your sleep clothes," I whispered and she pulled out a long, satin thing out of the top of the shopping bag that she'd sat beside her on the bed.

Right now, it wasn't about sex. It wasn't about me. It was about intimacy. It was about building trust and making sure that not only did she feel *safe* but that she knew her will with me would be *respected.* It was about respecting her and that was one of the core tenants of the MC life – *respect.*

It wasn't given. It was earned and earning that shit was slow going. Every one of us understood that.

It was no different from being a prospect. You earned your way, plain and simple, and that was one of the biggest problems with citizen culture. They were always looking to take the easy way out, always looking to cut corners and shit. Rejecting the road in front of them if it looked even just a little bit difficult.

I was all about the road less traveled and you didn't earn respect, or the love of a good woman, by cutting corners and noping the fuck out of things the second shit got tough.

This was the same as everything else. None of us got ahead by playing by the typical rules, and I was here to play by my own and my own rule was simple – put up or shut up. Practice what you preached or take a goddamned seat.

I eased her out of her bra, and let her cover herself with her arms. She looked up at me questioningly and I whispered, "Just wait right there for half a second."

I picked up her nightgown and took the knife out my pocket, flicking it open, using the sharp blade to sever the plastic filaments between the fobs holding the tags onto the garment.

The lace and satin were delicate fabrics, and I didn't want to ruin them ripping the tags through with my teeth like some fucking savage. Make no mistake, I could be a savage when I wanted to be, when I needed to be, but there was a time and place for everything and this was most definitely not the time or the place.

I found the front of the nightgown she'd purchase and gathered it in my hands, turning it and slipping it over her head. I gently guided it down over her and hooked her panties with my fingertips, dragging them down her long legs, letting them slip to a puddle on the floor, the nightie falling to her mid-calf and hugging her curves beautifully.

My jeans got mighty tight and uncomfortable in the crotch right then, but I ignored it. Again, it wasn't the time even if it was most definitely the place for that kind of a thing. I'd get mine later when it was just me and her.

I guided her gently around the bed to her side and pulled back the blankets and sheets so she could get in and was as good as my word. The perfect gentleman, tucking my lady in, kissing her softly, and whispering goodnight.

"Thank you for that," she whispered into the dark and I smiled.

"It was my pleasure, baby…" and it was.

I put the bag she'd brought in here with her, which still held a small pile of silk, satin, and lace in the bottom, and set it aside against the mirrored closet doors on their running track.

"You go on and try to sleep now. I'm going to make quick work of bringing the rest of your stuff in here and we'll work on getting it all put away tomorrow."

"Thank you," she murmured again.

"Again, my pleasure, baby."

She sighed out, and I slipped back out into the living room.

"Dahlia went nuts," Fen said flatly, dropping something fluid and fluttery into the top of one of the shopping bags on the coffee table.

"Like dropping a thermonuclear device to take care of your rat problem," I said.

"What?" Fen asked, looking at me like I'd gone nuts.

I rolled my eyes.

"Overkill," I explained.

"No shit," he said sucking in a long breath through his nose and huffing it out his mouth.

"She dragged my girl all over hell and gone," I said shaking my head.

"No wonder she'd like to fall asleep in her mashed potatoes."

I chuckled.

"Hand me this shit at the bedroom door, let's get it out of your way."

"Copy that," he said, and I took several bags up and with me. He followed and set them at the bedroom door and I quietly lined things up on the bedroom carpet, trying to remain as noiseless as possible.

The rest he set aside on the dining room table and that was fine.

"Night, bro," he said with a sigh and I gave a nod.

"Night."

I shut myself into my room with the gentle even breath of my girl the only interruption of sound in the quiet dark and I smiled.

I undressed quietly, took down my hair, and stood at the foot of the bed and watched her, cock throbbing, for several seconds. Maybe even a full minute.

I liked the cream satin nightgown she'd picked. Didn't bother putting anything on, myself, and got into bed behind her. She snuggled back into the curve of my body when I eased up behind her and the feel of her ripe as a peach ass pushing against my cock with that thin overlay of satin almost had me coming all over the brand-new material.

I sighed out, frustrated, anticipating the deep and abiding ache in my balls that was coming at giving myself no relief, but I didn't care.

None of this was about me tonight. It was about her. Tomorrow morning, though? Once Fen got the fuck up out of here? All bets were probably off. I don't know. We'd have to see.

CHAPTER TWENTY-ONE

*L*ittle Bird...

I woke to several sensations happening at once. The first was that I was nestled back into the curve of Dump Truck's much larger body and I had to say, I *loved* being his little spoon. The second was a slightly damp spot where my nightgown was sticking to my ass, the third was him grinding against my ass, and the one that I adored the most was the combination of his lips against my shoulder, his fingers gathering the material of my nightgown up, the satin warm and softly slick, working its way up my leg.

"Morning," he grumbled in my ear.

"Good morning," I whispered back.

It was just us, in this space. Just me and just him, his cock thick, hard, and hot against my ass. That damp spot likely a byproduct of his excitement. He did produce a lot of pre-cum, but I didn't mind that. Not at all. There was something incredibly hot, incredibly sexy about that physical representation of his arousal for me. It delighted me, actually, how much I turned him on.

I ground my ass back against him and he grunted, groaning, and I loved the sound. I felt so small and insignificant next to Dump Truck and there was something powerful and empowering about the fact that I could affect him so strongly. That I could bring this giant to his knees simply by writhing sinuously against him. All it took was a come-hither look and a wriggle of my hips and he was nearly undone.

I didn't fully understand it. Why I affected him so much, but he absolutely did the same thing to me.

"Oh, God," I gasped, as he worried that delicate spot on the side of my neck with his tongue.

The hand atop my thigh that'd raised my nightgown out of his way, bunching it around my waist, disappeared behind me and suddenly his cock was at my entrance, teasing my pussy lips apart, begging entrance.

"Yes, oh God, yes please," I whispered and he pressed at my opening, easing in slowly. I panted, making feral little noises as he pushed slowly into me. His hand returned to my hip, steadying me, keeping me still, with a gentle pressure – a reminder that if I took him too fast, I could hurt myself.

I didn't care, but I let him have this. I let him guide me. I let him have control.

When he was sure I would keep my movements small, and that I wouldn't rush to fuck him, he let go of my hip, his hand migrating in front of me, fingertips rubbing the top of the front of my sex in rhythmic circles in time with his slow and easy micro-thrusting. Each and every one of his movements, slow, small, and controlled.

My passionate roiling boil came back down to a slow, pleasurable simmer when it became clear he wasn't after a quick and dirty fuck before work. I whimpered, and he slid his other arm beneath my neck, capturing me across my chest, big hand cradling my chin and drawing my head back and around, guiding my lips to his.

With every slow, small thrust, I grew wetter, and he slid in a little bit further, working his way into my body to the root. I moaned, gave myself over to the feel of him in and around me, melted into his much bigger form, took shelter in his arms, against his chest, and let him love me.

He tore his mouth from mine and let out this gasping, growling moan of satisfaction. His chest rising and falling at my back as though he had conquered me, even though I felt as though I had tamed him. I smiled and decided why couldn't it be both?

"*Fuck*, baby, your pussy's so hot," he growled, and I smiled and leaned back for another kiss.

I don't know how long we remained like that, him holding me in the shelter of his body, loving me slow, working me up at this beautifully, exquisitely torturous pace that left me wild, breathless with a need to reach that climax. He shredded every last one of my inhibitions, until I was a writhing, panting, begging hot mess in his arms. Coming apart, on the verge of tears from just how fantastic it felt.

Pleasure coursed through my body, crackling along nerve endings and making things tighten. Dump Truck grunted and thrust hard into me, teasing my clit with his fingertips while remaining still for a moment. The pleasure mounted and the feral sounds poured past my lips, riding the air that was thick with attraction.

"Come on, baby. Come on," he urged and the warmth of his breath against my ear and the side of my neck, the tingling wash of sensation that elevated and at the same time drew me in, it was almost too much, too good, until with a wild cry I felt as though I went supernova. He held me tight, his arms around me, and thrust inside me as I came around his cock. I shuddered and whimpered with pleasure as it felt like everything rushed out of me and I lay weak as a kitten in his arms.

He grunted, and with a final hard thrust that sent me over the edge *again* with another, gentler orgasm, he stilled, drawing in a shuddering breath, arms locked around me in a protective embrace.

"That was hot," Fen said from outside the bedroom doorway and I froze in Dump Truck's arms having completely forgotten that Fen was here.

Dump Truck gave a dirty little chuckle and called out, "Fuck off!"

I covered my face with my hands and felt my face flame. I mean, sure, Fen hadn't *seen* anything, but he'd certainly been *listening*. How could I have forgotten he was here?

"Shhh, s'alright, baby. 's all good," Dump Truck soothed. His hold on me tightened and he rocked me, sort of, as well as he could, given the position we were laying in on our sides. He withdrew from me with a slight grunt and held me close.

"I am so embarrassed," I whispered finally.

"Why?" he asked.

"I mean, um, what we did was *private* wasn't it?" I asked.

"I dunno," he said, and I felt his massive shoulder rise in a one-sided shrug. "I knew he was out there. I just don't give a fuck. Wasn't about to resist the temptation of waking up with a beautiful woman in my arms." He kissed the cap of my shoulder, a gentle press of lips, and I felt my body loosen slightly.

"I don't know how I could have forgotten," I whispered and he chuckled.

"How about I'm just that good at sex?" he said, and I rolled my eyes as well as myself so I could face him, my nightgown tangling around my ribs.

The sparkle of joy and mischief in his deep brown eyes definitely did something to sooth the sting of my humiliation.

"Okay," I said, changing tact from what I was *going* to say. There was no denying he was good at what he'd just done to me with him looking at me like that. "You're amazing," I whispered. "I'll give you that. I'm just not sure my, um…" I groped for the right word to use… "Confidence, is quite up to that level of showmanship yet."

He nodded thoughtfully, a darkness chasing the light from his eyes and he put his forehead against mine. His eyes closed and he sighed out heavily.

"I'm sorry," he said and the apology, for only being two words, ran swift and deep.

"You're what?" I asked, although I'd heard him right. I mean, I did, I just… something about it was just not computing.

"I'm sorry if you feel like I betrayed your trust. I apologize," he repeated.

I pulled back and swallowed hard, my heart thundering in my chest at the magnitude of it. I don't think any man I had ever been with or even been *around* had ever offered up an apology to me about anything… ever.

"Thank you," I whispered and he smiled a bit ruefully.

"I ain't trying to set us back," he said. "If anything, I'm trying to set you to rights. You've been through so much," he said, eyes sliding over my face, fingertip gentle where he chased some of my sleep and sex-mussed hair off my forehead and behind my ear.

I didn't know what to say, so I said nothing. Instead, I put my arms around him and held myself close to the warmth radiating from his body.

"Tell you what," he murmured, holding me back. "Why don't you take your time in here, pick out something to wear for today, and I'll go out and keep Fenris company while you get a shower and get dressed. Maybe make us some breakfast."

"Okay," I whispered.

"Alright, now. Do me a favor and dress sturdy. Jeans and the like, would you?"

"Okay."

He kissed my forehead and when he let me go, I felt much better.

"Okay," he murmured in echo and he pushed himself back and off the other side of the bed, rising like a leviathan from the deep. Virile, strong, and yes even gorgeous. I smiled and pushed off the opposite side of the bed, nightgown slipping down to cover me. I smiled, feeling a bit like the phoenix rising from the ashes myself and so very beautiful by the way he looked at me. By the smile that painted his lips, half hidden by his beard. A secret smile meant just for me.

Without thinking, we both helped each other straighten the blankets and pillows on the bed and I felt a little more solid with the gesture, like we were back in synch, whereas just the moment before, I'd felt as though we'd fallen out of it.

He went to the dresser and opened it up, pulling out a pair of cut-off cargo pants, the strings hanging from the knees just below the side leg pockets would have tickled my legs and driven me nuts.

"Take your time, I mean it," he said. "Slip across the hall, take a long hot shower – relax. I want this to be a good start to your day."

I smiled at him and nodded saying truthfully, "It's the best start a girl could ask for."

He smiled at me bigger, pulled on the shorts and fastening the button and fly, slipped out the bedroom door, shutting it firmly behind him.

CHAPTER TWENTY-TWO

*D*ump Truck…

I hit the head, first. Taking a leak, brushing my teeth, that kind of thing before I stepped out into the living room.

"That was wild," Fenris declared dryly, taking a drink from a fresh beer he'd liberated out of my fridge.

"It's seven o'clock in the fuckin' morning," I said, crossing my eyes.

He laughed.

"You didn't set your coffee maker," he said, raising his eyebrows and taking another drink. "Tap water around here tastes like shit."

"You ain't lying," I said with a snort and set myself to work brewing a pot. He knew I was particular about my morning brew so he was wise to leave it be.

"She cool?" he asked.

"Yeah, just maybe the next time you hear something out of her don't make a comment. She got a little embarrassed."

"A little sensitive," he said and I fixed him with a look.

"She's got a reason," I said and I put some steel into my tone. He raised his eyebrows and nodded, like he'd forgotten about that little detail and sighed.

"Didn't think about it that way. Probably because *I* wanna forget," he said. I nodded.

"She does too. Way fuckin' more. Try to keep that in mind."

"Will do," he said and sighed giving a big stretch.

The door to the bedroom opened and then the door to the little hall linen closet. I could see her from the kitchen, but unless Fenris switched ends of the couch, he couldn't. She kind of stepped out of the hall so he could see her, a couple of towels clutched to her chest like she was hiding behind 'em and asked, "Does anybody need to use the bathroom before I take it over?"

"Nah," Fen said.

"You're all good, babe. Take as long as you like," I told her and she nodded not quite looking at either of us, her cheeks turning red as she quickly ducked into the bathroom and shut the door.

Fen winced.

"That's gonna take a while," he said.

"What, for the awkward to wear off?" I asked.

"Yeah."

"Probably less time than you'd think," I said. "She's a tough cookie. A lot tougher than anybody's ever given her credit for, I think."

He nodded and I opened up my fridge and sighed. I had plenty of shit for a balanced breakfast, I just didn't know what I wanted to make.

"Should make her some of that French toast you do," he said casually and I chuckled.

"You want French toast, French toast it is," I said. It wasn't a bad idea. I went to move the brown paper bag from last night and thought to myself it would keep until tomorrow.

"Got any bacon?" he asked.

"Jesus fuckin' Christ, what am I? A line cook?"

"Today you are," he said.

I laughed. "Fuck you."

"Don't spit in my food, you fucker," he said back and I had an even better laugh over that one.

The shower kicked on and I got to work. By the time I was setting the first plate of food down for Fen who was jumping up to come and get it, the hair dryer shut off.

The bathroom door opened and my girl peeked out, then rushed back across the hall wrapped armpit to knees in one of my big damn bath towels. I smiled as the bedroom door shut behind her.

"Jesus," Fen muttered and pushed a bunch of shit away from a seat at my little dining room table.

"Jealous?" I asked.

"Fuck yeah," he declared.

"Eh, someday if you're lucky," I shot back and Fen snorted.

It was his turn.

"Fuck you."

I chuckled and went back in the kitchen to start up a plate for my girl.

She came out several minutes later, dressed in the same jeans and boots from last night, only this time she wore a plain black tee and a ladies' plain black hoodie zipped up halfway.

"There she is," Fen declared.

"Only for the moment," she said with a shy smile. "Still have to do my hair and makeup."

She went for the bags on the dining room table and started to root through them but I stopped her.

"Shove those aside and grab a bite to eat first, for me."

"Oh, okay." She shuffled things off to the far end of the table, clearing a place for herself and for me across from her. Accepting the plate I brought around to her with a murmured thanks.

"Coffee or orange juice?" I asked.

"Could have a beer like me," Fen said, polishing his off.

"Beer with French toast?" she asked and cringed.

"Beer with *bacon* and a side of French toast," he corrected.

"Beer with bacon actually doesn't sound horrible, but I think I'll have a glass of orange juice for right now," she said.

"O.J. it is, coming right up," I said.

"Where did you learn to cook like this?" she asked me after a few bites.

"My mom. She wasn't sending no helpless man-child into the world."

"Mad props to your mom," she said softly. "I sometimes wish I'd learned certain things."

"No time like the present," Fenris said gruffly, polishing off his food. I shook my head. It'd been so long since Fen had any type of woman in his life other than a one-night hookup that I was starting to think he'd gone too feral and would never be able to settle. Of course, there wasn't exactly anything wrong with that.

I had an inkling, though, that my boy here was more than a little envious. That he wasn't so much jealous that I had this beautiful woman in my bed that'd let me bone her on the regular, as much as he might be jealous that this could be a forever kind of thing. I mean, I was hoping it was and if it turned out that way, I think I would be just about the happiest man alive – but I didn't want to get too ahead of myself. The chemistry was there, it was as real and undeniable as anything I'd ever felt before, but chemistry was only part of the deal and I knew that.

"So, what're your big plans for the day?" Fen asked after the ensuing silence. I glanced at him, checking who he was talking to before I went and made an ass out of myself. He was lookin' at Little Bird who was studying her food.

"Babe," I said gently and she looked up, startled.

"What?" she asked.

"Fen asked you what your big plans were for today."

"Oh, um, nothing that I knew of. I figured you had something in mind when you asked me to get dressed."

"That I did," I agreed. "Thought maybe you'd like to come to the shop with me, but if you aren't feeling up to it, you're more than welcome to stay here. Just don't want you feelin' like you're trapped."

"I ain't got shit else to do today," Fen said leaning back in his seat. "Happy to take you for a ride." He held up his hands. "No strings or any conditions or stupid shit like that."

"Actually, it might be nice seeing where you work and what you do," she said quietly, looking at me. I smiled faintly and made a mental note to thank Fen for the minor assist later. She looked like she was going to err on the side of staying cooped up in here but Fen's little suggestion of taking her anywhere was far enough outside her comfort zone to make coming with me look good by comparison.

If she hated it at the shop, I not only wouldn't blame her, I'd give her a ride back here at lunch. I just didn't want her sealing herself away. Hiding, letting the dark consume her. She was this bright, shining light to me and I felt it to the bottom of my soul. She'd been stained by shadow, but getting out there, sunning herself, so to speak, was what she needed.

I needed to see about making her more independent. Get her a cage so she could get out there on her own if she wanted, and truthfully, I was getting to the point with my leg that it might not be a bad thing to have a grocery getter around during the colder months. I'd likely still die on the back of my bike, but looking at my little bird across from me, her warm brown eyes taking me in, I wanted to die an *old man*. Probably for the first time that I could ever remember, I wanted a future and that was no small thing.

"Love to show you everything, babe. I can go on and bring you back here at lunchtime if you get bored."

That seemed to make up her mind for her. She smiled and nodded and got up, her plate mostly eaten, and said, "Let me do my hair and makeup and I'll be ready.

"That's my cue to get a shower," I said rising and Fen got up with me.

"And my cue to hit the road. I'll see you around, man." We clasped hands and brought each other in for a savage hug.

"Keep the shiny side up," I told him.

"Always."

He nodded in my girl's direction. "Little Bird," he said and she smiled.

"Be careful, have a good day," she said pleasantly, but the awkward was still there in the tight lines of her expression.

Fen grinned ferally and gave another nod, heading for the coatrack. I picked up his and my plate and headed for the kitchen. My woman followed me with hers.

"I've got it," she murmured. "Go get your shower."

I nodded and Fen went out the front door, shutting it behind him. I went over and locked it for her benefit before turning and making my way into the bathroom.

By the time I got out, ran a brush through my hair, and pulled it back, she had the dishwasher running and was handwashing the skillet I'd used to fry up the bacon. So she at least had some damn sense when it came to the kitchen. You never put cast iron in the dishwasher.

I went in and got dressed for the day in a pair of grease-stained Levi's and a faded and equally greasy but clean shop tee.

I sat on the edge of the side table by the couch to put on my boots, grunting some when I had to raise my bad leg.

"Need help?" she asked faintly.

"Naw, I got it," I said too soon, right as I caught a fuckin' cramp.

"Here, let me." She came over and kneeled, gripping my leg with surety through the denim of my jeans and kneading the afflicted muscle carefully and thoroughly into submission.

"Ah, thanks," I said between gritted teeth.

"The least I could do," she murmured. "You've already done so much for me."

I shook my head. "This ain't no tit for tat, baby. You don't owe me nothin'."

"I beg to differ," she said looking up at me. "I owe you everything."

I caressed the side of her beautiful face and smiled. I didn't want to argue about it and this was one of those stalemate kind of things so I just shrugged and said, "Have to agree to disagree."

She gave a wry little twist of her luscious lips and said, "Fine."

I chuckled.

I needed to be to work between seven and nine. Today, we backed into one of the spots at the neighboring Eagle's lot just at the stroke of nine. Mav was waiting at the open door to my garage bay with an eyebrow raised.

"I ain't late," I grunted.

"Didn't say that you were. Hello, Little Bird," he said with a cool and appraising look.

"Hi," she said shyly.

I half expected Mav to ask for a word, but he didn't. Instead, he made himself useful and cleared a box of rags off the seat in the corner of my workspace.

"Go on and have a seat, babe," I said.

"Thanks," she said, as much to me as to Maverick.

"No problem," he said.

"We got a problem, Boss?" I asked, hanging up my jacket and cut on this bolt sticking out the cinderblock wall over my industrial sized toolkit.

"Not at all, man," he said and it wasn't what he said, but how he said it. The curiosity in his voice letting me know he was curious about why I'd brought my little bird in with me.

"Got a timeline on the finish of this particular job?" he asked, looking at the bike frame and motor on my lift.

"Depends, you get those seals in?"

"While you were away, they're on your bench."

"Awesome, then I would have to guess tomorrow, maybe the day after for full assembly. I should get the motor running by the end of today for sure, though."

"Sweet deal," he said. "I'll check back later." He gave me a nod and left with a lingering look at my girl. I felt some of the guarded stiffness ease out of my shoulders when I caught the distinct worry in his eyes with that look. Not worry about her being here, but more worry for her being here in general. I could appreciate that. I could respect it even, but I had this. She was safe as anything, wherever I was.

"So, what do you think?" I asked, walking over to my bench and sorting through the different parts and fresh boxes on its top.

"A bit dreary," she said with a smile, taking in the stained concrete floor, and the equally stained cinderblock walls. Their base color was white – sometime a long ass time ago, but that hadn't been the case even ever since I started coming here.

"Yeah?" I asked with a chuckle as she extracted the book she'd placed in her new, crossbody handbag. Dahlia'd done real good by her. Had thought of everything. Even a wallet, although she had nothing to go in it.

"Definitely blue collar with a certain…" her eyes drifted over a tittie calendar on the wall. "Toxic masculinity chic," she declared and I laughed outright.

"We are nothing if not a pack of feral dogs," I agreed.

She laughed with me and said, "Shall I just sit here, then?"

"Unless you're cold. I can move you further back and I got no problem shuttin' the door if it starts rainin' on us."

"I like the natural light," she said and I smiled.

"Me too."

The lack of windows in here got to me sometimes and the lighting wasn't always too good. She smiled at me and opened her book, seemingly content just to read and be near me.

That did my soul all kinds of good. Almost as good, if not better, than opening up the bike full throttle on a lonely stretch of straightaway.

I got to work, some music coming on pretty quick, and the day got underway.

CHAPTER TWENTY-THREE

*L*ittle Bird...

I was fully engrossed in my book when the weather… well, turned gross. The rain started coming down outside the garage door and I jumped up with a squeal when the wind kicked up slightly and blew it in sideways, spattering the pages of the book I held.

That was no way to treat a book!

Dump Truck got up from his broken apart office chair he used as a rolling stool and limped over to the garage door's switch, hitting the button to lower it as I tried to blot the rainwater from the paperback with a clean, dry shop rag.

"Hey, Little Bird," Mav called over the dividing half-wall between us and the waiting area.

"Yes?" I asked, looking up from the water-blotched pages.

"C'mere a minute. It's slowed down enough I want to show you something."

I looked over at D.T. who nodded at me, letting me know it was okay. I was still more than slightly apprehensive, though. After Maverick's initial overly familiar greeting of the night before, I didn't know what to think about putting myself in proximity to him. Especially where Dump Truck couldn't see me. Once he sat back down, he was behind the little dividing wall again.

Still, he'd nodded at me, so with some trepidation I went around the motorcycle he was working on, on its strange lift platform thing, and through the intersection of aisles – the one leading from the front door of the building to the back, and the other from Dump Truck's work area, past the main sales counter on one side and the shelves of parts on the other. I didn't see it last night, but there was another door up this aisle, leading to a back room. I wondered if the restroom was back there but didn't ask.

I didn't want to inadvertently wander where things were none of my business, and I didn't have to go bad enough yet to warrant a trip to the bathroom so…

"Come around here, sweetheart," Maverick said with a casual wave to indicate he wanted me over near him. I went around the metal counter and found shelves under it, lined with varying parts with big file tags held on by a twist of wire.

Maverick eyed me from the stool behind the register, nearby it, rested one of the two landline office phones. The lines were quiet for now, but they'd rung fairly consistently for the first part of the day. I blushed faintly while he scrutinized me, his slow, calculating look more than a little uncomfortable.

"How's your penmanship?" he asked me.

"Um, like cursive?" I asked.

He shook his head. "No, more like printing."

"Fine," I said shifting uncomfortably.

He reached up and scratched a thumbnail across his bottom lip.

"You're here and handy. I want to pay you for a few days to help me with inventory," he said.

"Um… okay," I said. "Not that I'm looking a gift horse, or you know, a temporary job when I have no skills in the mouth but, why?"

"You're here, you're handy, and it saves me from having to do a bunch of writing. It will make this shit go faster and spares me from having to pull one of the guys off a repair or a rebuild to do it. In the long run, it'd be cheaper to put you on the payroll and pay you for a few days of work than it would cost me in lost repair and part pulling time to have one of these guys do it."

"Okay," I said, nodding when the answer wasn't something ridiculously sexist like I expected it to be.

"Okay." He reached over and pulled a clipboard with some pages attached, turned it sideways and handed it to me. I took it and looked at the smooth blank lines and empty boxes. "We'll start in here," he declared. "Just write down what I say and how many, and when we finish a shelf front and back, I'll show you how to input everything into the terminal up here."

"Okay," I said. "You do know that's a tablet and I could potentially input it directly with one of them as we go, right?"

He shrugged and said, "I like to do it old-school. Drop a clipboard and paper by accident, or set a part on it, it costs me pennies. Fuck up one of those tablets…" he trailed off and raised his eyebrows.

"Duly noted and touché," I said with a wry smile.

He smiled back and took my book from my other hand.

"Phone rings, somebody grab it!" he yelled out.

"Got it," Dump Truck called from his work area.

I followed Mav with a mild trepidation to the edge of one of the giant shelves.

"Here we go," he said and flipped one of the tags then swore. "Some of this shit is just trash." He sighed. "Then again, you never know who's going to call for what."

What came after was a word salad of years, makes, models, and part names I couldn't even begin to keep track of or pronounce. I dutifully wrote them down, Maverick pausing just long enough to go get some nitrile gloves for the both of us out of the back so that we could move parts around if need be.

He read, I acted as his scribe, but it still took *quite a bit* of time to even get through one loaded column of shelves, which were somewhere around seven shelves high, each shelf around four feet long and each individual rack of shelves around three to four racks per aisle.

That didn't count the milk crates full of parts sitting on the floor in front of some of them, either.

Some parts were larger, some smaller, but there were just so many of all of them. The acrid tang of metal, combustion, and used motor oil hung thick between the shelves and I had to be careful not to get anything on my new clothes.

It took us two hours for one column of shelves and I was nearly dizzy with how many of the same component they had over such a wide range of motorcycle types. From Honda to Harley, Suzuki to Ducati... I didn't think I would ever know the difference or be able to keep it straight.

Mav sighed, and I had several pages filled by the time we finished the one rack and I looked at him, twisting my lips in sympathy as he swore.

"I wish there was a more efficient way of doing this shit," he said.

"I mean, how bad is it?" I asked.

"No way to fuckin' know," he said. "This place has been run old-school for so fuckin' long, there's no way to tell how much of what they got on the shelves. Doesn't help no one's done any kind of inventory for fuckin' *years* and none of these fucks put anything into the old system before shelving it."

"What a nightmare," I commented dryly.

"That's why I'm doing it from scratch. The old system used a dot matrix printer from like, 1990 for fuck's sake."

I grimaced.

"And it still worked?"

"Yeah, surprisingly enough, it did – until, you know, it didn't."

"How new is the new system?"

"Brand new."

"You know how to use it?"

"For the most part."

"Does it have a user's guide?"

"Yeah."

"Can I see it?"

He smiled and nodded. "Sure."

I had always been a better book learner. Someone could show me how to do something a half a dozen time and for some reason, it wouldn't stick. It was frustrating. Maddening even. You handed me a book, or let me write myself a written set of instructions I could refer back to? You could just wind me up and watch me go.

I set the clipboard aside and dropped onto the stool behind the register as the phone rang. Maverick answered it.

"Ironheart Salvage, this is Maverick, how can I help?" He reached past me and plucked the fat, square, user manual for the shiny new terminal in front of me off a shelf to my right and handed it to me, turning back to the pad of notepaper and stealing my pen off my clipboard to jot some details down.

I dove in and started looking through the manual, clicking through screens and following the directions. By the time he got off the call, I was already clacking away on the keyboard and clicking through screens with the mouse, inputting the data we'd just gathered.

"Nice," he muttered and left me to it. I can't tell you how refreshing it was to not have him try to jump in and explain it to me or show me how to do it another way.

It didn't take me long to find a groove and a little shortcut or two to what I was doing, and I was simply left alone to do it for the most part. Mav only interrupted me once to ring a customer up.

I watched over his shoulder, frowning slightly when I realized he was entering the price manually. That was another thing… I had been entering inventory but there were no set prices going in with them. That was a problem. I mean, how on earth was there any consistency?

Before I knew it, my questions were bubbling forth.

"Honestly, I don't fucking know what anything costs," Mav said, stripping off his gloves and running a hand back through his wild hair, which by the expression on his face, he was ready to tear out.

"So, um, who does?" I asked.

"Old Rusty, out back," he said.

"Okay. Fair enough. Before I go any further, let's go bug Rusty."

"I'd better go with you, he's the oldest of the old-school."

"As in sexist to the point it's painful?" I asked with a slight smile.

"As in sexist to the point even I want to lay his ass out," he agreed. "But he's worked here longer than anyone and he knows the fair market value for everything right off the top of his head so…"

"So, let's go talk to Rusty," I said with an intrepid sigh.

"After lunch." I looked up and over. Dump Truck was standing just the other side of the counter wiping his hands on a rag that was honestly just as greasy as what he was trying to get off.

"Only after you wash those hands," I said sweetly. He chuckled and limped back toward the shelves we'd just inventoried. The door down the aisle he traversed led to a back room. I hadn't been in there yet, but it was full of different equipment and a workbench with vices from what I could see when I went by. It had another door in the room that led outside. I could feel the damp and smell the rain when I walked by it. The wall along the back had another door in it that led into a narrow bathroom that held a stacking washer and dryer, of all things.

Past that, in a tight squeeze was a toilet and finally there was a deep shop skin, a bottle of orange smelling pumice hand cleaner open on a metal kitchen rack to one side. They didn't even have paper towels, just a seriously old-fashioned dispenser thing that had a loop of blue cloth. You pulled down on it to get fresh, dry cloth, dried your hands and walked out. I'd never seen anything like it before but judging by the dented old metal case thing that was on the wall, it was *old*. Maybe original to the building old.

The bathroom was also less than impressive on the cleanliness scale, and the multitude of scratches, stickers, and graffiti did nothing to disguise that fact and everything to encourage me to do the time-honored female tradition of the hover when I'd had to go earlier.

When Dump Truck came back out, he looked at me and I gave him a slightly pained, tight-lipped smile. He immediately picked up on what I was thinking and said, "That bathroom is disgusting and no place for a lady. Where's the prospect?"

"Oh, God!" I cried and both Dump Truck and Maverick broke into wide grins.

"You wanna do it?" Mav asked and I sighed.

"No, not particularly but –"

"Sounds like a job for the prospect," Dump Truck said with finality and I sighed.

"What's his favorite alcohol? I feel like I owe him a bottle since it's at my expense."

"A fine gesture, but one of us would have realized it at some point and he would be the one to do it. You just brought it to our attention faster before it could get *really* disgusting."

I sighed and with a grin that was entirely too delighted, Maverick yelled, "Hey, Prospect!"

I felt my face scrunch in sympathy but, no… oh no… it was about to be far worse than I feared.

"Yeah, Boss!" Sauley came in from the back in a pair of coveralls.

"What do you want for lunch?" Maverick asked coolly. "We'll bring you something back."

"Shit, seriously?"

"Yeah, man. You and Rusty both," Dump Truck said, taking me under his arm.

"Uh, let me check and see what Rusty wants, I'll go for whatever he's having." He trotted off and I whimpered.

"You guys are so *mean*."

My heart went out for the guy. I mean, he immediately defaulted to Rusty, who I'd seen come in a time or two but who hadn't cast a look in my direction as far as I could tell.

He came back a few minutes later and said, "Porker's Pit?"

"Barbecue, good deal!" Maverick said.

"The usual for you two?" Dump Truck asked.

"Yeah."

"Cool, we'll be back. We're gonna take Little Bird out for some air."

"Good deal, it's still raining. You going to ride?" he asked, pointedly casting a look in my direction.

"Shit, naw, we'll take the truck," Mav said.

"I appreciate that," I murmured as Sauley tossed Maverick a set of keys. I waited until he was around the corner and back down whatever steps before I said, "A nice lunch and then you're going to make him clean the bathroom? That's just cruel."

"Oh, he's cleaning that bathroom," Maverick said, both he and Dump Truck fighting to suppress their giggles.

I heaved a great sigh and tried to wheedle with them. "Fine but can you be slightly less mean than making him clean it on a full stomach?" I asked.

"What do you have in mind?" Mav asked me.

"Wait until just before closing and tell him he can't go home or over to the club until it's clean."

Dump Truck nodded slowly and said, "It's a fair compromise."

"Still a dick move, but not as big of a dick move… I like it," Mav said. "Okay, Little Bird, have it your way… but you owe me one."

"One what?" I asked.

"That remains to be seen," he said.

I chewed my bottom lip nervously and stared after where Sauley had gone and with a sigh said, "Okay, fine."

"Come on, babe. Before you got us hanging flower baskets or some shit," Dump Truck said with a smile.

I let him guide me around the counter.

The truck was parked at the curb and was a tiny old black Nissan with a bench seat and the salvage yard's logo painted on the side – or maybe it was just vinyl lettering. It was hard to tell.

Sandwiched between Dump Truck and Maverick, there still was barely room to breathe in the tiny cab and my God, was it awkward. My feet were to either side of the hump in the middle of the floor and the gearshift to the standard was between my legs. All kinds of funny but wildly inappropriate jokes were made as Maverick drove, pretty much reaching between my knees to shift gears.

Between the two of them, I was laughing until I cried and my face just *flamed*, hot against my fingers where I tried to hide behind my hands.

"Which one we going to?" Dump Truck asked as we went down 15th, away from the direction we'd come from.

"Original, fuck that new West Seattle shit. It's too much of a pain in the ass to get in and out of. I'd rather go Fourth Avenue."

So that's where we went, all the way to Fourth Avenue, across from the Starbucks headquarters, to this outdoor barbecue place, Porky's Pit, that specialized in pulled pork sandwiches 'spiked' with hot links in them, if you so ordered it that way.

We picked up a big paper bag of sandwiches both spiked and regular, bags of chips, and sides of baked beans and piled back into the small pickup for the return trip, stopping at a gas station on the way back to get some bottles of soda.

The atmosphere during lunch was light and full of good humor, but Rusty turned a little tempestuous when Maverick said he'd like him to go through pricing with me for the inventory we'd already done.

"Tryin' to make me obsolete?" the older man demanded.

"Tryin' to bring this fuckin' place into the twenty-first century," Mav replied coolly but I could see he didn't like to be questioned. "Little Bird here is gonna go over everything with you, get prices. That's the end of the conversation," Mav said, raising his eyebrows. "The club is a democracy, this here? Is a benevolent dictatorship."

Rusty shut up, but he glared at me from under his wiry and bushy white eyebrows, his watery blue eyes full of piss and vinegar.

"Look at my woman like that again, old man, I'm gonna take it as a disrespect," Dump Truck said and I swallowed hard, and suddenly didn't want to look at anyone as the once warm and cheery atmosphere dropped by about forty-five degrees.

Rusty wisely didn't say anything and wouldn't make eye contact with anyone for the remainder of the meal.

After we'd all finished and cleaned up, I sighed and asked softly, "Do you want to do this now?"

Rusty nodded curtly and said, "Yeah, but you come on out back. No sense in stoppin' what I'm doin' just to chitchat."

I smiled and said, "Fair enough," and picked up my clipboard to follow him.

"Sauley, you got a minute?" Dump Truck asked.

"Yeah, yeah, what's up?"

"Need an extra set of hands over here," D.T. said, but his gaze was fixed on me from over the low dividing wall that separated his workstation from the customer area.

I smiled back at him over my shoulder as Mav answered a call, and I followed Rusty into the back room and out the back door.

CHAPTER TWENTY-FOUR

*D*ump Truck…

Rusty could bitch and grumble under his breath all he wanted, but in the end, I think my girl somehow managed to win him over. One, because Sauley never came in to get me like I asked him to if Rusty started hasslin' her, and two, because when Rusty himself reappeared at quittin' time to hang his coveralls on the pegs lining the outside of the office door, he didn't have fuck all else to say about it.

"Whoa, not you, Prospect," Maverick said as Sauley started to pull off his coveralls. "Bathroom is a fuckin' pit. You need to clean it."

"Right now?" Sauley asked.

"Right now," Mav affirmed.

"On it, Boss," he said shrugging back into the tops of his coveralls and snapping them closed.

Maverick rose an eyebrow and I chuckled. I'd maybe let Sauley know that my girl had taken one for him. Owing Mav a favor in order to spare him some drama. Sauley was a quick fuckin' study, so I had even money that he figured out right quick exactly what he'd been spared.

Gettin' out late versus cleaning that shithole with a belly full of fresh barbecue? I know which one I'd pick. He smiled at my girl and said, "See you tomorrow, Little Bird?" She smiled warmly and nodded.

"See you tomorrow."

"Good deal."

"You comin' over to the club?" Mav asked.

"Naw." I shook my head. "We got a shit ton of stuff to put away. I think we'll skip it tonight." I knew I'd made the right call when my little bird's shoulders eased down minimally from the tightness they'd held.

"Right, see you both tomorrow," Mav said, counting up the till.

"See you tomorrow, have a good night," my girl murmured as I put a hand to her back and led her out the door.

She sighed, her breath pluming the air.

"Good day?" I asked as we wandered slowly through the cool humidity toward the bike.

"Good day," she said with a smile. "It's nice to find some purpose. Even if it's tedious, it's some nice and honest work. I might even be sad when it's all over."

I chuckled. "Wait until you get to the buckets of relays," I said, and she laughed too and leaned into me.

"I still don't know how I'm ever going to thank you for this," she said. I shook my head.

"You ain't gotta thank me, babe. Best thing you can do to thank me, honestly, is to not only survive but to *thrive*. That's all I ask."

She smiled a bit sadly and heaved a big sigh.

"I'm trying," she said bravely.

"And that's all I can ask of you. For real."

We geared up and rode home.

I sighed when we stepped into the apartment. I liked things neat and orderly, and this scatter and clutter from her shopping trip liked to drive me nuts.

"Let's make you some room to start putting some of this shit away," I said. "And while you do that, I'll fix us some dinner."

"Deal," she said immediately. "I feel bad enough that I've seemingly taken over your entire life… this… this is just way too extra."

I chuckled and we divested of our boots and jackets at the door. She even hung her purse.

"You ain't taken shit over. I want you here. I *like* you here. You make my life better."

She scoffed. "I don't see how."

"Well, you don't have to. It also ain't about how you see it. It's about how I do, so put that in your joint and smoke it."

She laughed and shook her head ruefully.

"Where should I start?" she asked, putting her hands on her hips and twisting her lips, looking around thoughtfully. I pulled open some of the drawers that were empty in my dresser simply for a lack of anything I had to put in them. I didn't need much, and sure as shit wasn't any kind of a clotheshorse. Not like Dahlia. I wasn't sure how much of this was actually my little bird's doing.

"You can start here with some of your foldable and more delicate things." I opened up the closet doors and sighed. "I'll have to get hangers for you but use what's available and do what you can with the shelf up here. The rest, I guess stack neat on the dresser top or in the bottom of the closet here. Stuff the bags into as few as possible and I'll take 'em out in the morning."

"Okay," she said, readily agreeable, her smile a little wan but I honestly chalked that up to her being tired. A lot had happened for her in an extremely short amount of time. It was a mark of her inner strength that she just kept right on rolling with the punches. She hadn't fallen apart again. Not like she had that first night. She'd had her meltdown, had survived it, and she just kept getting stronger every day.

"Makin' steak and potatoes. How do you like your meat?" I asked.

"Medium-rare if it's not too much trouble," she murmured.

"No trouble at all, babe," I said with a smile. "I'm right there with you."

She turned and I said softly, "Hey, Little Bird." She looked up and I shifted on my feet nervously.

"A couple more weeks or so and you'll have your new identity and your first paycheck. You can go wherever you want, do whatever you want, and *be* whoever you want to be," I said. She stared at me in stony silence, and I drew a deep breath. "I'm just sayin', whatever you choose to do is alright with me. I'd just really like it if you'd maybe consider stayin' with me. Because you want to – not because you feel like you have to."

Her chin came up, her chin dropping as she went to speak and I said, "Don't think you gotta make your decision on that now." I was half afraid of what she would say. "I just needed to make it known, you know… that I like having you here."

She closed her mouth and smiled, and it seemed tremulous, her bottom lip trembling slightly as she nodded, shakily.

I didn't want her to cry. Or, maybe, depending on the type of tears, it was okay. Really, I think it was I just didn't want to see her cry anymore. So, I backed out of the room and went into my kitchen to cook us up some grub, leaving her to her thoughts and to put some of the pieces of her new life away.

CHAPTER TWENTY-FIVE

*L*ittle Bird...

"You're serious," I said. It'd been several good days of working at the salvage yard. The weekend was upon us, but Dump Truck wouldn't be here to spend it with me. I was beyond disappointed about that, but what was even more disappointing was that he wouldn't tell me *why*.

"As a heart attack, babe. I wish I could, but club business is club business."

"Which isn't any of mine?" I asked hugging myself, and he gave me an apologetic little smile.

"That's one way of looking at it," he said. "The simplest of ways."

"The more complicated one?" I asked softly.

"Is that the less you know, the safer you are."

"From?"

"A lot of things," he said and his voice had grown husky with an edge of darkness. I sniffed and wiped under my eyes, staring at the true-blue sky until I felt like I had things back under control and that I wouldn't cry or ruin my makeup. I looked down into the palm of my hand where the set of car keys rested and then past Dump Truck to the Toyota 4runner sitting in the Eagle's lot behind him. It was a 2010 in a metallic silver gray. It had a few dings, and a fair amount of miles, but it also looked sturdy and reliable and was in pretty good condition given its age.

It was also mine. I mean, it was registered under Dump Truck's legal given name, but he was giving it to me and said we'd fix the registration as soon as I had the personal identification to do it with. I was a little flummoxed and my high at looking at the car had been brought low in the next moment when he said he wouldn't be here to enjoy it with me.

"I just didn't want you feeling trapped in the apartment all weekend long. I wanted you to be able to go where you wanted to and do whatever you wanted to do." He tried holding out the decent sized wad of cash to me again and I stared at it.

He sighed and said in a low and cajoling tone, "Come on Little Bird…"

I took the money but reminded him, "I mean, I still can't *drive it*. I don't have a license yet."

He shrugged his shoulders and said, "That one's easy. Just don't get pulled over."

I gave him a withering look and he smiled.

I sighed and snapped, "Do you really have to rush making me so damn independent?" My anger was misplaced, though. I wasn't mad at him for *giving me a car*. I mean, sort of, like everything he had done so far, it was just too much. I was just scared and aching inside that I would be alone and without him for the next few days. I swallowed hard and fought back tears a second time.

God, did I love him? Yes, you friggin' idiot. Of course, you do.

"Babe," he said consoling, pulling me into his chest and I cuddled against him as he held me close. "I was looking forward to spending some time with you, just you and me, but you have to believe me when I say, *I gotta go*."

He sounded so earnest and I finally nodded, miserable, half embarrassed and said, "I just… I just love you. I don't want you to go," I said and sniffed, rubbing the tip of my nose with the back of my wrist.

"I love you, too," he murmured and pulled me back against him. "And I'll have my ass back home as soon as I can."

I swallowed hard and nodded.

"You know how to get there from here by now, right?"

I glared up at him and he held up his hands in surrender. "I was just checkin'!" he said quickly to cover his ass. I smiled; I couldn't help it, and he sighed.

"I don't know what I'm going to do with myself," I confessed.

"Take yourself to the spa, head out to a bookstore, go shopping for more clothes you don't need, go see a chick movie!" he suggested, sounding more and more desperate with everything he listed and I sniffed one more time and looked up at him.

"All very good suggestions," I lied. "Thank you."

He brought his lips to mine in a lingering kiss and sighed.

"I wish I were staying right here with you," he growled and I nodded. I could feel the truth of his words to the very bottom of my soul.

"Me too, but I guess I understand," I said.

"Thank you," he said, tension easing out of his big body.

"You promise me you'll be *careful*," I demanded ruthlessly.

"Now that I *will* promise," he said.

I nodded.

"When do you leave?" I asked.

"In an hour, maybe two," he said and I couldn't keep the stricken look off my face if I tried. "Gotta follow you home now and pack up," he said.

I blew out my cheeks and nodded. "Okay."

He took me over to the SUV and opened the driver's side door for me. I got in and put my hands on the steering wheel.

"I'll follow you," he said and I nodded, taking a few extra moments to adjust the seat and mirrors and to just sit in my new-to-me car.

He knew me so well. Knew that this would make a huge difference for me with his being gone. It was like, sometimes, he knew me better than I even knew myself.

I drove home carefully, keeping it right on the speed limit, making absolutely certain I used my signals. White knuckling the steering wheel every time I saw a King County Sheriff's car or Burien Police vehicle – which there were *a lot* of both. The area we were in was riddled with crime, criminals, and gangbangers. Hilarious, right? Since I was one of them… since I loved one of them.

"Oh, the tangled webs, we weave…" I muttered, pulling into the familiar covered space beneath Dump Truck's apartment, creeping up, inching, inching forward until I cringed; lightly tapping the cement wall at the back of the spot with the front bumper.

I put it in park and immediately jumped out and went to the front, relieved that it was just the license plate and there was no harm done. Dump Truck shut off his bike behind me and called out, "Everything all good?"

"Yeah!" I called back and went and pulled the keys and my purse with its fresh wad of cash off the passenger seat. I shut and locked things up and rejoined D.T. by his bike.

He lightly grasped the back of my neck and lightly kneaded with his strong fingertips. I sighed and felt my shoulders ease down.

"Come on, I gotta get packed," he murmured and I nodded.

"Time for a blowjob or a quickie?" I asked hopeful and he chuckled darkly.

"Afraid not, but you best be naked and ready as soon as I get home," he growled against my ear as I unlocked the front door for us. He nipped the edge of my ear and I squealed in surprise, clapping my hand over my mouth at the sound as he howled with laughter behind me.

I pushed in the front door and he followed right behind, closing it tight.

I hated that he went straight to work packing a bag while I hung up my coat with a heavy sigh.

"We'll be back sometime Sunday. No tellin' when," he called from the bedroom, his voice lowering when I propped a shoulder against the doorway, crossing my arms over my middle.

"Are you all going?" I asked.

He shook his head. "We don't all go one place at one time unless it's all on the up and up and we *never* take our women on club business without them knowing."

I perked up slightly at that. "So you *do* have occasion to tell us the full meal deal?" I asked and he shook his head.

"Only as much as you *need* to know," he answered.

I nodded my understanding.

"How dangerous is what you're doing?" I asked, raising my hand when he looked like we was about to disavow any more information. "I'm talking on a scale of a night in jail to the electric chair," I said.

He smiled and said, "Life in prison. There's no electric chair in Washington. Used to be lethal injection or death by hanging but now, it's just life in prison."

"Okay, consider me educated, now could you answer the question? I mean, at least give me that."

"I already did, baby," he said grimly and I thought back over what he'd said…

"Life in prison?" He pursed his lips and nodded and I took a fortifying breath. I went to him and curled my fingers around the lapel of his leather vest and stared up at him, throwing his own words back in his face. "Then don't get pulled over."

He smirked and shook his head, lowering his mouth to mine in a deep and lingering kiss.

"I promise you," he said swallowing. "I'll see you on Sunday."

"You better," I whispered.

He left within the hour, and I furiously scrubbed the already clean kitchen and bathroom while I cried just to give myself something to do that felt useful and productive. I was still working on coping mechanisms out of this self-help book I'd found in and among the multitude of books on every subject on the living room shelves. I mean, what could it hurt, right?

I finally let myself have a good long cathartic cry in the middle of the bathroom floor, complete with loud wracking sobs just to get all the fear, frustration, and *worry* out of my system as much as I could.

I couldn't believe how much I missed him and he hadn't even been gone two hours.

CHAPTER TWENTY-SIX

*D*ump Truck…

We hauled ass up I-5 riding in formation. This run was my typical border crew. Maverick in the lead, me his right hand, and Fen behind us. Just the three of us. It was all we needed.

We ran this shit in relays. First team up to the border, we'd overnight in this bed-and-breakfast, the backyard butting right on up to the Canadian border. We'd wait for the cover of night, would head to the drop point in the woods, and would pack that shit out. Next morning, we took somewhat of a scenic route back south. Typically, we met up with some of the Eastern Washington guys over near Steven's Pass and they'd pick up the relay for their territory.

That was pretty much shot to shit with so many of their crew up on charges, so now we could handle it one of two ways. One, we'd meet up with some of our own crew in Monroe or Sultan and they'd head over the pass and complete the stops over there, or two, we'd run straight through and do it ourselves.

This run was a relay. We were supposed to meet up with Blackjack, Deacon, and Tic-Tac, pass off the stuff for eastern Washington to them and take the rest of the western Washington lot with us to another drop point where Squatch, Nine, and Cipher would run some of it to distribution points on the way to Vancouver at the southern Washington border to pass what was left on to the Western Oregon crew for distribution.

Eastern Oregon and Idaho were trying to alleviate some of the load off of us with the vacuum left by the Eastern Washington crew by meeting up with our guys in parts of eastern Washington.

We rotated constantly with shit like this. Sometimes we'd run for the border, sometimes we'd be the ones taking the scripts on the next leg of the journey to the south or to the east. It all depended. It was also getting hella dicey to the point, Mav was thinking about tapping this small club in Tacoma we were buddies with. Those guys? Well, let's just say they were a bunch of fuckin' freaks.

I hated every fuckin' minute of the ride up to Blaine. We pulled into the driveway of the Bootlegger's Inn and parked. Manny, the inn's owner and one of our points of contact over the border, came out onto the front porch to greet us.

"Welcome weary travelers!" he called out, and I just smirked, hung my head and shook it as I pulled my cane from the clips holding it to my bike. Goddamn leg always gave me fits in the cold and there was a cold front bearing down on us from the great wide north.

"How's it been, Manny?" Maverick asked.

"Same ole, same ole," he declared.

"Everything on track?" Fenris asked.

"Yes, it is," Manny declared.

"Good deal. Let's get in there and get some sleep," Maverick said and Manny held the door to his place open for us.

He was an old hippy with a motherfuckin' axe to grind with the American Healthcare system. All the bureaucratic bullshit of insurance companies denying claims and putting him and his wife through the ringer had led to her eventual death through what was tantamount to medical neglect.

Manny, to his credit, had been pissed but rather than let his anger consume him, rather than taking his ass to the insurance company's main offices and opening up with a fully automatic weapon and a bevy of homemade improvised explosives like I would if someone took my little bird from me – he raised a good old-fashioned one-fingered salute and fuckin' bootstrapped a solution for as many people as he could fuckin' provide for.

He'd been using the Bootlegger's Inn for twenty going on thirty *years* now to smuggle lifesaving drugs over the border to go to the people who depended on them most at a fraction of the cost that United States drug companies were charging. He'd readily gotten into bed with the bag of assholes that was us to get those drugs going where they needed to be.

It was a symbiotic relationship so long as nobody got fuckin' greedy. Which as more came out about it, it sounded like the Eastern Washington's chapter had. To the point that Maverick had every intention of taking his ass to the mother chapter's next lake run to look into our options about bringing some club justice their way.

The Eastern Washington chapter had put us all in a bad spot by gettin' greedy and gettin' themselves onto their local law enforcement's radar. It was a real shitshow over there and we were going to be forced to clean that shit up. A lot of fuckin' people depended on it and not just *the club*.

There were people who depended on these drugs and as far as a lot of us were concerned, SHMC-EW had *really* screwed the goddamn pooch.

As soon as we got in the house, Manny asked, "Just how bad is it Mav?" He looked worried.

"Bad," Mav answered. "But we're handling it on our end."

"Good, good," Manny said but he still sounded troubled. Trust had been eroded and it took a lot of smooth-talking and reassurances out of Mav to get the ship back on somewhat of an even keel. The most important thing we learned? The Canadian side of things didn't know anything was amiss down here in America. Manny hadn't told him and we spent far too long convincing him that was the way to go. That we would keep everything 'business as usual' and that the drugs would get where they needed to go at the initial agreed upon prices.

If anybody could figure this shit out and had the mind and patience for the social engineering involved to get shit done, it was Mav. The real trick would be figuring it out to the point of keeping everybody fuckin' happy while simultaneously making sure no motherfuckers misunderstood our sudden perceived kindness for some type of weakness. They made that mistake; they'd have to deal with me and Fen and just because I may have somehow lucked into the love of a good woman did *not* mean I was any kind of softer for it. Not where business was concerned. Especially where business was concerned.

With the thing with my little bird, it'd just added a major extra layer of drama to the SHMC-EW bullshit. Our chapter was now massively strapped for cash from buying her a new identity and that cash needed to be replaced.

We could fill the holes the arrests made in Eastern Washington left behind for a while, but it was dangerous. Not only was it dangerous, because law enforcement was on a scent like the truffle hunting pigs they were, but also because we couldn't fuckin' fill those gaps *forever*. It left us stretched far too thin.

I looked over at Mav who sat with his head in one hand, a glass of whiskey hanging from the other where his wrist hung limp over the arm of the chair he sat in.

"Heavy is the head that wears the crown," Fen muttered.

Mav heaved a big sigh saying, "You got that fuckin' right."

"Hey. We're all good. We bought some time," I said.

"Yeah, but how much remains to be seen," Mav declared.

"Manny ain't gonna find a different distributor," Fen said and I nodded.

"We'd never done Manny wrong before. Hell, we haven't done him wrong *now*," I said.

"That's not why we would have to worry about him," Mav said softly. "Manny cares a lot less about himself than he does the people receiving these drugs. We're going to have to seriously eat it these first couple runs across the mountains."

"How's that?" Fen asked.

"How else are we going to regain trust?" Mav asked. "It's the people we gotta convince. Not Manny, not the Canadians, but the people on our side. The one's Rebel and his crew dicked the fuck over."

"You giving them a cut rate the first few runs?" Fen asked.

"Either that or a few straight up freebies," he said. "I'm going to ride along with the next relay. I need to take the temperature of the people myself," he said judiciously. "Once we pass things off, you two go on back home."

"Fuck, you would do this to me, wouldn't you?" I asked, running a hand over my face.

"Do what?" he asked.

"Make me chose between your smartass and my woman," I answered.

Mav chuckled. "Wouldn't that make me a dumbass?" he asked.

I shook my head. "Now *that* you'll never be."

He shook his head, expression sobering some. "There's no choice, there's no contest. I need you to run the shop in my absence if I'm taking a few extra days to run the east routes."

"Fuck," I swore.

"Don't worry about it, bro. I'll stick with our president."

"No, you won't," Mav said. "One extra, fine – any more than that and we'll stand out worse than a set of tits on a bull and end up just as fuckin' useless when they catch us with the stash we'll be runnin'." He took a sip from his glass. "No, you two will hand off and take your fucking asses home."

"Still don't like it," I said and Mav finally snapped at me, "I didn't say you had to like it, I just said you had to fuckin' do it!"

I tried not to let it get to me. He was stressed with all the interpersonal bullshit and outlaw politics. I couldn't say I blamed him, even though my first inclination was to tell him just how far off he could fuck with talkin' to me like that.

He huffed out an angry frustrated breath and said, "I'm sorry. You don't deserve to be talked to like that." Which is another reason exactly why Maverick was not only our leader, but the most respected one we'd probably ever had in the history of this chapter of the club.

"Ain't nothin' to apologize for," I said and met his eyes with mine.

He nodded slowly, picking up on the gratitude I put into my gaze for all that he'd done for Little Bird.

We didn't try to talk anymore about anything else. Instead, we went from Manny's parlor or whatever you would fucking call it, up to our usual rooms to rack out for as long as we could.

It was a full moon tonight which just made shit even trickier and more dangerous.

~

"D.T. YOU GOOD?" Maverick asked.

"I'm good, keep movin'," I growled. The underbrush wasn't thick, but it was mainly dried husks of thick blackberry vines so it liked to puncture and snag and was a bitch to navigate with no flashlights or anything else.

We didn't have to go too far in, though, and I was at the back of the line, closest to the Bootlegger's property line with Manny.

"Hurry up, now!" Manny whisper-shouted and with a crack of a stick we both winced. All of us froze and ducked down low. A rifle shot cracked the air, and I hissed between my teeth when somebody out there shouted.

"Mav! Fen! You alright!?"

"Yeah!" Fen hissed.

"Mav!?" I stood up straight and was prepared to lumber into the dark when he whisper-shouted down the line.

"Fucking poachers out here! I'm good!"

"Watch. Your. Ass!"

He laughed nervously and called back, "I do what I want!"

We all got really quiet and sank down to the ground, my leg screaming as voices drew near and someone called out, "Dang it! I swore I got it." A headlamp flickered to life some yards away, and I pulled out my piece from the back of my waistband. "Wait – here's some blood. It went this way!"

The light flickered out and I held my breath, heart thundering against the inside of my ribs when these fuckin' dumbass jack holes that were probably just tryin' to feed their fuckin' families moved off in another direction.

I think we *all* let out a collective sigh of relief when they moved off and didn't come any closer.

We waited until the noises of their departure grew even more distant and then waited some more. Finally, we heard a grunt and a scraping sound up ahead as Mav pulled the plywood cover off of the cache.

Then the work began. There was a pause, then the squeak of Styrofoam as Mav lifted the first cold-storage pack of insulin out of the ground and passed it back to Fen who passed it back to me. I hurriedly put away my piece and passed it to Manny who loaded it into a foldable off-road camp wagon in country camo, the white box disappearing up under the country camo tarp he had over it.

"Shit, there's almost twice as much as last time," Mav grunted and quickly kept passing.

"We callin' up reserves to come up?" I asked.

"Might have to."

We shut our mouths and made quick work of what felt like an endless supply coming down our way. The insulin chests, cold packed for 24 hours would need to be re-packed for the ride and would get refrigerated in Manny's basement as we re-packed coolers with fresh ice packs into the wee hours of the morning.

Boxes of antibiotics, heart medications, anti-depressants, and other shit I had no fuckin' idea what it did – I just knew it was needed by folks – came down the line and Manny cursed.

"What now?" I hissed.

"Out of fuckin' room in the wagon. I don't know why there's so much but keep stacking it. I'll bring it in."

Manny trotted over to his old cellar doors and the old-fashioned coal chute he'd fixed up next to 'em and started sending boxes of meds down the steep slide we'd refurbished and cleaned up, down into his basement.

The sound was minimal, but every second we were out here was a second more we could get fuckin' caught.

I was sweating bullets, stacking boxes, my mouth dry and finally there was the grate and shift of the camouflage out in the woods as Maverick slid the cover back into place. He and Fen materialized out of the trees and met up with me, and we started drifting across Manny's manicured back lawn through the fence's hidden back gate. As in, you looked at that back fence during the day and you'd never know there was a gate in it. Hell, it was so well hidden, you could walk along it up close and never see the latch or where it came open if you didn't know where to look.

It was tense moments getting it all across the yard and down the chute but we managed, bucket brigade style. Once it was in, then came the easy but tedious part of packing it for transport.

"What the fuck was that all about?" Fen demanded and Mav was like, "I don't fuckin' know, but I shit you not – there's a fuckin' note."

He scowled and went with Manny over to the dimly lit lamp on the corner of an old metal desk, turning the switch on the back to bring it up in brightness a couple of notches to read by.

Manny read it out loud. "Cardiac drug supply disrupted by manufacturer. Didn't want to disrupt patient supply so extra. Sorry – figure it out. Regards."

"Well ain't that just peachy?" Mav said sarcastically and Manny shrugged.

"I have contingencies for that," he said.

"Oh yeah? Let's hear it."

"False bottoms in the freezers," he said and jerked his head to the two deep freezers, the kind you could keep bodies in, against the far wall.

"Nice." Mav nodded then sighed. "Dig in, boys. Let's figure out what we've got copious amounts of and load the freezers up. The rest is business as usual."

"Let's do it," I agreed, and we started with unpacking the insulin into the fridge down here.

We pulled an all-nighter, separating out meds and traipsing it up through the house and out to the garage where our bikes were parked. Fen had a gutted travel trailer he and his pops had modified affixed to his pop's bike which he used for this. The Honda Goldwing was an old man's touring bike, a Barcalounger of the highways and byways but it was well suited to the task of smuggling for several reasons – storage capacity chief among them. Almost all the shit to be distributed south through Western Washington and Western Oregon went with him and he could do the south run practically by himself if he wanted to. Not that any man ever rode solo for anything during an operation like this.

Newer backpacks were loaded, stuffed around the outer edges of our cargo with tough bags of medical saline to disguise the lumpy and angular outlines of bottles and boxes. We didn't always take the six to a dozen bottles out of their box. It kept them together and neat.

The sun was coming up by the time we got done and we had just enough time for another short nap before hitting the road, which we took gladly. When we got up, Manny put some breakfast sandwiches in our faces and some caffeine in our veins by way of hot coffee you could stand a spoon up in it.

"Until next time, gentlemen," he said, opening up his garage door.

"Until next time," Mav agreed and we pulled out, our colors stashed under RUB gear and beneath the expensive-ass bougie Gore-Tex Eddie Bauer coats we wore. Our faces covered with balaclavas for me and Fen to hide our beards. Our usual half helmets were replaced with touring helmets, which for the most part were more comfortable, but god*damn* did we look like pussies.

It was actually a pretty masterful disguise. We looked like every other fuckin' tech worker, hipster-type, weekend rider douchebag Western Washington had to offer thanks to the resident titans of the technological industry that'd sprung up over the last ten to twenty years.

We rode south, hung a left on 405 and rendezvoused with our boys out back of a medical clinic in the little town of Sultan. Stocked them up, took our payday from them, and transferred shit from me by way of a backpack swap with one of the boys waiting for the proverbial baton pass.

They had more bikes, so we distributed things accordingly and got rid of the weight of the packs and the shit out of my saddlebags, making quick work of it. Fen just plain swapped bikes. Taking what needed to go south and letting the rest of that which needed to go east continue on with Deacon. Once the exchange was made, we were cut loose, free to make the next relay stop at a garage in North Seattle.

"You gonna stop and see Mace?" Mav asked and Fen and I, both divested of our bullshit RUB gear and back flying colors nodded.

It was always a kick stopping at the Monroe prison complex with the bikes loaded with illegal pharmaceuticals outside right under the guard's noses.

Yeah. We were those kind of assholes, but we were here and Mace was our brother serving out a sentence for assault with a deadly weapon. His term was almost up, though. He'd be getting out this year thanks to a decent plea deal.

"No *Fast Riding Awards*," Mav cautioned and Fen and I exchanged grins.

"Same to you, buddy."

We made the rounds and the guys each gave us messages to pass along to Mace.

I was just thrilled that I was going to get to be home a day early. That my little bird and I were going to get our Sunday together. I wondered as we rode back to Monroe what she'd been up to.

CHAPTER TWENTY-SEVEN

$\mathcal{L}$ ittle Bird...

I couldn't sleep. I tossed and turned, restless and missing the warmth and protection of Dump Truck's solid body. When I got up the next morning, I felt ramshackle and wrecked. I showered, did my hair and makeup, and dressed in comfortable clothing, which for me was athletic leggings and a warm, form-fitting long-sleeved top. I pulled on the matching jacket and lifted the laundry basket full of dirty clothes out of the bottom of the closet.

I went through all the pockets, stripped the bed, and with the basket mounded with bed linens and the week's laundry, I took it out into the living room. I perused the bookshelves and couldn't settle on anything to read and decided that I would pay the laundromat up by the Fred Meyer for their laundry service and would pick things up later that day. That a trip to the bookstore was in order.

I went to the laundromat and found a space right out front. I went in first to talk to the attendant, knowing that it was likely to be crazy busy on a Saturday and boy I wasn't wrong. It was a zoo. The attendant was nice and told me that yes, actually, I could get my basket done same day and to bring it in.

I went and got it, had it weighed, and she bagged it and gave me a claim ticket. I left and took my basket with me and felt a little bit guilty for the luxury of the expense but at the same time, I was tired, and a little distraught. I just didn't have the energy to be around so many people.

Dump Truck had gotten me a phone earlier in the week and had programmed everyone in the club's numbers into it for me, including Dahlia's. But as good as they all treated me, and as much as I was growing to love them all like family – I wasn't up to company today and just wanted to see how I did on my own.

Still, I kept the phone on me in case Dump Truck could call, and it did have its other uses – such as looking up bookstores in the area and a GPS map service to give me turn by turn directions.

I couldn't say I was overly familiar with this area, it being a poorer bluer collar area than my privileged ass ever had a reason to be in.

I had no desire whatsoever to go anywhere near the eastside. Not until I could shake the anxiety of potentially being recognized, so I wanted to stay close to my new home, close to safety. I looked for bookstores near me and there were several. One was a used bookstore here in Burien, but I was looking for something new, as in a recently published title. The other two were in Tukwila surrounding Southcenter Mall. One was a Half-Price Books, which again was a used bookstore but the other was a Barnes & Noble, so I headed there first.

Stepping inside and under the golden glow of their lights, eyes taking in all of those beautiful books was good for my soul. The sound of milk being steamed over in the connected Starbucks lured me like a siren's call and I drifted past the magazine and periodical racks to go stand in line.

I ordered my favorite and smiled when I finally got to wrap my hands around that warm paper cup.

I went straight for the romance section, looking for Timber Philips' latest title, *Love Springs Eternal* which should have just come out this past Tuesday. I found it readily, and snatched it up, hugging it to my chest.

One of the things that was quickly becoming a favorite of mine, was reading out loud with Dump Truck before bed. Each taking turns voicing every other chapter from the male or female point of view, which was how Timber Philips liked to write her novels.

My other love of reading was mysteries, and I headed there next, looking to see if there was a new Amber Eckart mystery by Eric Plume. Alas, there was not, and the sense of disappointment I felt over that was something I was still trying to get used to despite the fact it had been *years* of nothing new. I picked up a copy of the two available, *Margin Play* and *Naming the Hangman*, so that I could have them. I re-read them often… it was like spending time with old friends when I did, plus I could read them to D.T. on the nights he didn't feel like reading – which hadn't happened yet, but I loved these books and wanted to share them with him.

I picked up a few other old favorites and then went in search of something new. I sipped my coffee as I perused books and at one point, the growing stack in my arms getting heavy, an employee help-fully brought me a shopping basket.

I spent more than a few hours at it, even taking the time to cozy up in one of their leather chairs to read through another, different self-help book while I finished my coffee. It ended up in the basket, too.

The damage at the register came to almost two-hundred dollars, but I couldn't put a price on this self-care, and I happily handed two crisp hundred-dollar bills out of my wallet to the woman behind the counter – pleased when Dump Truck's phone number worked for the rewards program.

On the drive back to Burien, I was conveniently texted and notified my clothes were done and to come get them at my convenience.

I stopped at the Fred Meyer first and bought some candles and a bottle of wine as well as some tea before I went to get our clothes. I had the forethought to put those things into the car before I went and got the laundry, taking my basket in with me, and I was glad she handed everything over clean, but in a thin, clear plastic trash bag as the skies opened up outside in a deluge.

"Oh, wow…" she said open mouthed as we stared out the front windows together. "You should totally wait it out in here."

I smiled and laughed a little and said, "I think I will," as I took my change.

She smiled brightly, her blue eyes sparkling below her copper colored hair and I smiled back. We chatted a little and it was nice, mostly about books when I saw her pick up a thick Stephen King paperback from beside the cash register.

Her name was Kaylee, and she'd read the Eckart Mysteries, too, which excited me. Not many people had heard of them.

The rain petered out just as quickly as it'd started coming down and we parted ways but my mood from the small exchange was markedly elevated. I went through the Jack-In-The-Box drive-through on the way out of the parking lot and headed home, managing to get all of it inside in one load thanks to the laundry being in the big plastic bag. The rest I dumped in the basket and braced it on my opposite hip, washer woman style.

When I got inside, I dumped the clothes on the dining table and dropped onto the end of the couch to eat my chicken sandwich and fries, washing it all down with my Dr. Pepper.

Feeling fat and a little happier, I emptied the clothes on the coffee table to fold them up and put them away. I made the bed next, and generally neatened up, putting my wine in the fridge, setting out candles around the apartment, and lighting some of them up in the living room.

I cozied up on the couch, emptied the bookstore bag onto the corner of the coffee table and ditched the crumpled bags from everywhere I'd been in the kitchen trash.

With a deep cleansing breath, I looked around satisfied. The light outside was beginning to fail, fall quickly moving along toward winter. The holidays would be upon us soon, and I wondered briefly what those would be like from now on.

I thought about what Dump Truck had asked me, about staying, and sat on the end of the couch in the gathering dark and felt nothing but gratitude. I wanted that. To stay with him, so badly, and I couldn't tell you why I was afraid to say 'yes.' I mean, I really had no other plans, but wondered if I would feel different when I had all of my new identification.

I sighed, restless again, and went through my purchases that I'd made today. Finally, I settled on the self-help book and thought it would pair nicely with a candle-lit bath and a glass of wine.

Before I did that, though, I counted how much money I had left, feeling a little guilty at how free the guys had been with just handing me money. Wondering and even worrying at what cost in human suffering it came. Of course, I could say the same for my entire life thus far. My father's money was likely at a far greater cost of tears than the cash I held in my hands now. I just couldn't see D.T. or even the rest of the guys of the Western Washington division of their club hurting innocent people.

I put the remainder of the cash away in my wallet and the wallet back in my purse, letting it swing back against the coatrack it hung on.

With a great sigh, I went to begin drawing that bath, bringing towels from the linen closet into the bathroom with me, lighting candles, and clipping my hair up off my shoulders in a twist at the back of my head.

I started the tub to filling, and went back out to the kitchen, swearing when I couldn't find a wine glass and sighing when I couldn't find a corkscrew when I'd finally settled on the rocks glass I did find.

There was a crappy corkscrew keychain thing in the junk drawer and I made it work, though I had to go in and stop the bathwater midway through the ordeal.

Frazzled from my misadventure, I took my glass and my book into the bathroom and set them where they were safe, yet still within reach so I could strip down and get into the water, glad I'd drawn it a touch too hot. It was perfect by the time I finally got to sink into it and in perfect complement to the sip of cool, sweet wine that I took once I was settled.

"God, D.T.," I said, blowing out a breath. "I miss you."

I closed my eyes and rested my head back against the wall and took another sip from my glass, just trying to relax.

CHAPTER TWENTY-EIGHT

*D*ump Truck…

I took the Corson Avenue and Michigan Street exit with Fenris at my side, traveling through Georgetown and up and over the First Avenue South Bridge onto Highway 509. He waved at me and got off on the Myers Way/White Center exit to take Roxbury up to the club while I kept going, headed for home and my girl.

We'd stopped and saw Mace, met up with the southward bound crew at the garage in the Greenwood neighborhood in north Seattle and passed the rest of the shit off to them to deal with, and finally, we were on our way home… well, I was. Fen had other plans apparently. Booze or some pussy. Probably both. The club was a good place for either or on a Saturday night, but I didn't care.

I had something more important at home waiting for me. Not expecting to see me until tomorrow and the soul crushing disappointment in her eyes when I'd left her the day before told me that I had some making up to do. Not because I had to, but because I wanted to. I didn't want to hurt the beautiful, fragile creature that shared my bed.

I wanted so much more than that. I wanted her to share my life, but I didn't want to push, and I didn't want to pressure her so I had to keep that shit on lock. She couldn't know how desperate I was for her to stay.

I took the next exit up, Glendale, and made a right up the hill and around the curve, following it until I was in the thick of some residential neighborhoods. Houses built in the sixties and seventies lining the streets. I turned down the one that would spill to mine as soon as I crossed First Avenue and was glad she'd pulled all the way up, was making it a habit, so I could fit the spot behind her. Either that, or she hadn't gone anywhere today.

I hoped that wasn't the case and had some reassurance the moment I stepped into the apartment, the living room glowing with the muted light of candles, their sweet and spicy scent not unpleasant or overpowering. I turned my head at the light music of water hitting water coming from the bathroom where more candlelight flickered.

I quietly hung up my jacket and cut, toed off my boots with a wince when my leg twinged at me and threatened to cramp. I gripped the side of my leg and limped in my sock feet across the tired carpet that'd been tired when I'd moved into this place a few years back.

She was submerged, her knees up in the air, hair floating around her face when I leaned against the doorframe, pushing the long sleeves of my thermal shirt on up under one of my tees higher up on my forearms. She sat up, holding her head back, letting the water slick her long locks back from her face, pressing fingertips to her eyes to rub them as she sat up.

"Hey, baby," I said, and she jumped hardcore and let out a yip, her arms covering her chest. I bit my lips together and bowed my head, shaking it a little, trying not to upset her by laughing.

"What are you doing here?" she asked reflexively and I looked up grinning.

"Surprising you," I said and I came over, moving her book, towel, and an empty glass fragrant with the dregs of some wine off the closed lid of the john. Setting it aside on the counter and taking a seat, I grunted, weary from the hard riding and our little walk in the woods the night before, and eased my leg out in front of me.

She stared at me, eyes wide, hands pressed together as though she prayed, fingers pressed to her lips, speechless, and I worried for half a second I'd ruined her solitude and relaxing evening.

"Miss me?" I asked uncertain and she burst into tears, sitting up on her knees, reaching for me.

I got down on the floor on the other side of the wall of the tub and pulled her into my arms. I held her tight as she sobbed over my shoulder and didn't have a *fucking* clue what to do.

"I was… so… *worried!*" she managed between hiccupping sobs and the tension in my body eased.

"I missed you, too, which is why I busted my ass to get shit done and get back to you," I told her, sitting back and smoothing some of her wet hair back off of her face. I smiled and shook my head.

"I'm so glad you're home," she said sniffing, the storm past for now.

"Me too," I said. "I see you went out." I glanced around at the new candles.

"I cleaned, first. Had the laundry done, then I went to the book-store." I smiled.

"I'm so proud of you," I said. "Going out on your own is a big step."

She nodded and then her face scrunched into a frown. "I did Jack-In-The-Box on my way home. I didn't try to cook or think to cook… I mean I didn't expect you."

"Don't you worry about any of that none; I can make a sandwich." I let her go but not before I pressed a kiss to her forehead. She one upped me, grabbing my face and kissing me fiercely. I kissed her back and when she had her fill, she let go.

I needed a shower but it could wait, because now that she'd mentioned it, I was hungry.

"Take your time, babe. You want more wine?" I asked. She shook her head and smiled.

"Thank you, but I want to get out and show you what I got at the bookstore."

"Okay, love. Take your time, there's no rush. I'll be in the kitchen." I pushed to my feet with a grunt. "Excited to see what you got us, though."

"I'll be just a couple of minutes."

I went in the kitchen and got into the fridge. I heard the bathwater let and start to trickle down the drain and smiled to myself. It was a good way to come home and now that I knew she liked to take baths; I had some ideas about some future accommodations.

She'd made up her mind. I'd seen it in her face, had felt it in the way she'd had a death grip on me, could hear it in her lyrical voice as she sang to herself happily with no words as she dried off and combed her hair or whatever. I looked up from where I crafted me a sandwich – as she came around the counter, towel wrapped around her, her glass in her other hand and set down her book.

I picked up her bottle that was sweating on the counter nearby and tipped some of the fragrant liquid into her glass.

"Get me down a glass there would you?" I asked. She smiled taking a sip first, twisting a bit in an adorably impish way, practically vibrating with excitement. She went and got me down a glass as I polished off throwing together my sandwich and slapped the two sides together.

She handed me a glass and a small plate right behind it. I poured myself some wine first and plated my sandwich while she put the fixin's away.

I smiled, taking a sip from my glass and wondered at the pure domesticated bliss I was feeling. It was like she completed me some-how, even though I hadn't known I'd needed her and as desperate as I was to hold on to this feeling, to hold on to *her*, I wanted to see my little bird fly.

"What's that look for?" she asked softly, deep brown eyes fixed on me as she swung the fridge door shut.

"I love you," I said. "I'd be a fool not to say it or give you any impression otherwise."

She smiled, mixed emotions in her eyes but she came to me and hugged herself close to me. I held her and she whispered, "I missed you so much."

"I missed you too, babe." I'd missed her for the longest time. Since our first time.

"Is it crazy that I thought of you every day?" she asked quietly.

"No," I said back. "I did too."

She laughed nervously and tried to play it off. "Well, yeah. I can only imagine you would think about yourself. You're you."

I pulled her back and tipped her chin up with a crooked finger. She looked up at me startled and I let the seriousness I felt fill my eyes. Her eyes widened, her breath caught, and I dipped my head to put my lips against hers.

The little moan of surrender she made as she opened her lips to let me kiss her more fully… *damn*. So hot. She was incredible and she had no idea. I don't think anyone had ever given her the idea that she was anything other than beautiful on the surface. I got the impression she'd been little more than furniture to those rich fucks, and not just her Ken doll husband.

I pulled her close and kissed her fiercely, with every ounce of passion I held and she upped the ante, dropping her towel, and I suddenly had no desire to eat. I wanted to feast on her instead.

I pulled her tight against my body and she twined her arms around me, pulling herself even tighter, climbing my body like some beautifully flowering vine.

I led her around out of the kitchen toward the bedroom and she came willingly, enthusiastically, even. Giggling as I gave her a light smack on her bare ass, turning with her hands covering her rear, walking backwards ahead of me, her tits thrust forward and begging for my lips as I stalked her with a low, wolf-like growl.

I reached for her, playfully, threatening to tickle her and she shrieked, backing up faster until she hit the bed and fell back on it laughing and putting her hands up to protect herself, laughing and twisting, as I put my mouth against her fragrant soft skin. I pretended to eat her, covering my teeth with my lips, tickling her hip, her ribs, as she wriggled to get away and my cock rose to the occasion.

By the time I straightened up to pull my shirts over my head, she was breathless and glowing with happiness, relaxed and ready to take shit up a notch. She was a quick study in what I liked, laying back, legs coyly together, knees up, but her hands? They drifted over her silken skin, cupped her breasts, played in the light patch of curling hair at the top of her sex and it was *so* hot.

I pulled my jeans off, and the light in her eyes as she gazed on my cock, the way her head came up, the way her breathing deepened, the way she made that slow, sensual, slide into desire for me… it was a visual feast for the eyes and I wanted her like nobody's business.

I kneeled on the floor at the foot of the bed and wrapped my arms around her legs, sliding her ass to the edge, folding her legs back, separating them, so I could go down on her.

She was with me so far, gazing down her lush body, between the valley of her perfect tits that she massaged and fondled for my benefit as I sucked along her pussy lips and tasted her. She was fresh and clean, sweet with a slightly salty edge, the musk of her arousal making me throb against my stomach as I let my hands wander over her hips. Locking my hands to either side of her just above the flair of her pelvis to keep her in place, holding her against my mouth as I delved my tongue inside her and lapped at her.

She cried out in passion and writhed and I let her. Watching her dance for me was something next-level beautiful and caused my desire for her to just *rage*.

"Oh, *God!*" she cried, head dropping back, body arching, as I touched my tongue to her clit and teased it mercilessly. The way her voice deepened, the way she panted, those gorgeous globes of her breasts rising and falling, nipples stiff peaks, begging for my mouth's attention as soon as I could work her up enough to take me easily.

That was the ultimate goal here. Getting inside her, being with her, making our two halves a sensuous writhing whole. Hot, erotic, perfect.

I slid my middle finger up into her hot and ready pussy and teased around in there looking for that spot that would ignite her and send her up among the stars. She jumped slightly, voice a sudden expression of surprise, the cry feral and wordless and music to my ears.

Her body clenched, tightening up around my finger, and I increased the press of my tongue against her clit. Her hands flew to her sides, slapping the bedcovers, her fingers contracting into fists by her hips as her back arched and she fought to hold still, not to writhe, so I could get her there.

It was as if the universe held its collective breath, and I loved how when she was super close, *she* forgot to breathe, until finally with a sharp, earth-shattering cry, she collapsed back onto the bed. A wetness gushed around my finger and her pussy fluttered wildly around it and I couldn't wait to get my cock up in there – to feel the same thing.

I waited until the contractions around my middle finger slowed before slipping it free. I'd already given up with the tongue action so that I could watch her. She was tense, laying on the bed, and she slowly unfurled, as though she'd been thrown into a pool slow motion and she was on the rise back to the surface.

It was beautiful, how liquid, how full of grace she was without even trying as her head lolled back so that she could look at me through eyes hooded with euphoria. I loomed, climbing up her body, walking her back up the bed, putting myself between those silky thighs. She crab-walked back up the bed drunk on my love and damn it was a sight to behold.

I gathered her close, put myself over her, carefully lying so I wouldn't crush her as I eased my way inside slow. She sucked in a sharp breath, jumping slightly at the intimate contact, always like she expected it to hurt but that was the *last* thing I would ever do to her – unless, of course, she asked for it.

I smoothed the hair back from her face and put a hand to the outside of her thigh so I could lift her leg some, to gain some ground. I thrust forward and she moaned, raising her legs, wrapping them around my hips, her nails biting into my ass to urge me on and I smiled. *So it was like that, then.*

She felt so good, so hot, so slick; so soft around me. Electric shivers sweeping from my balls up over my ass, blushing up my back as though fate or pleasure itself stood behind me, blowing softly.

I was electrified and in no hurry, just taking things slow and easy, a long casual ride on an idyllic Pacific Northwest day – being with her was the same effect on my soul.

I guess it was saying something when you found a woman you loved to ride as much as your motorcycle. I mean, that right there made her a keeper, right?"

She was so responsive, so delicate where she writhed beneath me. I cradled her gently, an arm beneath her shoulder, hand cradling the back of her head and neck, the damp strands of her hair wrapped around my hand and lying against my arm in an almost loving embrace of its own.

I bowed my head to kiss the side of her neck and she tightened around me at the same time she sucked in a sharp breath. I thrust tight up into her and played that spot with my lips and light little flicks of my tongue, losing myself in her so completely, letting my body move on her through instinct and emotion.

I don't know how long we were like that, my leg miraculously cooperating, and I didn't question things. I just let it happen, let the sensations flow through me and over me, warming myself against her, sheltering her with my body, loving her wholly, thoroughly, and completely.

She held onto me, kissing me wherever her lips could reach – my chest, my shoulder, the side of my neck. She wasn't shy, her hands roving over my flesh, pulling me into her, holding tightly to me, and I let myself drown in the sensations of her love.

When she came again, arching into me, pressing her taut, beautiful body, pussy throbbing gently around me, hot slick walls pressing against me, the friction too much to keep my own self-contained, I came with her. Grunting, and thrusting as deep as I could go, spilling inside of her, and too spent to do much else than pant, I held myself off of her just enough so I wouldn't crush her, and to rest my forehead pressed against hers.

God, nothing matched the beautiful sight, the exquisite agony painted on her lovely face when I made her come like that, and I was a fool – so deeply, so completely, and so incredibly in love with her, I would probably lose a big part of myself if she didn't stay.

I would lose my heart, because wherever she chose to go, she'd take it with her.

CHAPTER TWENTY-NINE

$\mathcal{L}$ittle Bird…

I wasn't going anywhere. Not when he made me feel so whole, so safe, and so *seen*. I couldn't. It would be to deny all I had ever wanted and for what? To prove something I had literally no one to prove it to? That I could be independent and take care of myself. I knew, deep down, that I could do that. That I could be resourceful and that no matter what happened, I could take care of things – it would be folly to leave a man so wonderful and so good for a point of pride.

We cuddled for a little while, speaking softly, joking, and coming down off our afterglow slowly.

"I'm starving," he growled and came at me, growling and snarling, beard tickling my breast as I shrieked with laughter and pushed at his broad shoulders and chest. He smiled and climbed off of me and held down a hand to help me up. I stood and bit my bottom lip and said, "Meet you out there," making a beeline for the bathroom.

I used the restroom and cleaned myself up and passed him in the hall, both of us giving each other a kiss as he slipped past to go for his sandwich in a pair of cut-off sweatpants shorts that could barely contain his massive thighs. I slipped past into the bedroom and slipped my clean nightgown from my intimates' drawer and slipped it over my head.

He was on the end of the couch, sandwich balanced on his good thigh, both glasses of wine on the coffee table with the selection of books I'd bought that day.

"Come tell me what you got," he said and I smiled and went to him, settling near him and that was how we spent our evening. Talking books, favorites and genres. About trying new things and settling on what we wanted to read next after we finished our current selection.

It was the perfect and peaceful end to a beautiful evening.

THE NEXT MORNING we woke up, made love again, and stayed in bed past ten, until almost eleven, really. He made us coffee, we talked about lunch, and he suggested brunch at this little local spot in Old Burien.

We showered together, and though it was crisp outside, the sun was shining so riding was actually *my* suggestion. It was worth it to see him light up from the inside and I didn't bother to contain my smile.

We dressed to ride, me in my ill-fitting borrowed gear and he stopped me and said, "Would you be pissed at me if I suggested shopping after we eat?"

"Shopping for what?" I asked, laughing. "I already have everything I need."

He took a step back and roved me with his eyes and said, "Almost everything. Don't deprive your man of a trip to *his* toy store, now."

I laughed lightly and rolled my eyes. "I wouldn't dream of it."

"God, you're a woman after my heart," he said and pulled my forehead against his lips. I closed my eyes, melting. God, he had no idea how much I *loved* that he did that. I don't know what it was about it but it just *did things…* calmed me, soothed my broken soul and put it back together just a little at a time every time he did it.

"Come on, let's go."

We went to a place called *Classic Eats* which was a fancy modern dining establishment with a bar. It was on 152nd a couple of blocks down from Ambaum in a part of town that looked like it was an upscale version of some old main drag in a western. It even had a feed and general store on the strip just before the place we were looking for.

We'd missed the main rush, but the place was still *really* full and we had to wait for a bit. They had it set up buffet style along the bar and the food looked *really* good.

Dump Truck fielded a couple of calls from his phone that he liked to call his burner and which I suggested might sound a lot less under-world and illegal if he called it the 'club' phone out in public. He laughed and nodded and said I was right, then pulled me in to kiss me on my temple.

By the time he got off the call there was seating available in the bar and since we were the only couple without someone underage that were waiting, we took it.

I asked if everything was okay when we sat down to eat and he smiled and nodded. "Yeah, just checking in. A regular thing," he told me and I didn't feel the need to ask anything else about it.

Brunch was a delight, the owner of the restaurant coming by and greeting Dump Truck with some familiarity.

Apparently, the owner, a very athletic and extremely handsome black man, was big into youth activities for a lot of the underprivileged local youth. He worked on a volunteer basis to keep kids out of gangs and to get them into school sports programs. The younger kids without school programs, he got into things like pee-wee football sponsored by the Boys & Girls club or the YMCA and the like. They explained to me that the MC did a once a year charity run to raise money for the programs in support.

Dump Truck and Tony had a low and intense exchange, D.T. asking if there was anything the Sacred Hearts should know about. Tony made a face like there was nothing out of the ordinary going on, shook his head, and said, "It's all good, man. All good. Thanks for asking."

"Alright now, you just let us know. We like to keep it that way," D.T. told him, and Tony smiled big, and I mean huge.

"You know I appreciate you guys," he said and clasped hands with Dump Truck and hugged him.

"Likewise, man. You keep doing good things."

"It was nice to meet you," Tony said raising his eyebrows at me and I smiled, even though he hadn't gotten my name – which I would have told him 'Little Bird' anyway. I felt like 'Bianca' was a dead name. That that girl was dead, dead and gone, and I didn't ever have to be her anymore.

It was incredibly nice. Incredibly freeing.

"It was nice to meet you, too," I said, genuinely, warmly.

"Enjoy your food," he said and wandered away.

It was hard not to. The food from Tony's kitchen was *amazing*. The eggs fluffy and the sausage flavorful.

After brunch, both of us full and happy, we left the establishment, pinky fingers linked and arms swinging nonchalantly between us as we crossed the narrow street to the bike parked on the opposite side.

"I don't think I've ever seen you so excited," I said laughing and he grinned.

"It is my *favorite* store," he said. "All that new leather and chrome. It's a thing of beauty."

I laughed and he grinned. The ride was beautiful, and I decided I was *definitely* getting some sunglasses if they had any available that I liked.

When we went inside, a salesman immediately came out from around the counter and rushed toward Dump Truck.

"Hi, what can we do for you today?" he asked like an eager puppy.

"I'm actually here for my lady," D.T. declared. "I need to get her some proper safety and riding gear."

"Oh, yeah? Let me get my girl, Trinity, out here to help you all. She is the absolute best when it comes to women's riding gear."

I was quickly shuffled off into the capable hands of a bubbly blonde who definitely knew her stuff. She took me three times around the sales floor, through chaps, and jackets, boots, and helmets and was determined to get me into the proper fit for everything in a style that *I* liked, since I would be the one wearing it.

Still, I wanted to make sure that Dump Truck liked it, too, and he wasn't shy about telling me what worked and what didn't when I stepped out of the fitting room. Both of us smiling, my confidence rising every time he had me turn so he could check out my ass.

It was a good day, and I ended up leaving wearing some of the purchases made and he seemed much more relaxed now that I was in safety gear that he deemed appropriate. I think the thing that had been bothering him the most was my lack of a properly fitting helmet which had been the *first* thing he had insisted on remedying.

"Where to now?" I asked as soon as he had finished stuffing the saddlebags with the rest.

"How about just a ride for the sake of going for a ride?" he asked and I smiled.

"Sounds nice," I said when actually, it sounded *perfect*.

We went up 405 and hung a right on I-90 toward Issaquah. The sun beaming down, the wind and the fresh mountain air was heady. I was much *warmer* in the new gear which I was incredibly grateful for as we climbed into the Cascades from the foothills and I had no idea where we were going.

He took the exit in Snoqualmie, past the Snoqualmie Casino, but he didn't stop. I relaxed when he pulled into the lot next to the Salish Lodge and Spa and had a feeling we were here for the falls.

He put down the kickstand for the bike and leaned it over, shutting it off. I got off from behind him and undid the simpler catch on the chinstrap of my new helmet, taking it off. He took it from me and hung it from one of the handlebars before taking off his own.

I looked around, putting my sunglasses up on top of my head and breathed in.

"It's so peaceful up here," I said and I meant it. There was a stillness to the mountains and the trees rising up all around us.

"I like it up here," he agreed. "It's nice to come up here when you want a bit of stillness to think."

"That is a precise echo of what I was just thinking," I said with a smile and reached out a hand. He got up, unclipped his cane, and took my hand. Leaning on it, we went for the switchback cement trail to wander up to observation to see the falls.

"Today has been really perfect," I said. "Thank you."

"You ain't gotta thank me, Little Bird," he said. "If anything, I've just been taking you along for the ride."

I smiled faintly and squeezed his hand lightly. "We certainly make a pair, don't we?" I asked.

"Ah, yeah," he said grinning and nodding.

"You ever think about the future?" I asked. "I mean, like what's next?"

"I never used to," he said honestly.

"Why not?" I asked.

"Never felt like I had a future worth livin'," he answered, and it was a raw and stark answer that held no bravado. It couldn't be anything less than true, either, and that was somehow damaging, edging on devastating for my heart to hear.

"Why do you think that is?" My voice was soft, and he leaned down some to hear me over the dull roar of the falls that we couldn't see but we could certainly feel. A fine mist carried on the light breeze. We were almost there.

"Life just doesn't seem like it's worth living when you're alone," he said. "I never thought I would ever meet somebody like you. Never thought I would be part of a pair. I just didn't see it happening for me."

"When did that change?" I asked, genuinely curious.

He was quiet for a moment and answered, "When you stepped into my apartment and opened up that fancy coat with nothing on underneath it but that sexy lingerie."

I smiled and snorted a laugh but stopped when it hit me…

"You thought you had it all the way back then and then I just up and disappeared," I said. "You had my number in your phone. I mean, I called you so… why didn't you?"

"What, call you?" He lifted one shoulder in a shrug. "A woman leaves you while you're sleeping like that and leaves your contact information – well, let's just say I can take a hint."

I stopped, and he stopped with me and faced me. I looked him in the eyes, my own prickling with the beginning of tears and I said the only thing I could think of. The only thing that was appropriate for a situation like this one.

"I'm sorry."

He smiled faintly and searched my face, giving a nod, accepting it just like that, even though I couldn't stop myself from feeling *horrible*. Clearly, we both felt *something* for the other from that day, but equally as clearly, either he was more self-aware of his feelings than I was or had been, or he had felt far more deeply than I had in the beginning.

I laced my fingers between his as we got back into motion and made the turn on the last switchback on the gentle gradient leading up to the crest of the ridge so we could look down on the falls.

We stepped up to the railing just as a puff of fine mist wafted up to kiss our faces. The falls were beautiful. All of that *power*, flowing over, falling, roiling at the bottom and rushing out – it was precisely how I felt about him. I looked up at him, at the faint smile on his lips as he stared down at the falls and I felt *so strongly* for him.

I wanted to tell him. To open my mouth and *beg him* to let me stay with him forever, but it was like the words stuck in my throat and wouldn't budge because what if I changed my mind? What if having those identification papers in my hands changed *everything*?

"You alright?" he asked, not taking his eyes off the falls even though I couldn't take my eyes off of him.

"I'm fine," I said and aside from that one bit of turmoil, I was.

I cuddled into his side and he held me as we watched all of that water rush and churn. Until we felt as though it carried the last of our worries away with its raw, elemental power.

"Wanna check out the gift shop?" he asked and I smiled and nodded.

"Yeah, but I want to take some pictures first."

CHAPTER THIRTY

*D*ump Truck…

Maverick leaned back from the counter and looked after where my little bird had gone out back. I caught his eye from over the dividing wall and he got up and came around, walking hurriedly in my direction.

"Glass Jaw went and picked up your girl's papers today," he said and I let out an explosive breath.

"Good deal, man."

"We're tryin' to throw her a surprise party, get her on over to the club after work tonight."

I nodded. "Gotcha," I said and looked up at the sound of the back door opening up. She stopped in the middle of the aisle.

"Everything alright?" she asked.

"Yeah," Mav declared, rubbing his chin. "Club business."

"You need me to step back out?" she asked and Mav smiled, genuinely.

"Naw, you're good. We're all done."

I smiled at her, glowing with pride. She came up to the dividing wall and did what'd become a habit over the last two or three weeks.

She kneeled up on one of the waiting room chairs and folded her arms on the top of the wall.

"So, I know where I wanna go this weekend if you're game," she said with a hopeful little grin.

"Oh yeah? Where's that?"

"I got online and found a *list!*" she said with savage glee, and I threw back my head and laughed.

A few weeks back, we'd gone into the Snoqualmie Falls gift shop and they had one of those souvenir penny machines. You know the ones. Put in your penny, spend like fifty cents to a dollar, crank the handle and it flattens the penny out and puts a design or whatever on it? She'd become crazy about them, and the next weekend when I'd asked where she'd wanted to go, we'd ended up at the Space Needle where she'd gotten another one and a book to put them in.

Her obsession was beyond adorable, and I was on the lookout myself for the damn things tryin' to think up where they could be.

"So where we headin' this time, baby girl?" I asked.

"Depends, you have club business?" she asked.

"Next week," I said and she nodded.

"Well," she pulled out her phone, "there's *a lot* in Seattle. It could be like a treasure hunt!"

I laughed again and asked, "How much is a lot?"

"According to the list..." she trailed off and started to count. "Thirty-nine, but six of them are gone and some of them are marked 'moved' with no forwarding address but yeah – enough to keep us busy!"

"Alright," I nodded slowly. "Tell you what, plot a route and if it's nice, we'll take the bike and do a bunch. If the weather is shitty, I don't want you riding in it so make a backup plan. Pick a location where we can be indoors for a while but still get one and we'll take your cage."

She squealed in glee and quipped, "Thank you!" and not for the first time I marveled at how quick she seemingly had bounced back. I knew in my heart that she would see a setback at some point and that the hurt was just buried for now. My worry was it was festering.

I was relieved that her papers had come. It meant she could go on the payroll official, be paid for real, and put on the boneyard's health insurance policy so I could get her some help peeling back the layers and laying some deep healing on them.

That was, if she stayed. She'd been reluctant to talk about it, skirting the topic anytime it came up.

It was strange. She had no trouble planning a future with me, but whenever I even looked like I was going to ask about her *staying*, she'd clam up and just shut down. It hurt, vaguely, and kept me on rocky ground which I didn't like and wasn't comfortable with but I didn't pay it no mind. I'd been in situations far more painful and uncomfortable before and I was honestly more concerned about *her* and her wellbeing.

I put in the work, Squatch sticking his head in the door and looking left then right and when he realized the coast was clear asked, "Dude! Chocolate or Vanilla?"

"For what?"

"We're gettin' your girl a cake."

I chuckled and said, "Vanilla with some kind of fruit filling like strawberry or raspberry."

"Raspberry it is. Nine's allergic to strawberries."

"Oh, shit. That's right, I forgot about that," I said. "Good lookin' out."

Squatch shot me a little salute and backed out the door. I shook my head and smiled to myself. A sense of pride, a golden glow suffusing me at how much the rest of the guys had grown to like her. Well, except Tic-Tac, but that motherfucker didn't like anybody. Still, he'd even grudgingly admitted that while he didn't like my little bird due to her rich background, he didn't *hate* her, which for him was the same thing.

Around quitting time, Mav sent my little bird out back on some bullshit mission to ask Rusty something. Problem was, Rusty and Sauley were already gone. They'd come out the gate and had gone across to the club something like five minutes ago.

While she was back there, Mav and I did likewise, hauling ass across the street for the big surprise. I loped my big ass across and up the stairs before she could get back around front and laughed my ass off along with Mav the whole time I was doing it.

This was gonna be great.

We all gathered at the end of the hall from the back, in the main room of the club and waited. The cake in its pink box was put into my arms, the writing spelling out 'Happy Birthday Kestrel' while Fenris lit the candles scattered like stars across the top.

We all stood and waited, hearing her tread on the back stairs, shushing the shit out of each other as she called out, "Guys?" and I was so excited to finally give my woman her name.

CHAPTER THIRTY-ONE

Little Bird...

*K*estrel...

"Guys?" I called, my anxiety mounting, prickling along my spine, my throat squeezing tight as I hauled open the club's back door.

When I had come up front to tell Mav that Rusty and Sauley were nowhere to be found, he and Dump Truck were gone. The only logical place where they could have gotten to was the club, so I'd trotted across the street but it too was entirely too quiet.

I went in the back door and froze.

Dump Truck was at the end of it, a cake glowing with birthday candles tilted my way in his hands.

"Happy Birthday to you!" the guys crowded in from the sides and started singing as I crept forward, hands over my mouth, but when they reached the line where I expected them to call me *Little Bird* I was surprised.

"Happy Birthday, dear Kestrel..."

I burst into tears, Mav standing to the side with a telling manila legal-sized envelope in his hands.

They finished the song with a rowdy cheer as I blew out the candles on the cake, Dump Truck grinning.

"You guys are being ridiculous. My birthday is in April!" I cried.

"Actually, according to your birth certificate, it's today," Maverick said and handed me a sheet of paper from the envelope.

Kestrel Destiny Martin born October 18th, 1992. I was, apparently, twenty-seven now and I *loved* my new name.

I looked at my cake, *Happy Birthday Kestrel* spelled out on the white frosting and tears still dripping off my chin stood on tiptoe to kiss my man.

A round of 'awws' and whistles went up and I sighed.

"Somebody get this damn cake," Dump Truck said against my lips and it was slid out from between us so I could hold and kiss him for real.

Maverick handed me the envelope with the rest of my documents and it was all there –birth certificate for the state of Washington, a Washington driver's license, social security card, and even a US passport. I couldn't even begin to imagine how they'd done it but it was *all here.*

"Thank you," I said and my voice wavered to another round of 'awws.'

Dump Truck held me close, and as I held the documents in my hands, I realized they didn't make a damn bit of difference. I was right where I wanted to be, but now wasn't the time for a conversation as deep and meaningful as that.

"Hey, Prospect, go lock up the yard, would you? We're closing a little early tonight." Maverick tossed Sauley the keys.

"On it, Boss!" He went jogging down the hall and out the back door.

"Well hell, somebody get me a damn beer if that's the case," Rusty grinned and his missing teeth made it seem that much more ridiculously happy.

"Speaking of legal documentation, you'll find your banking info in there and here's your first check." Maverick handed it over. "I hope you'll consider staying on permanent. I could really use someone to answer the phones and ring up sales, pack up the shipping –"

"Absolutely, I'll consider it," I said with a grin. I wanted to talk to Dump Truck about staying first.

"Can we just fuckin' party now?" Tic-Tac demanded, and I grinned and nodded while everyone else got super rowdy again.

"How about you come open your presents?" Dump Truck asked me after I'd been handed some cake.

"You guys!" I cried in protest.

"Shut the fuck up!" Glass Jaw said. "It's your *birthday!*"

It certainly felt like it was.

IT'D BEEN RAINING as we left for work that morning, and it was drizzling as Dump Truck had put me back in my cage to drive myself home.

"Mav wants a quick word, baby. Club business. You go on home and be *careful.* I'll be right behind you."

"Okay," I murmured, and he ducked his head into the cabin of the 4Runner and kissed me soundly. I kissed him back and called out past him, "Don't keep him long, Maverick!" Then for D.T.'s ears only said, "I need you inside of me."

"Oh, I'm gonna be *right* home," he vowed, leaning back and shutting the door. I wanted to tell him, so badly. I needed to get the words out but I also needed it to be just him and me.

I drove home, my important documents on the seat beside me. My license in my wallet along with my new bank card.

I felt like a real person again and that was priceless.

I picked out the gift bags and open boxes from the back seat and carried my birthday presents upstairs with me. There were all kinds of things. From quarters and pennies from Fenris to candles to 'bath shit' from Nine because, according to him, *'every chick loves bath shit.'*

He cracked me up.

I divested myself of my purse, jacket and boots by the coat-tree after setting everything on the coffee table, and as soon as that was done, I wandered back over and picked up the manila envelope with all my paperwork inside.

I don't know how long I stood, staring at it sightlessly, thinking how stupid I must be for thinking it would or could make me feel any differently about this man who had done *so much* for me, but I was still standing there when he came through the front door.

I looked up, turning my head in his direction and he froze halfway in the door and met my eyes.

We stood for several heartbeats before he stepped the rest of the way through, shutting and locking the door behind him.

"What's up?" he asked, coolly, guarded, and it broke my heart.

"I don't know where the best place is for me to keep this," I said softly.

"You trust me to put it in my safe deposit box?" he asked me, just as softly.

I sniffed, the tears already starting to flow. "I would really like that," I said and he was there, striding for me, stripping off his coat, pulling his shirts over his head and I was just as hurried in trying to get myself undressed. Dropping the papers on the coffee table, walking backwards, his mouth on mine, leading him to the bedroom, leaving clothing like breadcrumbs in our wake.

I turned my back to him and dropped my jeans, shimmying my hips to sweep them down my legs along with my panties; stepping out of them and my socks while he appreciated the view of my ass and my sex that were exposed to him.

His big hands went to my hips, his thumbs stroking over my skin, back and forth, back and forth, as I grew wet for him and only him.

"Hold me down," I murmured, and he put his lips to my shoulder and kissed from the outside in, stepping up to me, his chest warm against my back.

"I'll never hold you down, my little bird. I'll only ever lift you up," he whispered and I snorted. While I appreciated the sentiment, that's not what I meant.

"No, I mean, *hold me down*. I want it, I want it rough," I said and ground my ass back into his dick.

"Oh, well if that's what my lady wants…" his hand went to the back of my neck, gripping me firmly, the heel of his hand pressing between my shoulders as he kissed the side of my neck like the beautiful savage he was. His other hand grabbed a handful of my tit, kneading it roughly as I pressed my thighs together.

I moaned and leaned back into him, his hand drifting from my breast down my body, his fingertips pressing roughly against the top of my sex, rubbing at my clit. I moaned, which died on a gasp, the sound deep and throaty, sensual, sexual, and caused him to growl.

Oh, shit that was hot… the sound rumbling through my back as he flung me down on the bed and he went for his pants to get them off.

"Don't you *fuckin'* move," he ordered, and I froze mid-motion from where I'd been about to push myself up to turn onto my back.

Yes. That's what I wanted…

He climbed up onto the bed, massive tree trunks for legs to either side of mine, keeping them tightly closed; one big hand splayed against my back at the base of my neck, pressing my upper body into the bed. The other he used to grip my hip, jerking my hips up and back towards him, putting my spine into a deep and sexy arch to expose my pussy to his questing cock.

Yes. Yes, yes, yes, yes, yes!

He slammed into me and I cried out, shoving back to meet his forward thrust and I swear to fucking God it hurt so good!

I begged him to fuck me. I begged him to fuck me so good, my cries wordless, my voice feral as he didn't disappoint, driving himself deep, fucking me with great enthusiasm, yet still with *care*. He was *rough* yes, but he was *never* careless. Deeply in tune with my reactions, backing off when my cries turned sharp with too much pain.

"God, yeah! Tighter!" He slapped my ass, the sting sharp and immediate, and I tightened my pussy in reaction even as I felt my skin begin to burn and welt up in the shape of his stinging palm print. Holy *shit*, the warring sensations!

So wonderful, so beautiful, so *intense*, the weight of orgasm wouldn't hold off or be denied. It rushed in with every forward thrust of his cock inside me and made my womb feel heavy. I clenched up again when he laid another smack on my ass, so lost in the sensations he was dragging and pushing me through I'd forgotten.

He grunted and I turned my face, looking up behind me. He was so virile, so intense, brow furrowed in concentration, chest glistening with sweat as he pounded my pussy raw, just like I asked, just like I wanted, and I loved, I mean I loved, loved, *loved*, that I could *trust him*. That I could trust him to give me everything I asked for and that I could trust him to never take it too far.

That I could trust him was everything and that, *that* was what made it so I came. That incredibly sexy, deeply emotional knowledge just tripped my trigger and sent me right over the high side, crashing into orgasm, crashing into a deep, irrevocable, unconditional love for this man who undoubtedly held the same depth of feeling for me.

I came back to myself feeling raw and gasping for breath, Dump Truck lying over the top of me and pressing me into the bed beneath me. His body over mine felt nothing but protective.

I panted and swallowed hard and asked him, "What is your name? Your *legal* name?"

"Casey," he said back, gasping. "Casey Martin."

I thought for a second and asked, "Is there a marriage license in that envelope?"

He laughed.

"No, a coincidence. I swear it."

"Oh," I said, vaguely disappointed by that. "You're going to have to fix that."

He laughed, stopped, gasped, laughed some more and said, "Sounds like a plan."

I couldn't help but smile. He had no idea how serious I was.

EPILOGUE

$\mathcal{M}$arisol...

They came once a month. Sometimes only once every couple of months, but we depended on them. Rough men in wind and rain-worn black leather, the chrome of their bikes sparkling cold fire in the sun or gleaming softly under the cloud cover depending on the time of year. They would ride up, their faces covered in red or black bandanas, a rooster tail of dust kicked up by the tires of their motorcycles behind them.

These outlaws were dirty from a long, hard ride and road weary; yet they only stayed for a few minutes each time. They were considered the very dregs of society – but not by us.

To us, they were heroes; and Maverick? Maverick was our very own Robin Hood. The men he rode with, their faces set in hard lines and casting menacing looks, were his band of not-so-merry men.

The arrival of the Sacred Hearts was everything to a girl like me. Their departure almost soul crushing. Their visits had become the stuff my dreams were made of over the years, and even more so now that it was *Maverick* and his men and not the ones that used to come before.

I wanted out so badly from my stifling life here. So badly, that their departure became a nightmare ending to what was a beautiful dream every time I heard them coming.

I always dreamed that someday they would take me with them, and yet they always left without even noticing I was here.

I was just the girl to bring them lemonade, or water, blending into the background, but then sometimes Maverick would catch my eyes with his deep dark blue ones and I would feel that little flicker of hope…

I could be so lucky.

ALSO BY A.J. DOWNEY

The Sacred Hearts MC

1. Shattered & Scarred

2. Broken & Burned

3. Cracked & Crushed

3.5 Masked & Miserable (a novella)

4. Tattered & Torn

5. Fractured & Formidable

6. Damaged & Dangerous

The Virtues

1. Cutter's Hope

2. Marlin's Faith

3. Charity for Nothing

4. Stoker's Serenity

The Sacred Brotherhood

1. Brother to Brother

2. Her Brother's Keeper

3. Brother In Arms

4. Between Brothers

5. A Brother's Secret

6. A Brother At My Back

7. A Brother's Salvation

Indigo Knights

1. Her Thin Blue Lifeline

2. His Cold Blue Command

3. A Low Blue Flame

4. His Wild Blue Rose

5. Her Pained Blue Silence

6. A Cold Blue Call

7. Her Reluctant Blue Cavalier

8. Forged Under Fire

9. Under A Blue Moon

Paranormal Romance (with Ryan Kells)

1. I Am The Alpha

2. Omega's Run

3. Hunter's End

ABOUT THE AUTHOR

A.J. Downey specializes in writing real and relatable contemporary romance stories. She's from Seattle, WA and loves the Pacific Northwest. She finds inspiration from her surroundings, through the people she meets, and likely as a byproduct of way too much caffeine. An avid reader all of her life, it's now her turn to try and give back a little, entertaining as she has been entertained.

Stalker Information:

Website
www.ajdowney.com

Sign up for her newsletter at
http://eepurl.com/dkQiIH

Facebook Group - AJ's Sacred Circle
https://www.facebook.com/groups/authorajdowney/

facebook.com/authorajdowney

twitter.com/authorajdowney

instagram.com/ajdowney

bookbub.com/authors/a-j-downey